Constance sighed, loc   t move is obvious, is it no

"It is?" asked Jack wa...y.

"Of course. I must travel to Fréhel, where I may find out for myself what has become of Selwyn."

"Well . . . hmm."

She turned a quick look Jack's way. "It *is* possible, is it not? There is, surely, no danger for English visitors to France now that the war is ended?"

"France is not yet, I fear, an entirely comfortable place for the English."

"Are you suggesting I should *not* go?"

He frowned. "Who would escort you?"

Constance's brows rose. "Escort me? Sir, I am of an age, surely, when I no longer require escort!"

"Do not look so much like an outraged kitten, or I'll pick you up and unruffle your fur and set you to purring."

He could have kicked himself when she blushed rosily, her eyes darting to meet his and rushing away.

"I apologize," he said softly. "That was outrageous, not that you do *not* tempt a man," he added still more softly.

And then, her blush returning, he promised himself that kick just as soon as he found himself alone. And yet, their eyes met, held, and seemed to draw each far into the other's mind and soul. . . .

***　　***　　***

Praise for Jeanne Savery and *Lord Galveston and the Ghost:*

"Ms. Savery's Regencies are known for having something extra special and this one does."

—Rendezvous

"Tickles the funny bone . . . readers will enjoy Ms. Savery's diverting plot and light touch."

—Romantic Times

Books by Jeanne Savery

THE WIDOW AND THE RAKE
THE REFORMED RAKE
A CHRISTMAS TREASURE
A LADY'S DECEPTION
CUPID'S CHALLENGE
LADY STEPHANIE
A TIMELESS LOVE
A LADY'S LESSON
LORD GALVESTON AND THE GHOST
A LADY'S PROPOSAL
THE WIDOWED MISS MORDAUNT

Published by Zebra Books

THE WIDOWED MISS MORDAUNT

Jeanne Savery

Zebra Books
Kensington Publishing Corp.

http://www.zebrabooks.com

ZEBRA BOOKS are published by

Kensington Publishing Corp.
850 Third Avenue
New York, NY 10022

First Printing: March, 1999
10 9 8 7 6 5 4 3 2 1

Printed in the United States of America

Chapter 1

Jack Durrant, or, as the high sticklers would insist, Major Lord St. Aubyn, stopped just around the corner from the main entrance hall to the Horse Guards. He stopped because he overheard a delightfully feminine voice say a name: Selwyn Mordaunt, a name no one mentioned. At least, not above a whisper.

Several years earlier Lieutenant Selwyn Mordaunt had been placed, at the man's own suggestion, in a sensitive position in an obscure French fishing village complete with a neat little harbor from which information could be sent across the Channel. Mordaunt's last report arrived soon *after* Napoleon was defeated at Waterloo. There'd been no hint that Mordaunt's identity had been discovered, but no more was heard from him. The war was over and Jack hadn't a clue to where the fellow had gotten to. . . .

He certainly hadn't reported in here in London, as he should have done!

And this time the war was truly ended, unlike after the

abortive Quadruple Alliance Treaty of '14, when Napoleon
was sent to Elba. At that time Mordaunt insisted there were
strong reasons for him to remain in France. The man
had been right, too, his suspicions justified by Napoleon's
escape and his unbelievably rapid return to power during
the three months and a bit before Waterloo.

But Waterloo was long over. Napoleon was incarcerated
where he would not again escape. And Mordaunt *should*
have left his post and returned to England.

Jack had been reminded of that fact only this morning
when a much delayed report arrived on his desk, water
spotted, ragged, and almost impossible to decipher. But
the existence of the report had roused Jack's curiosity
about his missing colleague. And now, not only was Jack
interested in Mordaunt's whereabouts, but it appeared the
young fool had a woman looking for him.

Jack peered around the corner and ducked back. What
a woman it was, too! Why, wondered Jack, would any man
stay away from that tall, dark-haired beauty a moment
longer than need be?

Unsquelchable curiosity was Jack's premier failing, and
this situation roused it to its full strength. The major eased
around the corner, leaned against the wall, and, quite
shamelessly, eavesdropped.

"But surely there is something you can do," insisted the
woman.

"I . . . I don't think so," temporized the young officer
whose current duty was to screen applicants who wished
to see a senior officer. His primary order, although implicit,
was that his superiors were *not* to be bothered by trivia.
"Mrs. Mordaunt, you must go through channels."

Although the boy's back was to him, Jack could visualize
the young and very green ensign to whom Mrs. Mordaunt
spoke. His face, thought Jack, would be one shade less red

than his uniform, his snub nose and round chin not at all improved by embarrassment.

At least, that was the case if Redfield's frequent mopping of his forehead was any indication! The lad turned, and Jack was pleased to see his powers of deduction were not lost. The young officer's eyes darted from one end of the hall to the other. Quite obviously, the boy longed for rescue. Jack wondered, rather cynically, what the young man's lot would have been had he been forced to face the French. Would he have been as inadequate on the battlefield as he'd been, so far, at the Horse Guards?

"Can you not at least allow me in to speak to someone who *might* do something?" wheedled Constance, using one of her deceased sister–in–law's much despised tricks.

"I . . . er . . . *channels!*" insisted Redfield, and he yet again ran his handkerchief over his forehead and the back of his neck.

Jack decided the poor fool had been punished enough for one day. Standing away from his wall, he moved briskly toward the couple. "Trouble, Redfield?"

The lad stood to attention. "No sir, Major, sir. Of course not, Major Lord St. Aubyn."

"But I heard a lady's voice requesting aid, did I not? This lady, perhaps?" Jack looked directly, challengingly, at Mrs. Mordaunt.

The attractive woman's chin rose a notch or two in response.

Jack grinned and brushed back the heavy layer of hair which would *not* stay off his forehead, no matter how his batman worked. "You *did* speak, did you not? To Redfield here?" Released from his raking fingers, the hair immediately slid forward. "You were asking about a missing soldier? Perhaps a relative?"

"I requested that this officer discover what he could

about Lieutenant Selwyn Mordaunt. When he admitted there was nothing *he* could do, I requested that he introduce me to someone who *could.*" Constance didn't succumb to temptation, but she felt like stamping her foot at the delays and lack of assistance. "I do *not* understand why everyone treats me as if I were—"

"A rose bush in the turnip patch?" interrupted Jack, quite certain he didn't wish to hear how the lady herself would end her sentence. "Perhaps," he added, pretending severity, "because you *are.* The proper course in a case such as this is to write a letter."

Constance pulled a thick batch of correspondence tied up in a ribbon from her reticule and thrust it toward him.

Jack's brows climbed upward. "Hmm. If that is, as it appears to be, correspondence with someone here at the Guards, I understand why you might have become a trifle impatient." He pushed at his hair, running his fingers through the thick mass, and watched her watching him.

Something deep inside him tightened, warmed.

Constance's eyes followed the movement of the major's fingers and suddenly her own itched to see if *she* might not have the knack of making that hair stay in place. She'd be willing, she thought, to put every effort into the project. She'd work for hours if need be!

Her eyes dropped at the blush–making thought and she saw that the officer's other hand was held toward her. For a moment she thought he wished to offer her a handshake. Then she realized he wished to see the letters. She handed them over.

And again she stared, this time watching long–fingered, strong–looking hands at work as they unfolded first one and then a second long, rambling, and totally unhelpful letter.

Jack held up yet a third letter, thoughtfully perusing it. Then he looked around, his gaze falling on the young officer. "You may go, Redfield. I am sure that, somewhere in this large and rambling building, duty calls."

It wasn't true, of course. The new and untried officer's orders were to stand just where he was. Still, although a neophyte, he wasn't so completely lacking in wits he didn't understand his superior officer wished him elsewhere. Jack waited patiently while Redfield blushed, bowed to the lady, saluted, and took himself off. Only then did Jack turn back to the woman.

He introduced himself. "I am, as I think that young idiot may have said, Major St. Aubyn. I feel compelled to apologize for the treatment you have received at the hands of my superiors." He waved the letters back and forth.

"I am Constance Mordaunt. I and the children have not heard from Selwyn for a very long time now."

What exceedingly bad luck that she is Selwyn Mordaunt's wife, thought Jack. Then he wondered why such a thought crossed his mind.

One look at the woman before him and he'd the answer to that particular question! Although not a beauty in the accepted sense of the word, she was exceedingly attractive. His hands trembled very slightly as he refolded the third letter, the heavy paper with its embossed crown at the top less stiff than it had once been. The letter had obviously been folded and refolded until the creases were limp.

Old Packway is a fool, thought Jack—and not for the first time.

The man had tried, in his bumbling way, to put this

Constance Mordaunt off with vague phrases and odder
hints, but very likely he'd only succeeded in intriguing her
still more. It was one more indication that Lord Packway
should have retired years ago.

"Tell me exactly what it is you wish," Jack said,
restraining the least hint of a flirtatious note with difficulty.

"I thought," said Constance, her tone etched by the
faintest brush of acid, "that I'd made that clear. I wish
to find Selwyn Mordaunt, lieutenant in the king's army.
Something over two years ago he was about to be decom-
missioned for a wound which wouldn't heal properly. That
was after the Battle of Vitoria in June of 'thirteen. In July
of that year we were informed he'd be returning home.
Then, suddenly, the decision was reversed and he didn't.
Return, I mean. Knowing Silly, I suspect he managed,
somehow, to talk someone into letting him stay in the
army, in Heaven alone knows what capacity. You've never
seen such an army mad idiot." She said it fondly, a little
smile playing about her lips.

Silly, she'd called him? She, his wife, called Selwyn Mordaunt *Silly*? Jack, remembering Selwyn's hey–go–mad
character, swallowed a burst of laughter which, under the
circumstances, was totally uncalled for. Especially since,
when they'd last talked, Selwyn seemed to have sobered
up a great deal. His near brush with death, perhaps?

The lady was sober, too, lifting large, eloquent eyes to
meet Jack's gaze. "We've never heard another word."

When he opened his mouth to respond, she held up a
gloved hand. He promptly closed his mouth, wondering
what she'd say next.

"Don't tell me he must have died, after all," said Constance severely, bringing Jack's thoughts away from those
eyes and back to where they belonged. "There would be
a record of it. And if for some reason we'd not been

informed at the time, there'd not be the sort of hemming
and hawing I've been handed these past few months. Quite
simply, I'd have been told of his death when I first asked,
along with an apology that I'd not been informed.''

She glared at him, very much, he thought, like an angry
little kitten—not that she was so little, he amended.

"Well?"

Jack again forced his thoughts back into a proper mode,
this time taking them away from her delightfully firm little
chin. "I cannot tell you he died, because I am equally
certain he did not," said Jack smoothly. "Mrs. Mordaunt,
I'll be frank. I recently began wondering just where"—he
grinned broadly, his gray–green eyes twinkling in a way
Constance had never thought such eyes could twinkle—
"Silly, did you call him?"

She nodded, a slow smile growing to match that of the
man facing her. A dimple appeared in her cheek and,
fascinated, Jack wondered what it would feel like under
his tongue. Something revealing in his expression had her
smile and the dimple fading.

"You were saying?" she asked, that severe note back in
her voice.

"Saying? Oh. Yes. Saying." Jack searched his memory
and remembered they were discussing this woman's husband. *Husband.* The lingering bits of his smile disappeared.
"Hmm. Yes. Lieutenant Mordaunt."

"Lieutenant *Lord* Mordaunt. He is *Baron* Mordaunt,"
Constance corrected.

"Baron? I thought . . . ." Jack shook his head. "No, never
mind. He has, I presume, recently inherited his title." The
major drew in a deep breath. "Mrs. Mordaunt, or I should
say Lady Mordaunt, as I began to explain, Mordaunt *was*
brought to mind."

Jack had to think quickly to repress the information of

Mordaunt's long delayed report and ignored a hesitant lifting of the lady's hand.

"Something occurred. I, too, have been wondering where he is. Now I've *another* reason to look into that question, and I promise you I will. Where may I find you if I discover anything of interest to you?"

His last words were somewhat brusque. The thought of meeting Lady Mordaunt outside of these halls instantly led his thoughts into forbidden paths. Paths into which they must not drift. Not when a married lady was involved. Jack avoided married ladies as he would the plague. Married women were, he believed, quite as dangerous as that dread disease.

"My lady?"

She hesitated, opening her mouth and then closing it again. Finally she said slowly, "We are staying, under sufferance, with a cousin. Mr. Wilmot Mordaunt. He makes it obvious to the meanest observer he wishes us to the devil." She frowned. "I should not have said that. Still, I've the impression he'd not approve of callers. Perhaps I might meet you somewhere."

She tipped her head a trifle to the side, and again Jack was led to think of kittens and wondered what it would take to make that dimple reappear.

Her expression changed to one of satisfaction at discovering a solution to the problem. "Or perhaps better— *you* might meet *me*. I take the children to the park for exercise twice a day, weather permitting. The poor mites," she said fondly. "They are used to so much more freedom than is possible here, but are behaving beautifully. I do feel for them. The city, I've discovered, is no place for children, Major." Constance spoke with a certain severity.

She'd mentioned children before. *This becomes worse and*

worse, thought Jack, and then wondered what he meant by *that* odd thought. "Children, you say?"

"Selwyn's son and daughter," said Constance proudly.

"Ah yes. A son and a daughter."

Jack thought back over Mordaunt's career. It was a record ill–suited to a belief that the man was a responsible married man. A quick calculation gave rise to another question, and he asked, "They cannot, surely, have seen their papa for some time?"

"Silly has *never* seen his daughter," said Constance simply, if a little sadly.

"That is a sad thing for both of them," said Jack somewhat absently. Then he drew in a deep breath and went on more firmly. "If it is true your cousin is at sixes and sevens about your visit, I agree it's best I come to you in the park." He grinned, again trying to brush back his hair. *"I've* no desire to run the gauntlet of a toffee–nosed butler who wishes to forbid me the premises! At what time do you usually walk out, and for that matter, in which park will I find you?"

Constance shook her head soulfully. "Such a skitterwit you'll think me."

She smiled the brilliant smile he'd already seen once. This time there was a touch of mischief in it and that lovely dimple drew Jack's gaze for the second time.

"Of course there is more than the one park in London," she explained. "We go to *Green Park* after breakfast, and again sometime after two. My cousin's house is far too grand for children, so it is just as well that it lies conveniently along the Piccadilly side of the park and not far from the King's old ice–houses, which is where they play."

"Green Park, is it? I must tell your boy the tale of a duel held there many years ago. He'll enjoy that if he is anything like most little boys I've met."

"A duel," repeated Constance.

"Hmm. A young Italian and an Englishman are said to have met there, the latter pinking the former quite nicely in the arm. The Italian is quoted as saying, 'My view is that Ligonier'—his opponent, you know—'did not kill me because he did not want to, and I did not kill him because I did not know how.' " Jack grinned again. "I have always thought that the height of the Continental's odd sense of humor."

Much to Jack's regret Constance did not smile, and the dimple remained in hiding. In fact, she went so far as to frown. "I hope," she said, "that it is no longer common for duels to be fought there."

"Of course not," he said. "The area was nowhere nearly so well populated then as it is now. In our era one couldn't guarantee privacy for the purpose." He waved, a dismissing gesture. "Besides, dueling is no longer legal, so it is irrelevant, is it not?"

Constance gave the officer a long, steady look. Then she smiled a trifle wryly when a streak of red colored the tops of his ears.

Jack cleared his throat. "I think from your expression you would suggest that duelists still duel, despite the law. I'll not argue that, but I hold to the notion they no longer do it in Green Park."

Again their smiles grew, and again Jack found her dimple far too intriguing for his peace of mind. Still again, he cleared his throat. "I shall see what can be discovered, and will join you in the park one day soon." He bowed. "Good day to you, Lady Mordaunt."

Again Constance almost said something but closed her mouth before she spoke. Instead, she curtsied, thanked him, and turned away. As she approached the door a severe-looking though plump and rosy-cheeked woman rose from a hard bench and joined her. The maid asked a question. Lady Mordaunt sighed, shook her head, and walked on.

At least, thought Jack, *she did not come here alone, as I'd feared.*

Then, remembering that dimple and wishing she were the sort who would allow him to satisfy his curiosity concerning the feel of it, honesty made him add a mental caveat.

Or perhaps, that she'd come alone is exactly *what I'd hoped?*

"Did I hear that officer call you Lady Mordaunt?" asked Miss Willes. They were settled into a hack called for them by a very attentive young officer, who had taken one look at Constance and instantly asked how he might serve her. Only Miss Willes's famous glare had kept the young man from entering the carriage after them and escorting them all the way home. "Why did you not contradict him?" she added when Constance nodded.

"You will think me missish, but I remembered something Ada Wright said when I visited her just before we left home. Willy, she insisted I'd be treated with far more respect if I allowed the world to believe I was Silly's wife instead of his sister. I pooh–poohed the notion at the time, but somehow, when that officer assumed . . ." Constance drew in a sharp breath as, once again, she wished she might run her fingers through the hair dropping over the Major's forehead.

Miss Willes nodded. "You thought it wise to allow the assumption to stand. Yes. I see. It isn't exactly a lie, I suppose. You did not *tell* the gentleman you were a married lady."

"Willy," interrupted Constance, her eyes dancing with

laughter, "you will *not* lecture me on my moral decline, just because you are uncertain whether it would not have been more proper if I'd instantly contradicted the man." She pretended to glare. "Well, my dear Willy, I am no longer in the nursery, and I will not have it!"

"To the contrary, my dear," said Miss Willes with a smile. "Rather than give you a scold, I meant to congratulate you on your good sense. It is very true that young and unmarried women are not always treated well. Especially when they are well looking and I cannot deny that, despite the very great age you've achieved, you have a certain look that men like." At the reference to Constance's twenty–fifth birthday, which she'd recently celebrated, Willy slid a sly smile toward her old charge.

"I believe that is a compliment," said Constance pertly.

Constance didn't *feel* particularly pert. She was recalling her last visit to her friend, Ada Wright. Upon hearing Constance was to go to London, her friend had told her a tale she still found difficult to believe. Ada was *not* a widow, as all in their small Cornish village believed. And her darling little girl, with her red hair and mismatched eyes, was the result of Ada's downfall. Her family, Ada revealed, had set her up with a new identity and an annuity, and then deserted her. And that when she'd been no more than a child of sixteen or seventeen.

Given her background, Constance didn't wonder that Ada insisted she should pretend to be Selwyn's wife. Why, though, when the Major assumed exactly that, had Constance not contradicted him? She'd insisted to Ada that such subterfuge was surely unnecessary in her case. Constance brooded on the oddity of her own behavior all the way home.

Constance and Nurse Willes returned home none too soon. Just as they were given entry by Lester, Wilmot Mordaunt's oily looking butler, Val and Venetia raced down the stairs at a dangerous pace. White–faced, the children threw themselves against Constance and Willy.

Wilmot Mordaunt, cane in hand, waddled into view at the top of the impressive flight of stairs only moments later. "Where are those devils?" he yelled in a voice hoarsened by age and drink. "Just you wait 'til I catch those imps of hell! I'll kill them, I tell you!"

There was something in his tone that had Constance straightening her back, her hands going to cover Val's soft, dark curls so very like her own. "Cousin Mordaunt," she said, "I apologize if the children have somehow disturbed you. They were supposed to be entertained in their rooms by one of the maids until we returned."

"My maids have work to do," growled Mordaunt. "You are not to order them away from their duties." He scowled at her, almost attaining a certain dignity as he glared down his rather red nose. "I'll not have it, Missy. You hear me?"

"I hear. And it should be unnecessary to ask for such help in the future." She drew in a deep breath and added, "I am almost certain we'll be a burden on you for only a little longer."

Wilmot, about to roar out further complaints and orders, closed his mouth. "Why not?" he asked peacefully, although his faded blue eyes glittered in an odd fashion.

Constance hesitated. She'd confided her business to him upon their arrival and been told he'd attend to it. She did not wish to appear to find his efforts inadequate, though that was exactly her feeling.

Constance, however, had great difficulty telling lies successfully. So she didn't. "I visited the Horse Guards today. It was very kind of you to offer to help me, but I wished to discover for myself where my brother has disappeared to."

"Hasn't disappeared," said the old man promptly.

Perhaps too promptly? Constance was alarmed by the glitter snapping in his cold, blue eyes. Since they'd arrived in London, she had decided that that particular expression cued one that the man would begin lying through his teeth. She certainly didn't believe his next comment.

"Didn't wish to upset you," he asserted. "Was trying to think how to break bad news. See I should've said it right out. Little lady, Selwyn's been dead for years. Merely a mistake you weren't informed of it. I was told immediately when I asked."

Constance, standing perfectly still, remained silent for a moment. He lied. But *why?* The major's revelations supported her belief that he lied. Still, having lied, he would expect her to return to Cornwall . . . and perhaps *that* was his reason?

But she couldn't. It was necessary that she discover what that very interesting major had to say concerning her brother.

"I see," she said at last. "Cousin, you give me bad news indeed."

"Never you mind," said the old man, his jowls shaking. "Must have guessed it long ago," he added, his eyes narrowing.

"I admit I've wondered," said Constance. After all, she had asked herself if it were possible. Immediately, on each such occasion, she'd decided it was not. They would, at the very least, have received a letter from the Horse Guards saying Silly was missing. The army did not misplace its officers and not question that loss.

"Hmm." The narrowed eyes squinted down at her. "You'll be wishing to go home then."

It was as she'd feared. "Cousin," she said feeling her way, "I realize we're interfering in your life and I must apologize for that, but it is exceedingly unlikely I'll ever again have an opportunity to see something of London.''

That much was true. Could she make him believe she *wished* to see it?

"So, if it would not put you out *too* much," she went on, "I'd like to spend no more than another week with you, during which I'll visit some of the important sights." She had a sudden notion. "And a London *modiste* for just *one* up-to-the-knocker afternoon gown. I believe I can afford that, and just think how envious my neighbors will be when I return to Cornwall and show it off.''

"Frills and frippery. Hurumph."

It was, thought Constance hopefully, something her rather dense cousin *might* believe of a woman, that she'd be interested in what he'd just called frills and frippery.

And it seemed he did. She held her breath while Cousin Wilmot searched his mind for a reason to deny her the treat. Obviously he didn't find one. "Just don't you go off and leave those brats alone again. Can't stand children," he growled. "Should never be seen. Or heard. Not 'til they reach an age of reason."

"Age ... thirty-five, cousin?" asked Constance, her brows arching and the dimple appearing.

"No no, not such a great age as that." He frowned, obviously considering the question she'd asked in jest. *"Twenty*-five would do. For lads. Girls ... maybe a trifle younger. Girls seem to gain *some* sense of their place in this world at a far younger age than boys do, don't you know?" Then he glared down his nose at her. *"Some* girls, at least," he suggested meaningfully.

"Oh, yes. I understand you. Perfectly. Having very nearly reached the quarter century myself, I know exactly what you mean." She leaned down and whispered into Val's ear. "I haven't a notion what you did, but you *must* behave, my boy. I cannot leave London just yet. Now go off quietly with Nurse Willy. *Quietly,* " she added softly but sternly when the boy opened his mouth. Reluctantly he removed himself to the nurse's side and took her hand. "I think you'd better take them up the back stairs," she added to Miss Willes, who nodded silent agreement.

Miss Willes took Valerian by the hand, turned little Venetia around so that she stood by her other side. Head high, she moved toward the baize–covered servant's door which would lead the trio back to the steep stairs which debouched near their rooms on the third floor.

Constance watched them go, but looked up in time to see her cousin glaring at Val. She blinked, wondering what the boy could possibly have done to deserve such . . . enmity? Not mere anger. Something worse.

Something in that look frightened Constance. Once before she'd felt, intuitively, that Mordaunt must hate her nephew. Then she'd scolded herself. Surely it was a stupid reaction to whatever it was she saw every time the old man stared at her nephew. Still, there was *something* there. Something which made her wish to pick Val up and carry him off and hide him.

And she'd just seen it again. Constance decided she'd not stay in London one more moment than necessary.

Later that afternoon Ensign Redfield faced his second Mordaunt of the day. "But Mr. Mordaunt . . ." began the young and untried officer for the third time.

"No need, I tell you. She's got bats in her belfry on the subject, and no one can get them out. Just forget she ever came by, don't you know?" said the old man with seeming joviality.

But, thought Redfield, *there's something nasty hiding behind the man's smile.*

Mr. Mordaunt, your cousin spoke with Major Lord St. Aubyn." Redfield managed to get the words out in a tone which was heard. "I'll take you to the major's office, shall I?"

"A major, hmm? Brass–faced hoyden actually managed to talk to someone with rank, hmm?"

"I did not find the lady at all coming. She behaved in nothing but the most acceptable of manners!" said Redfield with the firmness he'd just discovered actually seemed to get through to this awful man.

Major St. Aubyn would have appreciated knowing that it was only when facing women, young and pretty women, that is, that Redfield became flustered.

"Come this way, if you please," he finished, and moved off briskly.

Mordaunt was forced to move a trifle more quickly than was agreeable to his sense of dignity. "Not a hoyden, hmm?" Mordaunt managed a rather evil–sounding chuckle despite his tendency to pant. "Just a green young man, *you* are," he added slyly. "All you young ones ever see is the curly hair and blue eyes, and immediately you forget what lies behind the pretty face. I tell you boy, she's so cracked that she has the whole family at sixes and sevens, not knowing what to do with her, you see." Mordaunt said the last in a confiding tone, but Redfield cast him such a disbelieving look the old man sighed.

Mordaunt hoped he'd have better luck convincing this major he was to meet that his cousin was not to be cosseted in any way. No telling what might be found if they went prying into the records. Of course, they might find the boy had *absconded,* in which case he'd be outlawed for desertion and unable to return to England. *Ever.*

That would be all right in its way, assuming one could prove him dead, of course—not *too* far into the future. Terrible thing was that they might discover something far more dreadful. Like where he was this very moment, and that he'd simply over-stayed his mission, whatever that might be. And then they might order him home. Which must be avoided.

Mustn't have the drafted boy home. Not now. Not just when he'd put into motion his most brilliant plot ever!

Lieutenant Redfield introduced Mordaunt to St. Aubyn and left the senior officer's office with far more alacrity than he usually displayed. Redfield had made something of a hero of the major and he usually did his best to linger in the older officer's presence.

Mordaunt didn't like the looks of the man standing behind the desk. The major was politely if a little impatiently waiting for Mordaunt to explain himself. That impatience didn't bode well. Besides, Mordaunt had never liked tall, strongly built men. They always made him feel, well, somehow, inadequate. Which was ridiculous. He'd more brains then a dozen bovine-muscled, thick-headed young men.

"Thought I'd save you some effort," began Wilmot. "My cousin, you know. Told me she came by?" He gave the major a questioning look.

"Yes?" said Jack.

The old man shook his head, adopting a patently false look of sadness. He next cast his gaze toward the ceiling in what he obviously thought a pious manner. "Don't know what we're to do with the poor child. May have to lock her up."

Mordaunt sent a quick, slicing glance in the major's direction, his eyes glittering in that way they had, to see how this comment went over. He was pleased to see the officer stiffen, his eyes narrow, tension radiating from the man.

"Wouldn't care to reveal her troubles to a soul, of course," Mordaunt said confidingly, "but this is a busy office, don't you know?"

Again Mordaunt chanced a glance. Again he noted the stiff expression which, somehow, even so, expressed curiosity.

"Can't have busy officers wasting their time on nonsense. No need to bother with her. You see? Just her nonsense." His voice trailed off.

Have I succeeded? wondered Wilmot.

After a moment in which his guest didn't continue, Jack, his face now a perfect blank, asked, "Nonsense?"

"Oh, quite definitely nonsense." Wilmot nodded several times. "You know, requesting information about Selwyn Mordaunt which is"—this time he looked sharply at the major, his eyes rather prominent, staring—"what she did, did she not?"

Jack nodded, his face a stern mask which revealed nothing of the thoughts teeming behind it.

"Dead, you know. Long dead. Gel won't admit it." Mordaunt shook his head. "Can't have her going around bothering busy, important men when all's clear and tidy." He once again tried the confiding tone. "Just thought I'd come by and drop a word in someone's ear."

"Dead?" asked Jack.

"Long dead. *Years* dead," insisted Mr. Mordaunt, expansively.

"You are saying," asked Jack, wishing to be absolutely certain he'd understood, "that your cousin, Lieutenant Lord Selwyn Mordaunt, is dead?"

Again Wilmot nodded several times.

"I see," said the major slowly, wondering just what the

fat old fool had up his sleeve. Again he waited, and again there was silence. He asked, "Are you perhaps suggesting I forget the lady's request that I discover the lieutenant's present whereabouts?"

"Got it in one," declared Wilmot, breathing more easily. He gave the major a hopeful look. "Already dead, so no need to bother, don't you see?"

"I see," said Jack again.

Jack wasn't sure exactly what it was he saw. The impossible old clunch was up to something. But what? Why did he insist Lieutenant Lord Mordaunt was dead? Because, as of the end of the war, the lieutenant had *not* been dead, not so very long ago. Months, certainly, but not *years*.

Jack looked his visitor up and down, not liking what he saw. That the man was fat as a flawn with creaking corsets was nothing about which one could cavil. After all, the Regent himself, the future king of England, was no less obese, and his corsets no more silent. No. It was something in the beady eyes. *Beady eyes*, thought the major, *should not be blue. Certainly not a faded, somewhat watery blue.* It didn't fit. They should be black, or at the very least a very dark brown.

Jack sighed. "Poor woman," he said, when his visitor seemed to wish more from him than he'd said so far. "Never know how grief may take our womenfolk, do we?"

"Grief," said Mordaunt with a certain fervor. "That's it. Took her bad, you see."

"Turned her mind, you would say," suggested Jack, curious as to how far Mordaunt could be led.

Mordaunt nodded his head several times in that odd way he had. "That's it. Bright as a new penny, *you* are." Mordaunt looked around, his eyes widening. He lowered his voice. "Know you won't voice her trouble around, hmm? Hmm?"

"I wouldn't think of telling anyone such a pretty young woman was not quite right in the head."

Because, thought Jack, *it wouldn't be true, so why should I suggest it? One must wonder, however, just why you have done so.* Jack's eyes narrowed ever so slightly.

"Good. Good. Trust you not to say a word." Again Mordaunt tried casting a sad look upward "Poor lady. Sad case. She'll be returning with the children to their home in Cornwall now. Probably tomorrow or the next day."

He's lying again. Why is he lying? But Jack pretended to accept that. "I see. Then certainly there is no reason for me to waste my time looking into the situation, is there?"

"No reason at all." Mordaunt struggled to heave himself from his chair. "That's all right, then. All right and tidy. Just thought I'd give you the hint," he said, panting slightly.

He bowed. The corsets creaked mightily and Jack wondered if it would be necessary to help the old man straighten up.

"I'll just be off, then," finished Wilmot, wheezing. He put his hat back on his head and turned to the door.

Suddenly he turned back, studying the major's expression. Something in the look had prickles crawling up Jack's spine. He thanked his lucky stars his training had been good and that his expression hadn't changed. At least he hoped it hadn't, because, obviously, Mordaunt had given him that one last look for no other reason than to check his reaction.

The situation smelled. Mr. Wilmot Mordaunt smelled, both literally and figuratively. Mr. Mordaunt was a bad fish if Jack had ever seen one. What did he expect to gain from his lies? At the extreme, just what evil might he contemplate? And why was one so thoroughly convinced the man plotted evil? Jack watched the door shut, reseated himself, and picked up a memo from the pile on his desk. Rather expecting what happened next, he was pretending to study it when the door was quickly and suddenly reopened. He waited. After a moment he looked up.

"Mr. Mordaunt?" he asked, putting surprise into his voice. "You forgot something?"

The old man smiled broadly. "No, no. Nothing like that. Or maybe yes. I forgot to thank you for treating my little cousin so kindly when she came by. Poor dear. Needs kindness. Maybe time will heal her trouble and she'll be the happy little lady she used to be. Just wanted to thank you." Mordaunt bobbed rather than bowed, and the door once again closed behind him.

Jack leaned back in his chair, a thoughtful look on his face, and stared at the door. This was the second Mordaunt he'd met that day. Not half so attractive, but, in his own way and for utterly different reasons, rather interesting. Yes, quite interesting.

"Mr. Mordaunt," said Jack softly as if to his departed guest, "I believe you have just handed me an antidote to the boredom I've suffered for some months now. I do believe my days as a spy have not quite ended, after all. You, my not–so–good sir, are up to something. And I would know exactly what . . . because what I *do not* believe is that it is to Lady Mordaunt's advantage!"

Early in his military career it was discovered that Jack St. Aubyn was exceedingly good at solving mysteries, at putting together odd facts and coming up with answers, at knowing the questions which must be asked so they *would* add up. Jack had achieved his desk at the Horse Guards because of that talent and, even while he knew the importance of what he did, he'd enjoyed every minute of it. Unfortunately, when the war ended, his bag of tricks had no longer been needed, and Jack had been bored very nearly to death.

Boredom. It was something he had never acquired the knack of handling, no matter how much he'd been forced to practice. And recently, he'd been practicing a lot. Jack pushed back the hair falling across his forehead and grinned. What a relief to discover that he'd not die of boredom quite yet! Not until he solved the problem of the missing Selwyn Mordaunt.

Boredom might await him in the future, hover around some corner, waiting to pounce and gobble him up. But now, with this problem before him, he might manage to get through the remaining weeks before he was allowed to resign his commission and take up a new career with the foreign office. He would use the time to solve all the little mysteries the Mordaunts had presented him!

Jack remembered the existence of a certain dimple in the cheek of one of those Mordaunts. He wondered, again, what that dimple would feel like under his tongue. . . .

Playing with his pen, he leaned back, allowing himself to daydream about dark hair let down from under a lace trimmed cap after the home-trimmed bonnet had been removed. He dreamed about a deep dimple which faded far too quickly and wondered how—or if—one could bring it into existence at one's slightest whim.

A daydream or two would hurt no one, but before totally giving way to the dreaming, Jack sternly reminded himself that one must never forget that dreams and reality were two separate things!

Oh yes. Quite different.

Now what, he wondered, closing his eyes, would that dimple feel like if he were to . . .

Chapter 2

Early the next morning Jack Durrant strolled away from the Horse Guard's parade and down a convenient path through St. James's Park toward Green Park, which abutted it at the far corner. He'd nearly reached the Mall when he noticed a rabbit–faced, flashily dressed man. Biggens was a man his espionage office had reluctantly used as a spy against the occasional Frenchman living in London during the war. The man had no sense of right or wrong that Jack had ever discovered. He did whatever he'd been hired to do and did it well, but he did it for money and no other reason.

Curious about the obviously heated discussion between Rhino Biggens and a man dressed in the typical fashion of an upper servant, a butler or perhaps a valet, Jack left the path. Who in Mayfair, he wondered, would require the services of a man like Biggens? Moving from tree to bush to hedge, he quickly closed in on his prey.

Rhino had been given his sobriquet because of his obsession with money, which was called, among other things, rhino in the thieves's cant prevalent in the London slums. At the moment, the fellow's close–set eyes were almost crossed due to his frown, and the tips of his over–large front teeth were firmly set against his lower lip. He shook his head decidedly.

"Nowhere near enough," insisted Rhino. "In the regular way I'm no miller, and this job's worth a sight more than *that* piddling offer. Even if it only be a tad, and easy like."

"I cannot offer more. I've been given precise instructions."

"Then you just go back and get yourself instructed all over again. Or I'm off."

The servant sighed. "You cannot know how difficult it is to admit failure to my principal. He has such a temper. I do not *like* things thrown at my head."

"That's your look–out, see? I'll not do it for a penny less than a monkey."

The upper servant looked horrified. "Five hundred pounds! He'll never agree."

"Then you'll find yourself another boy. 'Tisn't him what'll land in sheriff's picture frame if'n he's caught crashing the tadpole, now is it? You tell him that."

Sheriff's picture frame? The *gibbet*? The eavesdropping major frowned.

"I'll tell him you fear the deadly nevergreen, all right and tight," said the butler, who stifled a high and unpleasant titter. "Sorry, Mr. Biggens. Can never think of the gallows without thinking of the hanging I was took to see when I was but a nipperkin," he added, revealing his origins as his language returned to that of his youth. He swallowed hard before returning to more prissy tones.

"Will you meet me here tomorrow so that I may inform you of my man's decision?"

"I'll come," said Rhino, a threatening note quite incompatible with his rabbity appearance creeping into his voice. "But you better not be wasting my time. Time is val—u—able. Time is mon—ey. I like the rhino—and—ready more'n most, so don't you go a wastin' my val—u—able time."

Rhino held his hand cupped in a suggestive manner and glared. Something in his manner made the butler pull out a large handkerchief and mop his face. He then carefully patted his head so as to not disarrange a limp tress swirled in a complicated manner which did its best to hide his balding pate.

"Well?" growled the slum—born villain, jiggling his hand suggestively.

"I've no desire," said the nervous servant, "to waste your time, or my own for that matter. I'll . . . I'll give you a sixpence now and another tomorrow, so that you cannot say you've wasted it."

"A yellow boy."

"A guinea! No, no. A shilling, then. A bob's all I can possibly afford." The butler, assuming he *was* a butler, found courage from somewhere and managed a fairly convincing scowl. "You can't bleed me for more than I got!" he said, thrusting his chin well forward.

"A measly borde," said the flashily dressed cove, shaking his head. "What I've been brung low to!" Rhino grimaced. He scowled fearsomely when the butler winced. "Shouldn't do it for less than a crown, but—your own purse?"

The butler nodded.

"Very well," said Rhino, disgusted.

Rhino held out his dirty hand. Dark circles decorated the ends of his fingernails, nails which were rough and broken. The butler, keeping his own well cared for, white—skinned fingers clear of the grimy palm, dropped the promised coin into it and hurried away.

"Ah," muttered Rhino just loudly enough so that Jack could hear him from his hiding place behind a nearby bush, "A very fine gentleman *you* be—I don't think!" The slum—born, rabbity man stared thoughtfully after the servant. "Just hope this'll be no Flemish account like the last po—si—tion I took up." He sighed gustily. "No more easy pickings, I fear, now the war done ended." He sighed again, shaking his head, before turning and wandering off in the direction of his home in St. Giles—if one could call the room he shared with several others a home.

"Flemish account?" asked Jack a moment later, pushing back his hair and resettling his hat. He strolled on toward the Ice House and, with luck, a rendezvous with Lady Mordaunt. "Never heard *that* one," he muttered and asked himself two questions: Who was attempting to hire Rhino? For exactly what purpose?

So . . . more mystery to explain? Deciphering thieves's cant was occasionally more guesswork than he liked. Jack decided he didn't have time to delve into it, although he'd warn the runners Rhino was negotiating payment for a child—murder. That *was* what he'd meant by *crashing a tadpole,* was it not? The Runners would check it out. He'd enough on his plate just now, helping Lady Mordaunt find her husband.

Lady Mordaunt! Blast it all, why did such an intriguing woman have to be married and, because of Jack's well developed sense of self—preservation, beyond his touch? Of course, Mordaunt had been at war far more than he'd been in residence. Had they reached an arrangement whereby each was free to follow his or her own interests?

But, in fact, hadn't it been quite otherwise? Hadn't she, if anything, been overly correct in her behavior?

Irritated, Jack frowned. There'd been not the least sign of such an agreeable marital bargain. There'd been no hint of a flirtatious nature or anything in her deportment which suggested she might willingly indulge in a little dalliance.

Fortunately.

Because, if she'd shown the least sign of it, he'd be strongly tempted to break his rule against married women.

Jack approached the Ice House obliquely, wondering if he'd find his quarry there. A peal of childish laughter, coming from beyond the corner of the building, convinced him that someone had brought their children there, so he'd hoped he'd not wasted his time coming by. He thought of Rhino's concern about wasted time, and grinned. Rounding the corner, he stopped, his smile growing and his eyes sparkling as he took in the lively scene.

A boy of perhaps seven was attempting to roll a hoop which stood taller than himself. A girl, somewhat younger, stood nearby, jumping up and down and calling encouragement. Following behind the boy, her skirts raised in one hand to a delightful if slightly scandalous level, ran Constance Mordaunt.

Lady Mordaunt, he reminded himself.

Occasionally the young woman reached out with her own baton and gave the hoop a glancing blow to keep it going. She laughed. From under one side of her bonnet a lock of heavy dark hair dropped down, forming a fanciful curl which bounced against her shoulder. And then, her chest rising and falling as she breathed deeply, she stopped. Placing hands to her hips, she watched the boy carry on without her.

Suddenly the lad looked over his shoulder. His eyes widened. "Connie!"

"Yes?" she called, laughing.

He turned, letting the hoop go. It wobbled on for a space, tipped, coiled around and around on the ground for a moment, and finally lay still. The boy looked from it to the woman. "You promised to help me," he accused.

"But I did, Val. And then you did so well all by yourself that I thought I might take a moment to catch my breath."

"I was doing well?" asked the boy hopefully, his eyes as dark a blue as Constance Mordaunt's. "Truly?"

"*Very* well, Val. Don't you agree, Venetia?" She held out her hand and the little girl raced to take it. "Venetia? Don't you think Val did well?"

The child nodded. "May I try?" she asked shyly.

"The hoop's a trifle large, I fear. Perhaps you'd best take care of your new baby, instead," suggested Constance cheerfully. She pointed to where a miniature baby carriage stood. "Have you checked that she's still well covered?"

The child ran to the carriage, peered in under the umbrella–like structure hanging over the basketwork body, and glanced back. "She's sleeping."

"Very good."

The boy returned then, carrying the hoop ahead of him. "Will you get me started again? Please, Connie?" he asked.

"Perhaps I might help," said Jack, striding forward. "I was once a dab hand at the hoop. Good morning, Lady Mordaunt."

For just a moment Constance stilled. Then, grimacing slightly, she nodded. "I suppose that *would* be the proper form, would it not? Nevertheless, until Selwyn is returned to us I'd prefer a simpler style."

Without a hint of coyness, she reached up and worked

the wayward curl back up under her bonnet . . . much to Jack's distress.

He forced himself to concentrate on words rather than actions. "You are very certain he *will* return."

"I've faith nothing has happened to him." Her lips tightened and her eyes narrowed as she stared at nothing at all. "I know Selwyn. He will have found some excuse not to return immediately. The war is ended, however, and he must. He has responsibilities." She looked significantly at the children. "They need him and so, too, does his estate."

"And you do not?" asked Jack softly.

"I?" For a moment she looked blank, then she colored delightfully. "Oh, I don't count." The boy approached her and put his hand into hers. She looked down at him. "This is Valerian Mordaunt, Selwyn's son, and that shy young miss rocking the carriage is his daughter, Venetia. Children, make your bows to Major Lord St. Aubyn."

The lad stepped forward a pace and made a credible bow. The girl put her finger in her mouth and bobbed. Jack smiled from one to the other. "I've young cousins very much your age. I'd guess you must be . . . eight? Almost eight?" he asked the boy.

"I was seven only last month," said the boy, crowing because this stranger thought him older.

"Ah." Jack stepped to the carriage and looked into it. "And you, my dear—what a very nice baby you have there. Are you six, perhaps?"

Venetia held up five fingers.

"Ah. Five." Jack nodded solemnly. "I've a cousin who is just five. She hasn't quite that nice a baby, I think. Do you take good care of her?"

Venetia nodded shyly, but the finger came out of her mouth and she smiled. Constance smiled, as well. For a reason she didn't wish to delve into, she was quite satisfied by how quickly Lord St. Aubyn conquered her shy niece and managed to stand well with her nephew.

"Very good," said Jack. He touched the child's curls for a moment. "Now for the hoop, my young gentleman. I don't believe I've totally forgotten how to make the things go."

For perhaps ten minutes he helped Val roll the hoop, giving the boy some pointers for keeping it upright and rolling without wobbling. When the boy appeared to have caught the trick of it, he returned to where Lady Mordaunt was seated on a bench watching Miss Mordaunt undress her doll. The child carefully lay each item of clothing out on the grass or hung it from the branch of a nearby bush.

"Will she be able to get all those bits and pieces back on her doll?" he asked, seating himself.

"It depends on whether she's feeling independent or in need of comfort." Constance Mordaunt gave him a straight look. "Tell me what you discovered about Selwyn."

Jack grinned. "How do you know I've discovered anything at all?" His eyes followed the boy as he turned a curve in the walk. Soon, Jack decided, young Valerian would be out of sight, and that wouldn't do. He rose to his feet. "Excuse me. I'll go turn the boy around . . . shall I?" he said, belatedly asking permission.

The dimple appeared and nearly distracted him but when she nodded he remembered he'd set himself an errand, and went after Selwyn's son. He was soon back, the boy following along behind with the hoop.

"Now, then," said Jack, returning to his spot near the intriguing Lady Mordaunt, "we were saying?"

"I asked what you'd discovered about Selwyn," she scolded, but she smiled with it.

"And I wondered how you thought I'd found news so soon!" he retorted, pushing back his undisciplined hair.

"But you have, have you not?" When she looked up at him this time, her bright blue eyes had darkened with concern. "You see, I cannot find excuses to remain much longer with my cousin, who did not wish my intrusion in the first place. His letter was barely cordial when he agreed to my visit. Somehow I'd not made it clear I'd bring the children, and he has not ceased glowering since he set eyes on them—or perhaps he just naturally glowers and it has nothing to do with our visit." She tilted her head to one side.

"I think he may glower easily," said Jack thoughtfully, "but I do not think, myself, that it is so often or so consistently as you suggest."

She turned a wary, suspicious look his way. "When we first spoke, you did not tell me you knew our cousin, Mr. Wilmot Mordaunt."

"I did not tell you for the simple reason that, at that time, I'd not made his acquaintance. Now I have. Briefly." He felt a muscle jump in his jaw and forced himself to relax. "He came to my office yesterday. An hour or so after I met you."

Her frown deepened and, once again she stared at nothing, obviously puzzling something out. "I see," she said.

"You do?" Jack chuckled, and she glanced up at the wry sound. "It is more than *I* do," he said. "You see, your cousin attempted to convince me that you have bats in your belfry." A touch of red tinged his ears. "What I *meant* to say is that Mordaunt insisted that you refuse to admit to it although Lieutenant Lord Mordaunt died years ago, that grief has turned your mind, you see."

Constance stared at him. She opened her mouth to

speak and then closed it. Trying again, she managed, "But . . . that's nonsense."

"Of course it is. I've clear evidence that Selwyn Mordaunt was alive and well and had every expectation of remaining in good health very shortly before the war ended."

"You do?"

Jack nodded. Her eyes glowed, and for the first time he thought she looked as a married woman should look when discussing her husband.

"Oh, I am so *glad.*"

Constance's growing smile lit up her whole face, and she seemed to the watchful Major to be illuminated from the inside out. The dimple flickered in and out of existence.

"I was dreaming up all sorts of horrors, you see, when no one would tell me where he was or what he was doing. I even feared he'd been court–martialled for some disobedience."

She cast him a worried look.

"Not, you understand, that he'd have done anything wrong from *disloyalty,* but he might have decided his way was best, or gotten carried away or some such thing."

She glanced at the major, and saw that he was frowning.

"Oh dear. *Did* he do something he shouldn't? He wouldn't have meant it that way, I assure you," she said earnestly. "I know him so well, you see. I know he'd never do . . ." She trailed off when Jack raised his hand to stop the flow of words. She drew in a deep breath. "Perhaps I should let you explain instead of babbling on in such a scatterbrained way?"

"Mordaunt has done nothing which need embarrass you. As you know, he was wounded back in 'thirteen. When he recovered as much as he ever would—his limp, I'm

told, isn't pretty, and is, it is feared, quite permanent—
he was informed he'd be invalided home. The order was
reversed when he came up with a . . . a scheme. His notion
was relayed to the proper office here and we agreed to
it." His brows arced up under the shock of hair falling
over his forehead. "That limp, you see. It made his plan
feasible."

"His plan? A way he might remain in the army, of
course." She sighed, then bit her lip, again staring off into
space. "Not that I'm at all surprised."

Jack *was* surprised. *He'd* never have searched for reasons
to stay away from this woman. "Mordaunt has carried his
idea through with all the verve and *èlan* of his fearless
nature."

"Fearless nature!" Constance turned an impatient look
Jack's way. "Bah. Silly is simply too stupid to believe anything might happen to his precious skin!"

"But it did, did it not?"

She looked flustered for a moment. "Ah. You refer to
his wound. Yes, I guess it did. But I still maintain he can
be foolish to the utmost degree!"

Jack grinned, relieved, although he couldn't quite have
said why. Not at that instant, at least. It had something to
do with the fact that Lady Mordaunt's words did not sound
like those of a loving wife. For some reason that was becoming more and more important.

Jack gave Constance a rather speculative look. For the
first time, he put words to the emotions teasing him: *Perhaps*
he thought, *she would be interested in a brief affaire? Would
indulge the two of us in exploring where our senses might take
us?*

He closed his eyes. Such thoughts were wildly out of
place! *Partly* because of his rule against seducing married
women. *Mostly* because, for some reason, the idea of a *brief*

affaire didn't appeal. There was something quite wrong with the thought.

Not that he didn't wish to *bed* her.

Jack shook his head, dislodging the whole subject. He was here to discuss this woman's husband, *not* to seduce her for his own pleasure, however much that delightful dimple drew him. He noticed she was watching him warily and smiled at her.

She spoke a trifle diffidently: "You thought me lacking in proper feeling, did you not? When I suggested Selwyn can act foolishly? It is my opinion that the desire for glory and fame, which occasionally overcomes even the most sensible of men, is a quite stupid urge. I won't apologize even if you feel differently."

"I've known many young men with just that attitude. I've often thought them stupid to be so careless of their persons!" He grinned. "In this case, however, Mordaunt *has* covered himself with a certain amount of glory, although very little fame. Not that the fame might not follow eventually. If his story is ever told."

"Can you explain that to me? I don't entirely understand, you see."

"Of course you don't, and I've teased you unconscionably, have I not? It is this way. Mordaunt volunteered to go into France and take up a certain difficult but important position there. In his words, he'd be the spider in the center of a web, collecting and collating information gathered within French borders—information concerning Napoleon's troop movements, stores of supplies, where they were stored and when they were moved, all those details necessary to second guessing an enemy's intentions."

"You say he went into *France!*" Horror widened her eyes.

"But I've heard that all able–bodied men . . ." She put her hand to her mouth and pressed back more words.

Jack grinned. "Yes, Napoleon demanded service of every *able–bodied* man, but you haven't thought it through. The lieutenant was *not* able–bodied. He was too badly wounded to be conscripted into the French army. He set himself up as an innkeeper. The inn covered the comings and goings of our spies. Information was left with him. He arranged it and organized future projects and sent reports on to my department."

"A dangerous position indeed. And *just* like him."

"His description of himself as a spider lying in his web is apt. I will not fib to you about the danger. It *was* dangerous. But up to a week before Waterloo he was alive, and it is my belief he still lives. I do not know why he has not come home."

"But *where* is he?"

"Assuming he is still where he bought the inn, he is in Fréhel on the coast directly south of the Channel Islands."

Constance sighed, looking into the distance blindly. "Then my next move is obvious, is it not?"

"It is?" asked Jack warily.

"Of course. I must travel to Fréhel, where I may find out for myself what has become of him."

"Ah. Well . . . hmm . . ."

She turned a quick look his way. "It *is* possible, is it not? There is, surely, no danger for English visitors to France now that the war is ended?"

"France is not yet, I fear," he said carefully, "an entirely comfortable place for the English." Jack lifted his hat and brushed the hair back off his forehead. "Napoleon's Grand Army has been disbanded, of course, but Frenchmen quite understandably resent the English, who were foremost in beating them all hollow. Then, too, traveling through France is not easy, even where that attitude does not exist."

Constance stared off into the park, then turned to look at him. "Are you suggesting I should *not* go?"

He frowned. "Who would escort you?"

Constance's brows climbed her forehead. "Escort me? Sir, I am of an age, surely, when I no longer require escort!"

"Do not look so much like an outraged kitten or I'll pick you up and unruffle your fur and set you to purring."

He could have kicked himself when she blushed rosily, her eyes darting to meet his and rushing away.

"I apologize," he said softly. "That was outrageous, not that you do *not* tempt a man," he added still more softly.

Then, her blush returning, he promised himself that kick just as soon as he found himself alone. Their eyes met, held, seemed to draw each far into the other's mind and soul.

Constance, who had been thankful to feel her blush fading, felt it return at the warm look in his eye. She forced herself to look away. Needing distraction, she glanced around, wondering where the children had gotten themselves to. Venetia was quietly dressing her baby. Val was nowhere in sight. The boy was gone.

Instantly and completely free of the odd compulsion his gaze ignited deep within her, Constance rose to her feet. "Val! Where has that dratted boy gone?"

"I'll look."

"We'll both look," she said in a firm, no-nonsense voice. "You go that way, please." She gestured toward St. James Park. "And I'll take Venetia down that path." She pointed. "We will return here to see what has been discovered."

Without waiting for agreement, she hurried to Venetia and helped the child put her dolly into the carriage. She encouraged the child to hurry. As they moved off, he heard her mutter, "Drat that boy. *Just* like his father! When I find him, I'll . . ."

Jack sighed. Children were something of a nuisance. Everything was going so well. Or should he, he scolded himself, thank his lucky stars that children *were* a nuisance? He debated both sides of the point as he strode off himself, his ears on the prick, his glance darting every which way on the look-out for a seven-year-old boy with a hoop.

For Lady Mordaunt's son.

A glimpse of sparkling blue caught his eye. He lengthened his stride. It occurred to him that, if the lad had gotten himself this far, the Serpentine would be temptation far beyond the power of any normally adventurous boy's ability to resist!

It didn't surprise Jack, therefore, that moment's later he heard a squawk followed almost instantly by a splash. He set off at a ground-eating run. As he rounded a well-trimmed hedge, he saw a man in a black coat hurrying up a path. *Late home,* thought Jack cynically as he strode on. He idly wondered what tavern enjoyed the servant's patronage and how soon the fellow would find himself dismissed by an outraged householder, thereby joining the unbelievably huge number of servants who were out of a place.

Yowls of outrage came from the direction of the water, and Jack put the hilarious sight of a scurrying upper-servant from his mind, rushing on near enough to see the boy lose his footing on the slick bottom mud, dunking himself, obviously not for the first time.

Valerian came up sputtering and attempted to wipe his face on his dripping sleeve. He looked up. "You pushed me!" accused the lad.

"I was nowhere near. I just got here," said Jack pacifically.

The boy scowled, his lower lip pushed forward. "*Somebody* pushed me."

"Very well, you were pushed."

Jack wondered if the boy's accusation was an attempt to excuse the fact he'd fallen in. Was it possible he had been pushed? Absurd, he decided. Why would anyone push a small boy into these shallow waters—the lake was not particularly deep and not particularly dangerous—unless, of course, the child panicked. But why, in any case, would someone push a child into danger?

"Come along, now. Lady Mordaunt's worried about you."

Jack held out his hand and lifted the dripping boy onto the bank. Dangling a trail of muddy weeds, the hoop appeared as well.

"Very well done, lad. You did not let it go. That was excellent thinking on your part, my boy."

Val looked at the hoop and grimaced. "I lost control of it," he admitted. "I'd just reached it when I was pushed." He gave the major one more suspicious glance, but seemed to decide he wouldn't accuse him again. "Connie will be angry," he added as he looked down at his exceedingly wet self. "So," he said and sighed, "will Willy."

"Who is Willy?"

"Nurse Willy. She's a great gun. Mostly." He held out his arm and took another look at his soaked coat. "Willy'll lock me up and throw away the key, I fear."

Jack studied the boy, who had a tendency to sound older than his seven years. "No tutor yet?" he ventured.

"Connie helps with my Latin. Willy is good with sums and such like." He shrugged. "Next year I'll go to the vicar to start Greek and more advanced Latin. In a couple of years I'll get to go to Winchester."

"Winchester, hmm? Your father's school?" The boy nodded. "I'm an Eton man, myself."

Val gave him a disparaging look. "That's too bad," he said in a patronizing tone.

Jack smothered a laugh. "I rather liked Eton," he said, and found he had to curb a defensive note.

It was a wonder how a very young boy could imbibe such a deal of school spirit even before attending his school. Jack searched his mind, trying to remember if his cousin's son was anything like so precocious, and decided the boy was not. He was pretty certain Mary's boy wouldn't begin Greek until he was ten or eleven, and Latin wasn't usually begun until a child was well ahead with reading and writing English.

"Does your mother teach you your letters as well?"

"She did." The boy shivered.

About to ask who taught them to him now, Jack berated himself for keeping the child standing around. They needed to get him home and into dry clothing before he caught a chill. Or worse. "Come along, now." He lifted the dirty hoop from the boy's limp grasp. "We need to find your mother and get you home."

The boy gave him a sharp look, but trotted along docilely enough. However, when he saw Constance and his sister approaching he broke away and joined them. Jack came up to them as he was telling how his hoop had gone into the water and that when he was reaching for it someone pushed him in.

"I didn't mean to get all wet. Truly, Connie."

"Some boy pushed you, you mean?"

"I don't know. Didn't see him, did I?"

A flashing mental image of the scuttling upper-servant crossed Jack's mind and, his mind working in its usual complicated fashion, he connected that to the conversation he'd overheard between Rhino and a servant.

He gave Val a sharp look. Then he reminded himself that Rhino had been nowhere near. Besides, why kill this boy? If his father were not alive it would make a difference to the heir presumptive, whoever that might be. Wilmot Mordaunt, perhaps? Was he heir presumptive? He hadn't liked Mordaunt. Not at all. But he'd no proof . . . and besides, as he'd already calculated, with Selwyn still alive it made no sense to kill the son.

Jack pushed such thoughts to the back of his mind. He looked at Lady Mordaunt and said *sotto voce,* "Very likely just fell in, don't you think? And doesn't want to admit it?"

"Val is normally a very truthful boy." Constance frowned. "If he says he was pushed—"

"But why would anyone do such a thing?"

Constance briefly considered her cousin's threat to kill the boy. Surely that had been bluster, one of those things said in anger, but not meant literally. At least . . . no, surely not.

"I haven't a notion," she said sharply, refusing to look at Jack. "I'd better get him home."

"There is the chance, of course, that another boy pushed him in, but I saw no one around when I reached the lake, and I wasn't much more than a moment getting there after I heard him call out as he went in."

"You speak of me as if I were not here," said the boy, widening his stance and glaring. "I *was* pushed."

"All right," said Jack amiably. "You were. If we get you home and get you changed, then, very likely, no harm done. Shall we go?"

A stray breeze crossed their path and the boy shivered. "Yes. I think we should go, Connie," he said. Then he turned, bowed toward Jack and said, politely, "Thank you kindly for helping me with my hoop, sir, and for giving me a hand out of the water." That done, he turned back to Constance. "Can we go now?" he asked a trifle plaintively.

Jack met Constance's eyes and found there a smile to match his own. He wondered at the way he felt so attracted to a married woman, something he'd avoided since he'd become old enough to have any sense.

Married women were trouble, and he didn't need that sort! Still, he couldn't stop wishing he *were* the sort of rake who lightly took a married woman into his bed. It was commonly enough done. After all, most marriages were mere contracts made to provide an heir, and were planned around property arrangements. There was little motivation for loyalty to one's spouse. Far too many women were bored once they'd produced the heirs required by their husbands. Add to that too many men ready to take advantage of such boredom, and the results were not surprising.

But he'd already decided this woman was not such a one. And long ago he'd decided he was unwilling to become the sort of man he'd always rather despised.

"I'll escort you to your residence," he said gruffly, angry at himself for the thoughts running through his head.

"That will not be necessary," she insisted, giving him a sharp glance at the tone of his voice.

"I think it is. A woman should not walk the London streets alone, whatever one does in your Cornish village."

She didn't argue, but neither would she take his offered arm. "You are something of a tyrant, are you not, Major St. Aubyn?"

"Do you think so? Just because I worry about your safety?"

"Is *that* why you wish to escort me?"

The fact he also wished to know exactly where Mordaunt

House was situated, was, he felt, irrelevant. He could discover *that* information in any one of a dozen different ways! "Of course," he said virtuously, hiding any slight feelings of guilt behind what he recognized was nothing more than rationalization.

"Then I must offer you an apology. I fear I must have misinterpreted a certain look I noted in your face a moment ago."

If he'd allowed his thoughts to appear in his face, then she had reason to be wary, thought Jack ruefully. "I am an honorable man, Lady Mordaunt. You need have no fears of any sort when in my company." She stopped and he halted as well, turning to her. "You live here?" he asked, glancing at the narrow gate set in a high wall which nearly hid the house.

"This is the side gate, of course. I cannot allow Val, in his present condition, to cross the hall. Besides, if we enter from the back I may order up a hot bath for him." She gave the boy a worried look. "I do hope there were no miasmas in that water which will lay him low. Caring for a sick child in Cousin's Mordaunt's house would not do. It would be the final straw, I believe, for our cousin!"

"Connie," said the boy scornfully, "I merely wetted myself. I did not *drink* the nasty stuff."

"Not at all?"

"You think I've forgotten how to swim just because we're in London a few days?" asked the boy still more scornfully.

Jack laughed. "Good lad. Now, off with you and allow your Willy to care for you." He dropped to his haunches. "Good–bye, Miss Mordaunt," he said to Venetia, and again touched her curls lightly.

The little girl looked up at Connie, back to Jack. She put her finger in her mouth.

"Come dear. Give the gentleman your best curtsy,"

urged Constance, wishing the proprieties over so she could get Val inside.

The girl obediently bobbed.

"And good day to you, Lady Mordaunt." Before replacing his hat he automatically brushed back his hair. "Please don't make plans for going to France alone. I've a notion which I'd like to discuss with you. Perhaps we might meet tomorrow at about the same time and in the same place?"

Constance paused for an instant, then nodded. She opened the gate. "I must take Val in. Good–bye, Major, and thank you for finding out about Selwyn."

"Silly Selwyn, for staying away from you a moment longer than he must," said Jack softly, forcing a lightness he didn't truly feel. Selwyn *was* behaving in a ridiculous fashion.

She pursed her lips, obviously repressing a smile, and shook her head. The door shut, but for a moment he could not bring himself to move away. Did she, too, feel that odd connection which seemed to bind them together for better or for worse?

Jack turned away, strolling to the corner where he stopped short. The butler–type he'd seen in the park with Rhino was coming out the entrance of Mordaunt House. As the major strode back toward the Horse Guards, his mind churned. For a moment Jack pictured the back view of the servant running away from the lake and wondered if possibly . . . oh, surely not.

But if the butler were willing to try himself, why talk to Rhino? Or had it been mere chance, coming on the boy just then?

Oh, of course not, but still . . .

Jack forced his circling thoughts to behave. It *was* the man he'd seen arguing with Rhino. That was definite. For a moment Jack reviewed what he'd heard pass between the upper servant and the scum–ragtag to whom he'd been talking. That bit of scum was not one with whom a man of honor would deal. Not that this particular servant looked particularly honorable, of course.

But what they'd discussed! Had it truly been murder, as he'd thought at the time? Jack grimaced.

He'd better brush up his thieves's cant. Perhaps he'd also set an old acquaintance who lived in the same slum to listening for rumors concerning Rhino's newest doings. Yes, Jack decided, he'd set Marrow onto it. Marrow was one of the few residents in St. Giles who actually *preferred* to pick up an honest wage.

And he mustn't forget to drop a word in the Runner's ears. Rhino must not succeed in this particular bit of evil, whether the tadpole involved was Valerian Mordaunt or some other child. And he *wouldn't*. Not if Jack had anything to do with it.

The next question was whether or not he should warn Lady Mordaunt that he believed her son was in danger. Would she believe him? Jack set himself to analyzing the situation and decided that the boy would not be harmed while inside Mordaunt's house. Mordaunt wouldn't want to be associated with any hanky panky.

So?

The danger, if danger there was, would be when the boy left the house . . . and that could be countered if guards were set to watch him. Now, whom did he know who would take on the job of seeing to the boy's safety? *Still more important,* someone who would not bungle it.

Chapter 3

Jack grinned when his cousin, Lady Mary Grinnel, glanced up from her sewing, a sharp look questioning his request. Seeing the grin, Mary tipped her pretty nose into the air. "I do not see how you can expect me to actually invite this . . . this *woman* into my home," she said.

"It is the *children* I wish you to invite. Did I not say so?" he asked, forcing a teasing note. He wondered if he had the patience to cajole his cousin, as would be necessary if he were to smooth over her rather wobbly self-esteem.

"And just how may I invite the children and leave this . . . this *woman* in her place."

"Since her husband, as I told you, is a baron, I do not understand why you continue to call her"—Jack's voice rose to a falsetto—"this . . . this *woman.*"

Mary giggled. Dropping her sewing, she raised both hands to hide a smile. "Is that what I sound like?" she asked from behind her hands.

"*Exactly* like. Our well remembered but sadly unregretted neighbor could have done it no better."

"Really, Jack, you shouldn't make fun of the dead." Mary put on a prim look. "It is not at all polite."

"You mean it is the same as talking about someone behind their back? They cannot defend themselves? Hmmm . . ." He pretended to consider. "Perhaps there is something in what you say, but how could our long departed neighbor have defended herself against the charge of snobbishness when it is true that she was just such a one?"

"Yes, she was," sighed Lady Mary. "I think she rather gloried in it. You are very right to warn me against such a despicable trait. Still . . ." A wary look in her eye, she glanced sideways through long, silky lashes at the cousin on whom she'd showered her first feelings of young love. "Jack, you haven't done something truly silly and, well, hmm—" She broke off, pouting. "Jack, you are laughing at me!"

"If I am, Mary m'girl, then you richly deserve it. You are, are you not, accusing me—or, should we say *attempting* to accuse me in your unique and stammeringly charming fashion—of having developed a *tendre* for Lady Mordaunt?"

"And if I am?"

"Pish, tosh, and fiddle," said Jack promptly.

That he was strongly attracted to Constance Mordaunt, he vowed silently, did not suggest a *tendre*. Besides, even if it were to grow into one, it was none of his cousin's business.

"Truly, Jack?" asked his cousin wistfully.

"Truly."

That Mary had, at an early age, married another and much more suitable man, did not mean she must relinquish her belief that she had ownership of her big cousin, in some vague and undefined way, a situation of which he was well aware. So, although his use of the old nursery words, the pish, tosh and fiddle, almost soothed her, they did not, quite, do the trick. He wondered just what he *could* say in order to convince her.

Again Mary eyed Jack. "What is she like, this"—she stopped at Jack's incipient frown—"this Lady Mordaunt?"

"Taller than you are by a good hand's breadth. Hair which I believe would be nearly dark as night if one were allowed to see it, but she covers it with caps and hand—trimmed bonnets. Some might say she has the face of a minx, including the requisite dimple, but," he finished thoughtfully, "she's very near to, if not already past, the quarter century."

"All of twenty–five?" asked Mary, pretending shock. She was all of twenty–six herself, when she could bring herself to admit it. "Dear me."

"But she would have to be, would she not?" argued Jack. "The boy told me he was seven and the girl is five. Even at twenty–five, she would have been a mere child of seventeen when she wed."

Jack knew but ignored the fact that Mary was a month or two less than seventeen when *she* wed. Nor did that fact interfere with Mary's nodding in a portentous manner.

"All of twenty–five," she repeated. "Poor thing, to have seen so little of her husband. Why, he'll have been at war nearly the whole of their married life, will he not?"

"Very nearly. I doubt if they were together a full year in all, although he must have been home at least once beyond their marriage trip. The girl is, as I said, only five."

"You are very much the tease, Jack, are you not?" asked Mary archly, again eying him through her lashes, this time with a testing sort of look.

"In what way do you suggest I am teasing you?"

"You know very well," she said, with an airy pretense at a sophistication which hadn't quite a true ring to it, "that it is not exactly necessary for the *husband* to have been home." She lowered her lashes and looked at him through narrowed lids.

"*I* am aware," said Jack, suddenly austere, "but it is not necessary that *you* know of such things."

Mary giggled, but a touch of embarrassment was to be heard, assuming one knew her as well as her big cousin did. Jack rather wondered at it, but put the question aside when Mary, putting on a spurious dignity, scolded, "You forget I am no longer a mere child, Jack. I have been about the world now for ever so long. You must not think me still wrapped in cotton wool. I hear *all* the *on dits,* and have for *years.*"

"Oh. Merely an *on dit.*"

He relaxed, allowing himself to ignore the odd notion that his cousin was involved in an *affaire* or was thinking of becoming involved—something he could not approve, whatever his own behavior had been or might be again with certain females of his acquaintance. Certain *unmarried* females.

"In *that* case," he added for good measure.

"You thought that *I . . .*" Lady Mary rose from her seat and flounced over to the window, where she turned. The light behind her making of her short blond hair a halo, she pointed a stern finger at the door. Raising her nose in the air, she intoned, "Go!"

Jack, unimpressed, crossed his arms and stood his ground. "Not until you agree to invite Lady Mordaunt and her children here for an afternoon."

Mary recalled that Jack had never been taken in by her more dramatic performances and returned to her seat, a frown marring her brow and a plaintive note in her voice. "But Jack, I do not know this woman. *You* say it's an excellent Cornish family and an ancient title, but surely in that case they would have come to town, and I'd have been introduced. The only Mordaunt I've met is not at all the thing, and I'd not have met *him*, except that he thrust himself upon us in the park one day." She wrinkled a fastidious little nose, then tipped her head, curiosity filling her gaze. "I think, although I do not *know*, that he wanted something from dear Grinnel." Silently, she asked a question of her older and more knowing cousin.

"Did he now?" said Jack slowly, new notions running through his head. He must, he thought, have a quick conversation with Mary's husband. "That Mordaunt would be the cousin with whom they are staying, of course. Lady Mordaunt told me he is not happy with her visit and wishes she would depart. I think," he added casually, having realized he'd said too much and hoping to curtail Mary's questions, "that he must be something of a screw if not an out and out outsider."

"Jack, you will not use such language in my drawing room!"

"Very well. If you insist." Jack adopted a formidable air and struck a pose. "Mordaunt," he intoned, "is, at a minimum, a miser, but may be worse. It is therefore not unlikely he has put himself beyond the bounds of polite society." He strolled closer and looked down at his cousin, his eyes twinkling in that way that could still make Mary catch her breath. "You'll write Lady Mordaunt an invitation?"

"Oh, all right." Mary hunched a shoulder, turning slightly. "I think I've a free day next week. If not, then the following." She waved a hand, limp at the wrist.

"Oh no, my girl!" He caught the wrist, holding it a trifle

firmly. "None of your tricks, now. You'll see her tomorrow or the day after at the latest. I have said that Mordaunt wishes to see the back of Lady Mordaunt and her children. You will not dillydally and put it off until my new friends have left town!"

"You're cruel, Jack. What if it is discovered this woman is not what she seems?"

"You are the cruel one, my dear, not *I."* Jack stared down at her. "Actually, Mary, I am rather shocked."

Mary squirmed under that look until she took herself in hand and remembered she was no longer a schoolgirl whose every effort went into pleasing her cousin. She primmed her lips and, once again, turned her head away.

"Mary, please do this for me. I've a reason. Or, at least, I fear I *may* have a reason. I cannot get it out of my head that Mordaunt's man . . ."

Jack shook his head, wondering what it was that made him a gabble grinder in his cousin's presence when it would be better for everyone if he shut his mouth and kept it so.

He drew in a deep breath and began again. "I wish for you to know them, particularly the children, and discover for yourself that they are a delightful young family much in need of your patronage."

Jack didn't often ask a favor of her, and Mary discovered that somewhere within her there was still just a trifling bit of that old need to please him. She sighed. "Tomorrow, then. I am off to Richmond Park and a picnic party the following day. I'll write the invitation now, shall I?"

"Please do. You do that and I'll deliver it myself, if you'll trust me with it."

Mary rose and moved to her writing desk.

"Is your exceedingly efficient and knowledgeable husband at home?" he asked as she sorted through the clutter for a pen whose point had not been splayed beyond use.

"Grinnel?" She decided the one she held would do and uncapped her tiny cut glass bottle of ink. "You surely know I'm not the sort of wife who insists on keeping her husband in her pocket!" She set pen to paper and then added, "You must ask Lummy."

Jack chuckled. "I wonder where your exceedingly odd butler ever got such a name."

"Where does one ever get one's name?" she asked crossly. "One is born with it."

"In our circles, that is true. But in his? I wonder."

"Jack, you have the most suspicious nature of anyone I've ever known . . . except, of course when you *should* be suspicious," she finished tartly, with a meaningful look at the note she was sanding and about to fold and seal. She glanced from it to him.

Jack sighed. "Mary, if you refer again to my new acquaintance, then say so. I believe you will find Lady Mordaunt as delightful as I do, but perhaps not, of course."

"I have invited her here, and her children, for a nursery party, but I need not pretend to make her my friend."

"You put on that Friday face, m'girl, and she'll turn tail at the sight and never again come near you."

"I believe you are using more of that nasty language," she said, twisting aside.

"Friday face? Turn tail?" He gave her an incredulous look. "Mary," he scolded, "you are becoming a bore!"

She swung around, turning a look of horror on him. "I am not!"

"Then refrain from acting the prig," he suggested in a kindly tone. "I'll just have a word with Grinnel before leaving." He chucked her under the chin, plucking the invitation from her lax fingers. "Come on, girl. Give Cousin Jack a smile," he coaxed.

She scowled fiercely. "You are mean and nasty and over-bearing and always lecturing and—"

"Hmm," he interrupted. "As I recall this tactic, it can go on forever, listing all my many faults, beginning from when I was at Eton and you in the nursery. I hope you do not try that one on Grinnel, my dear. You'll catch cold at that, I think!"

Jack exited before she could do more than look around her for something to throw. Why, wondered Lady Mary, settling back into her seat, had she ever thought herself in love with that . . . that . . . She could think of nothing bad enough although she searched her memory. Suddenly she grinned, her mercurial emotions doing a complete turnabout. What she needed, of course, was her cousin. Jack would know exactly the proper thieves's cant for which she'd vainly searched her mind.

Why, she wondered, rising to her feet, did he wish to speak with Grinnel?

Jack strolled into Grinnel's library. "Got a moment for me?" he asked.

Frowning, Lord Grinnel looked up from the speech he was to give in the House of Lords that evening. "Oh. You," he said. "What can I do for you?"

"Such a gracious welcome," grinned Jack.

Grinnel chuckled. He sat back in his seat and ran strong fingers, a sprinkling of hair along their backs, along the stiff edge of an old–fashioned goose quill pen. A goodly supply of sharpened quills stood in a wide–mouthed vase before him, and he reached to move it from between himself and his visitor.

"You caught me at just the wrong moment, Jack. A certain phrase simply will not come right." His brows rose and he raised one hand, forestalling Jack's offer to help. "No sir! Don't even suggest it! I'll never again ask *your* aid! I well remember the ridiculous suggestions you made the last time this happened when you were near. I got to that part of my speech and forgot my carefully coined phrases, *yours* filling my head, you see. I burst out laughing, much to the disgust of my fellow peers. Worse, I'd no way to justify myself for doing so. It was most embarrassing. I was forced to sit down in disgrace. So, instead, you tell me what *I* may do for *you*?"

Jack pushed a stack of books aside and sat on the corner of the desk. "You may tell me what you know of a certain Wilmot Mordaunt."

Grinnel grimaced. "Discovered he filled war contracts with shoddy goods, have you? I can't say I'm at all surprised. The man's a rank outsider," said his lordship, unknowingly confirming Jack's opinion.

"Tell me."

Grinnel nodded toward the decanter set on a side table. "Pour us some of that Madeira, and I will. Yes, I know you'd prefer a canary or some lighter wine, but I prefer the heavier reds. Be a friend, Jack, and bring me a glass."

When both men had settled back with wine and cigars Grinnel told Jack how Mordaunt had first scraped up an acquaintance with him at his club. "And I'd like to know who brought the man into it, too," said Jack's host with a frown. "Ah well, water over the dam, I suppose. In any case, he wanted me to put in a word for him. Some contract for gun barrels. Seemed he had an interest in one of the new foundries. I managed to squirm out of that, but later he accosted Mary and myself when we were walking in the park. Now you must understand this was some years ago, and poor Mary was not yet up to snuff. It became quite obvious that once he'd forced an introduction to her, he would make a nuisance of himself and Mary would not know how to snub him. In fact," added Grinnel, frowning, "now I come to think of it, the knave went out of his way to give me that impression!"

Jack thought of the obese creature who had come to his office. Disbelieving, he asked, "You can't mean he's a rake?"

"Oh no. Not *that* sort of nuisance. I could easily enough have dealt with that. No, he's the sort who inserts himself into private conversations and then makes it impossible for one to ignore him, unless one has a cast–iron skin, which my Mary does *not*. Poor dear. She'd have, reluctantly of course, been introducing him right and left from then on whenever he found her with someone he wished to meet, a situation I very much wished to avoid."

"So?"

"So I told him I'd see him at our club the next afternoon. It was a different contract that time, blankets, I think, and I said I'd do what I could for him on one condition. It would be only that once, and he would never come within yards of my wife, ever, in the future."

"And he shrugged," suggested Jack, "said there are plenty of fish in the sea, and agreed to your condition."

"He said something very like that." Lord Grinnel, who had been squinting through his wine at the sun streaming in the study windows, gave Jack a sharp look.

"*Has* he come nosing around?" asked Jack.

"I believe not."

"Hmm."

"Why do you ask, Jack?" asked Grinnel, watching his guest's changing expressions through a few moment's silence.

"Hmm? Why? Oh, just a whim, I believe."

Grinnel chuckled. "Which means you do not mean to tell me. Very well. But if you are going all broody on me I do wish you'd do it elsewhere, so that I may get on with my speech." He tapped the plumed end of his quill on the papers spread out on his desk.

Jack nodded, finished his wine in two swallows, rose to his feet, and strolled toward the door. "Thanks for the information, by the way. It gives me some notions which I must mull over. But as you requested, I'll do it elsewhere." He grinned.

Jack collected his hat and cane, had a few words with the butler Lummy about an upcoming pugilistic battle, and went on his way. After a prime beefsteak at his club, *his way* led to the park, where he waited only a *seemingly* unbearable time before he was able to deliver his cousin's invitation into Lady Constance Mordaunt's own strong but beautiful hands.

Jack's decision to hand deliver the note required little explanation. Ignoring the fact it was an excuse to see her again, he didn't trust Wilmot Mordaunt's butler to give it to her. At least, not without first showing it to Mordaunt. And he didn't want that fine gentleman aware that he was still taking an interest in the family in spite of—perhaps *because* of—Mordaunt's insistence he not bother.

Besides, delivering his cousin's note personally allowed him another opportunity to talk to an intriguing woman. Not that that was relevant, of course.

The next day Constance took an extra good look at her niece and nephew. They were neat and, for the moment, clean, their cheeks rosy and eyes sparkling with the thought of the treat before them.

Constance hoped very much that it *would* be a treat. The major, when he'd handed over the invitation, had said in a casual, offhand manner which immediately set her on the alert that she was not to be put off by his cousin's manner when first they met. She was to ignore it if Mary were to seem a trifle starched up. Mary, he insisted, would come down off her high horse soon enough if Lady Mordaunt simply acted in her usual comfortable and common-sensical fashion.

Constance wondered if Lady Mary would also have hoity-toity notions about how children should behave. Constance's mouth compressed into a thin line. If Lady Grinnel thought she could condescend to a Mordaunt, she'd find herself much mistaken. Constance wouldn't put up with it.

If Lady Grinnel *did* try it on, the visit, Constance decided, would very likely turn into the shortest on record. She certainly *would* act simply and common–sensically, just as Major Lord St. Aubyn suggested: She'd simply and sensibly *leave* at the least sign of distress to the children.

So, although she hid it well, Constance arrived at the Grinnel townhouse with a very small, in fact so small as to be invisible, chip on her shoulder. And, when Lady Grinnel would have casually sent the children up to the nursery with a maid, Constance sensibly suggested it might be well if they were to accompany them, just until the Grinnel and Mordaunt children met and were comfortable together.

Constance didn't wait for a response beyond the blink of surprise she noted before she turned away and followed Val and Venetia up the stairs. She wondered what her hostess would do, but didn't pause in her determination to ascertain that the children would not be made uncomfortable with their new acquaintances.

There was a long silence in the hall below, and Constance would dearly have liked to turn and ascertain the expression on Lady Grinnel's face. If it were half so startled as Constance thought it might be, then it would be a precious sight indeed. Constance sternly suppressed a smile, but the tightening of her cheeks brought the dimple into existence, anyway.

The maid, children, and Constance were nearly to the top of the first flight of stairs before Lady Mary decided to follow. She must have hurried a trifle, because she caught up with them just as they finished climbing the third flight and were about to turn down the hall.

The day nursery door was open. Inside was a stern woman wearing a well-starched apron, neat gray sleeves covering heavy arms, and large red hands holding the tiny paws of a child on either side. Constance ignored the nanny and looked at the children, smiling.

"Hello," she said softly.

As Mary moved into the room one of the children, the girl, tugged loose from her nurse's hand and ran forward to hide her face in her mother's skirts. "Child," said Mary warningly, pushing the girl away. "You must not muss your mother's gown!"

Constance blinked, repressed what she would love to have said at this further proof Lady Mary knew nothing about children and looked at the older Grinnel child. "May I introduce Venetia and Val Mordaunt to your notice, young sir?"

The Grinnel heir tipped his head, but he frowned slightly. Tugging his hand free of his nanny's hold, he stepped nearer. "My name is Lord Antony. I am eight. That is my sister, Lady Rosalind. She's still a baby," he finished scornfully.

"I'm five!" said Rosalind, peeping around from behind her mother.

"And Venetia is soon to be six. Perhaps you would like to see her new baby?" Constance pushed her niece, hugging the doll, out a little farther. "Do you have babies?"

"I have dolls," said the girl somewhat scornfully for a five–year–old, but her curiosity was roused and she stepped around further so that she could look the stranger over. Venetia immediately put her finger in her mouth and looked at her toes.

"I have toy soldiers," said Antony.

"Do you?" asked Val politely, showing a proper amount of interest. "May I see them, please?"

Antony looked up at his nurse and Constance finally looked at the woman, as well. What she saw did not please her. The woman was obviously a martinet who wanted nothing happening in her nursery which she did not order and direct.

Before a negative could come from the nurse's pursed mouth, Constance moved a step or two nearer. "Would you show us, please?" she asked, looking down at the boy. She turned toward Lady Grinnel, an act which presented a shoulder to the nurse. "My Val would be fascinated. He has a few lead soldiers which were his father's, but not so many as to make a proper battle formation—or so poor Val tells me often and often!" She chuckled that warm inviting chuckle which was hers alone.

"It's true," said Val softly to the boy.

Mary capitulated to the stronger personality of her guest. Either ignoring the signals radiating from the nurse, or, more likely, actually not noticing them, she traipsed lightly across the large sunny room to a cupboard.

"Come, Antony," she said. "I'll help you bring them out."

Antony, shrugging loose from the nurse's attempt to hold him back, followed his mother, calling to Val to come along. "We'll have a right old battle. And I," he said slightly belligerently, "will be the English!"

The boys squabbled about that for half a moment before Val backed down. "I am your guest," he said stiffly. "I will be the French. And although they did not win at Waterloo, I will win *our* battle. You'll see!"

Lady Grinnel was helping the boys get started, so Constance looked from one shy little girl to another. Opening her oversized reticule, she pulled out Venetia's favorite book. "Shall I read to the two of you while the boys play?" she asked.

Venetia at once plopped down on the floor. Rosalind looked at her as if she were quite mad. But when Constance, too, arranged herself on the floor and held out her hand, the girl didn't even glance at the nurse for permission. She came at once and sat at Connie's other side, looking with interest at the book.

"Do you know this one?" asked Constance.

The child shook her head.

"Then you will have the pleasure of hearing it for the very first time." Constance forced herself to send a bland look straight at the servant. "Nurse, since both Lady Grinnel and I are here, perhaps you may have a little unexpected rest. I suggest you adjourn to the kitchen for a cup of tea, if that meets with Lady Grinnel's approval. We will ring when we are ready to leave, so you needn't worry that the children will be left alone."

Nurse looked to where Lady Grinnel, her arm around her son, was on her knees at a low table watching the boys set up their armies. Her ladyship had just asked why her son put a man on horseback well away from all the other soldiers.

"That is Wellington, of course," said the future Lord

Grinnel as if his mother should have known. "He must see all of what is going on so that he can give his orders."

The lad looked across the table to where Val was carefully arranging a long line of blue-coated soldiers. The two boys' eyes met.

"Women," mouthed Antony, obviously disgusted. Val nodded sober agreement.

Constance, after noting that bit of by-play, returned to helping the girls become comfortable with one another. It was obvious the boys, united by their opinion of the distaff side of life, were already well on the way toward forming a firm friendship!

Chapter 4

Some little time later Mary and Constance went down to a first floor salon. "You are very good with children," said Mary just a trifle wistfully. "I have often and often wished to play with mine in just that fashion. She pulled her lower lip between her teeth and cast a worried look toward Constance.

"I know. That nurse! A tyrant, is she not?"

"Hmm." Mary nodded, relieved that Lady Mordaunt was so understanding. "I have never liked her."

"Then why do you not find another?" Constance paused only a fraction of a second, a trifle of color warming her cheeks. "Pardon me. I spoke quite out of turn. It is likely she is an old retainer, and those are exceedingly difficult to be rid of. I know exactly how it is. We've a housekeeper with whom I've battled for years. She and I see eye to eye on practically nothing, but she came to Mordaunt Hall well over thirty years ago and there is no moving her."

Mary sighed. "That is not the case with our nurse. I

think I was too young when Antony was born for me to assert myself, and have since merely allowed myself to be intimidated by her. That air she has of always being right, of always knowing what is best!'' Mary shook her head.

Then she realized she'd lowered her guard with this woman whom she'd been determined to prove a mushroom. Knowing it would look very silly if she were to return to the cold and austere manner with which she'd intended treating Constance, she sighed again, this time in self–disgust.

''You are something of a surprise,'' she said, in lieu of the snubbing she'd meant to give Constance, given any opportunity at all.

''Oh? And how is that?''

''I don't know how it is, but somehow you do not seem married.'' Mary noted Constance's glowing cheeks. ''Oh my stupid *tongue!* Jack *will* scold. Besides, he explained you've had very little time with your husband. Of *course* you do not seem married in the way I mean. Do forgive me.''

By this time Constance had regained her countenance, but could think of no way short of embarrassing herself to disabuse Lady Grinnel of the notion she was married. Having impulsively but quite deliberately allowed Major Lord St. Aubyn to believe that she was, she decided she was stuck with it.

Instead of explaining she said, ''I can't think what you mean, but if you believe you require forgiveness, then, of course I forgive you. And I thank you, as well.'' Constance's smile faded. ''You cannot know how happy I was to receive your invitation. My cousin, Mr. Mordaunt, is unhappy with children in his house. He makes that clear not only to me but to them, as well. They are unused to such an ugly reaction from an adult, and are unsettled by it. I take them into the park as often as I can. It is to give them exercise, of course, but more to get them away from the odd atmosphere which pervades Mordaunt House." Constance gave a quick smile. "I do not know how it is that I have run on so, but there! You are very easy to confide in."

Mary was delighted at the compliment. "Do you think so? I've had little practice as a confidante, but I believe I know the rules. I will not discuss with anyone anything you confide in me."

Constance laughed. "Then you would make a good friend, I think."

Forgetting she'd ever suspected this woman of being an adventuress who would attempt to steal her Jack, Mary immediately made of her her bosom bow. She was instantly ready to confide *her own* most secret fears and hopes and disappointments and every aspect of her whole life, and *would* have done if Constance had not carefully steered the conversation into safer channels and done the trick so deftly poor Mary never knew how easily she was led.

Constance was about to suggest that the children had, perhaps, played enough for a first visit, when the double doors opened and the butler intoned, "Lord Temperance, my lady." Lummy bowed and faded back as a medium tall young man with wildly curling, red hair strode into the room. The door closed slowly, the butler peering through the crack for as long as he could do so.

However slowly they were closed, the doors latched just as his lordship approached the couch on which Lady Grinnel sat. The gentleman clasped his hostess's hand and placed something more, Constance thought, than a polite kiss upon it.

Nor was his look, intense and straight into Lady Grinnel's eyes, quite one which she'd have thought acceptable between a man and woman who were neither engaged nor, preferably, already married. When her ladyship turned a lovely rose shade she was sure the gentleman had overstepped himself, with or without the permission of the lady involved.

Constance cleared her throat.

Lady Grinnel, blushing still more furiously, turned a startled look Connie's way. "Lady Mordaunt! Do forgive me for allowing myself to become flustered by this arrant flirt and forgetting the niceties! Do allow me to introduce Lord Temperance." She giggled. "A more badly misnamed peer does not exist," she added, coyly teasing and flirting with a quick look up at him, which he didn't catch.

The gentleman was preoccupied with miming a pretense of surprise just as if he'd not previously noticed Constance. Her eyebrows arched derisively in response. His lips quirked, but he did not give over his outrageous behavior by one iota—even though he knew she saw through it, and that she knew he knew she had. Instead he grasped her hand, lifting it slowly with both of his strong, long–fingered hands, his eyes never leaving hers.

Lord Temperance halted the motion of hand to lips when Constance's mouth gaped and, she stared at him quite rudely in utter astonishment. Her gaze moved from his eyes to his hair and back to his eyes which she again, and quite obviously, compared one to the other.

"Yes, they are shocking are they not?" he said softly, and grimaced. "Not only misnamed, as my lovely hostess has proclaimed, but also mismatched!" He referred, of course, to the color of his eyes, the one definitely blue and the other a changeable hazel.

"Perhaps not so surprising to me as they might be to some who see them for the first time. I, sir, know an exact match to them," said Constance sternly. She pulled her hand from his loosened grip and frowned ferociously. "I believe we have nothing more to say to each other."

He straightened. "An exact match?"

Constance compressed her lips.

After a moment, when Constance would not look at him, Lord Temperance turned back to his hostess. He did not relax, however, and there was strain to his voice. His flirtation, with that touch of seduction about it, was neither quite so lighthearted nor half so seductive. He didn't stay more than the correct quarter hour for a morning call, and in that time he never once attempted to speak to Constance, nor she to him.

"What is it?" asked Mary when he left, her ladyship's gaze following him, rather wistfully thought Constance, all the way to the door. "Why were you so rude to him?" She turned back. "He is a harmless creature, I assure you," she said earnestly, "all talk and no action!"

Constance had to clear her throat before replying. "I would rather not explain, Lady Grinnel, if you will be so generous as to allow me that privilege. It is not my secret, you see. Will you *not* pry, please? Let us just say that we'll have to agree to disagree about your . . . cicisbeo?"

"Oh, he isn't!" exclaimed Mary. Then her face fell into sad lines. "I only *wish* he were. It would be such a *coup* for me. You see, no one captures Lord Temperance. He is a sly one who flirts and flirts but never settles to one lady for more than a moment. But isn't he delightful? And his is *such* a romantic story. . . ." Her voice trailed off.

"Romantic?"

"*I* think so. He was a fourth son, if you can believe it. He was in the army and fought in many a battle with never a wound, although he's been mentioned in dispatches for bravery. *He* wasn't touched, but an influenza took the earl, his father, and *two* of his brothers inside of a ten–day. His remaining brother inherited, of course, but he'd had no expectation of doing so, as, indeed, had not *our* Lord Temperance. In any case, that one, the last brother, became wild as bedamned—''

Lady Grinnel used the shocking curse so earnestly and with such innocence Constance decided her hostess was quoting someone.

"The men in that family often do, I've heard. Well! He went on a rampage in Tottinhill Fields which is a low vicious slum, you know, and, while he was drunk out of his mind, he was''—Mary's voice dropped to a whisper—''stripped naked and, because it was the dead of winter he froze to death! It was a terrible scandal. If it hadn't been for that red hair and a touch of those odd eyes, nothing so obvious as *our* Lord Temperance's eyes, he'd not have been identified.'' She sighed. "Ah, but *our* Lord Temperance is such a charmer, and nothing like so wild—unfortunately.'' Lady Grinnel rolled her eyes suggestively.

Again there was a touch of the wistful note despite the droll look. Constance spoke quickly before she could receive confidences she did not wish to hear. "A romantic story, indeed.'' She stood. "When he arrived I was about to suggest that the children had perhaps played together quite long enough. Perhaps one day you might bring them to the park.'' She smiled a quick self-deriding smile. "There I go again, assuming you will know exactly where I mean, as if there were only one small park in all of London! To *Green Park* near the Ice Houses, where they may run around and not worry if they shout or get overly excited? I would invite them, and you, to Mordaunt House, but, my cousin—''

"Do not explain. I have met Mr. Mordaunt.''

Mary, her gaze meeting Contance's, grimaced. Constance matched her look with a grimace of her own, and both smiled.

"The park sounds a lovely idea," said Mary, thinking it would give her an opportunity to talk again with this delightful young woman.

They arranged a time as they returned to the nursery. After promising the disappointed children that they could play again in the morning, before Lady Mary must prepare for her picnic, Constance told Val he must help Antony put away the soldiers and that Venetia must, quickly now, help Rosalind to put all of Rosalind's babies back to bed.

The nurse, who had been scowling mightily, unwound her arms from across her starched apron front, and watched, mouth agape, as these unwanted strangers quickly and without argument did as they were told, actually doing most of the work. Her own perfect charges weren't quite certain what it was required of them, never before having been asked to do such a thing!

"I shall bring my own nurse to the park tomorrow so that you may give yours time off, Lady Grinnel," said Constance firmly, not looking at the dragon she'd taken in dislike.

The nurse was about to respond that that would not be necessary, when her mistress spoke.

"What an excellent notion," said Mary. "Nurse, you will like to have an hour or so to yourself, I am sure." She began the comment firmly, but trailed off slightly toward the end, having made the mistake of looking into the woman's eyes. "Now, Nurse—"

"You will like to go shopping," interrupted Constance quickly, and the woman's mouth snapped shut on the scold she'd obviously been about to give. "Everyone needs time, occasionally, do they not, to get those little things one is always running out of, tooth powder, for instance." She smiled brightly, still not looking directly at the nanny.

"Children. Have you finished? Val, under the table? Yes. Just there. And Venetia? Ah, what a lovely family Lady Rosalind has. Have you your baby, Venetia? I see you do. Have you said thank you to Lady Grinnel? Yes, I see you have. Then, let us be off."

She smiled, said her own thank–yous as they went down the stairs, and breathed a sigh of relief when the big front door closed behind her. She wasn't even certain *why* she felt relief, except that sometime during her visit the notion had crossed her mind that a friendship with Lady Grinnel might prove a trifle exhausting. Likely it was simply that the complicated maneuvering to avoid intimate subjects and unwanted confidences would tire anyone.

Having suggested that Lady Grinnel and she become friends, though, she would now, she supposed, have to bear the consequences. It would take some doing, for she really did not wish to hear confessions of love for the wrong man or tales of past conquests, assuming the Grinnel marriage was of that order. Or complaints about Lord Grinnel's behavior if he strayed, making Lady Grinnel unhappy.

It will be necessary, she decided, *to continue doing my very best to continue avoiding confidences!* Constance's thoughts were brought to an abrupt halt as Lord Temperance stepped away from the wall and right into her path. "My lord?" she asked coldly.

"I must ask for an explanation of what you said to me inside."

There was nothing of the flirtatious gentleman about him now, but Constance was determined to give this rake a wide berth. For Ada's sake. For her abandoned friend who had been seduced and left to suffer the consequences. Constance supposed that it might have been one of his dead brothers who . . . but enough speculation. This man or another, it was not a family with which she wished to become acquainted.

"I suppose I cannot stop you asking," she said coldly, "but I have informed you *I've* nothing to say to *you.*" She attempted to move on, but again he stepped in front of her.

"Please listen to me," he said, speaking quickly. "The eyes are a family trait. They are more obvious in some than others. At the present time there are none so obviously mismatched as my own. If you have seen such, then I must know of it. A child, I presume? Perhaps, if you'll forgive the reference, a left hand offspring of my family and, if so, perhaps, in need?" He drew in a deep breath. "In which case, you'll surely admit I've a responsibility to see to that need."

"That is admirable, I suppose. However, the child I have in mind is not in anything approaching a desperate condition. Good day." It *was* admirable, if true. Constance backed down *slightly* in her mind, if not outwardly. She would write Ada Wright and ask her wishes. If Ada wanted this man to know of her plight, then Constance would inform him of it. If not, then not.

"Please do not leave me in ignorance."

The voice came from behind her. The words were simple and unaccented and somehow more impressive for being so. Constance found herself rather liking the man, as she had *not* when she'd observed his flirtatious manner in the drawing room.

"I will ask my . . . acquaintance . . . if I may tell you." It occurred to her that she might be leaving London before she could receive a reply from Ada. She turned. "Perhaps you will give me your card so that I may communicate her decision?"

Lord Temperance immediately patted his pockets and,

as he repeated the movements a streak of red touched his ears. "I seem to have forgotten my card case. May I ask where you are staying?"

"No. Give a card to Lady Grinnel. She will give it to me."

There was silence as he stared into her uncompromising visage. After a moment he sighed, stepped back, and bowed. He returned his hat to his head and watched them walk away from him.

Constance turned herself and the children, and Val tugged at her hand. "He looks like Clary," said the boy, speaking for the first time.

"Yes, he does. It is possible, Val, that he is a relative. Since Mrs. Wright is not in communication with her relatives or other members of the *ton,* then I think we will not mention Clarissa's existence to him?" She looked down at her nephew. "Do you understand, Val?"

"There is a secret and it is not ours to tell," said the lad promptly in his sometimes overly adult way.

Constance stared at him for a moment as she did whenever he came out with one of his pronouncements which hit a nail on the head quite sharply.

"Yes," she finally managed. "A secret. That is it exactly. Now come along. Willy will have a luncheon for you in the nursery, and then you must play quietly for a time while I go to a fitting for the gown I've ordered. Can you do that?"

"Cannot Willy take us to the park?"

"I don't know if she should be asked to. You become very wild in the park . . ."

"We'll be good," said the children in chorus and looked at her with big hopeful eyes.

Contance chuckled. "Well, in that case—"

The children whooped, and Constance gave an embarrassed glance to a passing couple. A word from her and the two again walked sedately at her side. For a while. Then, his eye caught by a particularly fancy rig and pair coming down the busy street, Val lagged a trifle behind.

What happened next happened in an instant. Val shouted, an anxious note in his voice, and Constance swung around. She discovered Lord Temperance was pulling Val back from a fall into the street.

"Val!"

"I was pushed!"

"He was, you know," said Lord Temperance. "I doubt it was deliberate, of course, but that man stumbled and bumped into the boy." He pointed to a short nattily dressed fellow weaving a rapid way between pedestrians farther down the street.

"And you caught him. Thank Heaven you did," said Constance, but there was a question in her eyes as well.

"You are wondering why I was near enough to do so." Lord Temperance's ears turned bright red. "There is no point, I suppose, pretending I was not following you. You see, I cannot allow you to disappear. I must know about this child. How old, where it may be found, everything you know."

"I wish I'd not allowed you to observe my surprise," said Constance, scowling fiercely.

He bowed, tacitly agreeing she'd erred in allowing him to discover she had knowledge he required.

"I can see," she continued, "that you are the sort who will make a great nuisance of himself." Her own ears took on the rosy tint of embarrassment. "Not that saving Val from harm as you just did was a nuisance, of course. Quite the contrary. But I cannot, without permission, tell you what you wish to know."

He sighed. "I will escort you to your home. I do not

think that funny little man deliberately tried to harm your boy, but I cannot be absolutely certain. I will see that nothing more of an untoward nature occurs.''

Constance gave him a steady look. ''And, of course, as a consequence, you will know where we stay.''

He grinned a quick slashing grin, a touch of the insouciant rake returning to his countenance. ''There is that, of course,'' he said a trifle airily.

She chuckled, unable to dislike his self–deriding tone. ''You, I think, have had your way far too often. But I know of no way I may forbid your accompanying us, so shall we continue?''

Constance collected the waiting children. She quickly determined that Val had not been overly shocked by the near accident, although the mere memory of seeing him about to fall under flying hooves and heavy wheels made her own heart tumble in a painful fashion. She started on down the street toward Mordaunt House and her temporary home.

Her very temporary home, she hoped.

In fact, she rather wished she'd never written her cousin, never informed him she was coming to London. Instead, she should have spent hard–saved money and, however against custom it was for a woman more or less alone, taken rooms at a hotel.

Chapter 5

"Well, Marrow," said Jack, studying the ill–dressed man who stood before his desk, hat in hand, "if that's all you know, that's all you know. But you'll find out more if you can, will you not? Rhino is up to something, and I fear it's a pretty nasty something. Unfortunately, he got used to living high during the war. I fear he's been spoiled."

"Rotten. *Always* rotten. Can't spoil a man more than rotten," said Marrow laconically. "I'll get you what word I can, but don't know if'n I'll find anyone willing to unbutton about our Rhino Biggens."

"You'll do your best." Major Lord St. Aubyn handed over a purse which clinked gently. "This may open sealed lips."

Marrow nodded, secreting the purse in a nimble–fingered way that set Jack to wondering how Marrow made his living when he couldn't find honest work.

"That will be all," said Jack.

The man fidgeted briefly with his hat, straightened only

a little from his slouching posture, and made a shambling progress toward the door.

"Ah! One moment, Marrow," Jack added, remembering Rhino's phrase. "What is a Flemish account?"

Marrow turned, his eyes narrowing in wry humor. "What you'll never deal in, Major. Means gettin' less than agreed, the Flemish pound being worth less then our own, ye ken—or, worse, getting nothing at all!"

Jack sighed. "In that case, having lost his *last* earnings, Rhino will be more than willing to do whatever he must to get the dibs in tune. He asked for a monkey, but I doubt he got so much."

Marrow's instant startlement quickly disappeared. "I'll see what I can see," he said with his usual blank expression, "but if you know those involved you might want to set a guard about them."

Jack met Marrow's unrevealing gaze. "Yes," he agred, "there are few things Rhino could do which would be worth quite that much money, are there not?"

"Not many," agreed Marrow in his usual laconic manner. "I'll be going, then."

"Normal channels will reach me," said Jack absently, his mind already worrying at the bits and pieces he'd seen and heard.

It occurred to him to wonder just how many lives stood between Wilmot Mordaunt and the Mordaunt title. Two questions were required to discover the answer, the first to discover *whom* to ask, and the second for the *asking*. The answer roused Jack's concern for Lady Mordaunt's son to the point that he instantly left the Horse Guards for a second visit to his cousin.

"I believe I'll swoon," said Lady Grinnel, her hands pressed to her bosom in a melodramatic fashion. "The sight of you again so soon gives me palpitations."

"Cut line. You met Lady Mordaunt?"

She bounced slightly in her seat. "You were *quite* right, Jack, and I was *quite* wrong. She is a delightful lady and my newest friend."

Jack gave cursory thought to all that would be involved in being admitted to his cousin's friendship, and wondered if he owed Lady Mordaunt an apology. Putting that from his mind, he spoke tersely, "I've a new request."

"To do with Lady Mordaunt?"

"With her and her delightful children. You are about to leave for Kent, are you not?"

"Yes." Mary pouted. "*I'd* prefer to stay in town the whole year round, but Grinnel says we'll do much better in the country. The weather has become so very hot and nasty, you know, so we leave next week." She sighed.

"Could you put your move forward?"

"Put it forward! Have you run mad?" Mary's bulging eyes relaxed and she giggled. "No, of course you have not. Manlike, it is far more probable that you simply haven't a notion what is involved when one moves from one house to the next. It will rush me to leave on Tuesday."

"Mary, Lady Mordaunt and her children must leave London immediately. I do not wish the Mordaunts to remain under their cousin's roof while I am gone, and it has become necessary for me to travel into France on an errand for the army. It is a leftover bit from the war which must be put right before I take up my new work."

"Just what business is it of yours where Lady Mordaunt and the children reside?" asked Mary, her suspicions once again aroused that she might be losing her cousin to *Another*.

"It is her husband I go to find. He should have returned to England at the end of the war. He did not. I must discover why."

"It is necessary that *you,* a *major,* find out why?"

Jack eyed her. "Mary, how much do you know or suspect about my work during the war?"

She bounced in her seat again, displaying an unladylike degree of amusement. *"You,* my dear cousin, were a *master spy."*

"The devil you say!" It had not occurred to him she knew half that much.

His reaction left Mary chagrinned, but she covered it with anger. "You will *not* use such language in my drawing room, Jack, or you will cease to be welcome here." Arms crossed, she turned away, the pout returning.

Sternly, Jack turned her face back to him. "Just where did you learn so exactly what it was I did?"

"I will not have secrets in my home, Jack," she said primly, but she eyed him a trifle warily.

"I should have known better than to speak of anything important when under any roof you occupy. You listened at keyholes!"

"I did not!" Her lips compressed into the mulish look he knew from old.

He was aware that she never lied to him. So, if she had not listened at the door when he discussed his work with her husband, how had she learned so much? He eyed her suspiciously and asked another question. Nevertheless, however he tried, he got no more from her on that head. So, instead and still sternly, he demanded to know how often she'd spoken of his work.

"I do not tell others things which should remain private with ourselves, Jack, but I will *not* be kept in the dark."

"Have you any notion of the damage you'd have caused if word *had* gotten round?"

"But it did not, did it?"

Once again he eyed her. "It is your saving grace, Mary,

that you can keep a secret. However, since you know so much, you will guess that Mordaunt was a field man. A report came just before the war ended. Another, a long lost one, has just now emerged from somewhere, but *he* has not." Concern tinged his voice. "We do not know what happened to him."

"You think ... something ... happened at the last instant?" Once again it flitted through Mary's mind that Lady Constance Mordaunt, rather than a *friend*, might be a *rival*. "He is *dead*, then?"

"I doubt it." Jack formed a quick flashing smile, briefly revealing even white teeth. "Selwyn Mordaunt is the sort who always falls on his feet. Nevertheless, there is a mystery." His brows formed a vee. "Why do you smile like that?"

"It is true that *I* cannot bear that there be a secret I do not know," she said pertly, "but *you* cannot bear that a mystery remain unsolved. I see why you will go to France. And you wish Lady Mordaunt and the children in Kent so they'll be nearby when you return with news, am I correct?"

"Yes. In part." He frowned again. "It is also true I want them out of that man's house as quickly as maybe. Tomorrow, if not *today!*"

"Why?"

"He ..." Almost Jack told her the truth, but, just in time, remembered he wished to keep her innocent of the true situation. "He makes the children unhappy. And they love the country. Besides, I must leave just as soon as I may organize my journey."

Mary eyed him for another long moment, but again decided to ignore the question of what he felt for Lady Mordaunt. "Perhaps you might escort them into Kent? It is not as if I would be long arriving." She frowned. "I suppose I *might* manage to leave Monday."

"If you write an invitation, I will take the Mordaunts down to Grinnel Manor and go on from there to the coast."

"You are very sure Lady Mordaunt will go with you."

"I will see that she does," he said.

He spoke with such unexpected grimness it instantly aroused Mary's suspicions. She wondered what new secret he would keep from her. *How* she detested secrets! Well, she decided complacently, she would uncover this one as she had all the rest. "I will speak with Lady Mordaunt myself, if you will escort me to see her."

Jack pulled the watch he'd inherited from his grandfather from his fob and opened it. "She will soon be with her children in the park."

"Then I will take my own children to the park to meet them."

Jack blinked. "You will *what?*"

Mary scowled blackly, partly at his tone and partly because of the guilt that tone roused. "Do not look so astounded. Do you think I cannot?"

"They are yours and of course you may, but that you ever *have* I doubt very much indeed."

"Then you are wrong!" she exclaimed, happy that, for once, *he* was at fault.

"I am?"

She ducked her head, blushing. "Not so *very* wrong," she admitted, in a rather small voice, "but I *have* taken them."

He still looked disbelieving, and after a grimace of irritation she confessed.

"Day before yesterday," she said. "We met Lady Mordaunt and her children there. Nurse was angry when we came home with Rosalind's skirts crushed and dirt on Antony's unmentionables." She glanced sideways. "Well, you see, his knickers were not exactly pristine after he and young Valerian had an, hmm, *argument* while playing marbles. I believe there were grass stains as well as dirt.''

"Surely it is her duty to care for the children's clothes. Why should she complain?''

"Absurd, is it not? I have asked Grinnel if I may find a new nurse.''

"And?''

Again she blushed, but this time it was the deep red and mottled flush of anger. "He questioned me about her and then scolded me for keeping her on for so long when I do not like her, which is very bad of him. He himself found her, before Antony was born, you know, and told me she came very highly recommended and I was to listen to her advice at all times!''

Mary's lower lip slipped between her teeth and her eyes got a bruised look Jack did not like. It was a look he'd seen often when she was young and, again and again, had not come up to her mother's high standards. It had been a long time since he'd last observed it.

Was Grinnel less tolerant than Jack had thought? He'd assumed the two well suited, but if Mary were unhappy . . . Ah! He could not think of that now. Mary's problems, if such existed, must wait until he sorted out Lady Mordaunt's situation and until he could be assured her son was no longer in danger from the man next in line for the barony.

"While you ready your children," he said, "I'll have a word or two with Grinnel.''

It occurred to him as he strolled toward the library that his cousin had rushed up the stairs with far greater alacrity than was usual, her normal languishing manner precluding any activity requiring such quickness. Suspicious, putting together what he recalled of the house's architecture and Mary's recent omniscience, he cheerfully greeting his cousin by marriage as he entered the library.

Grinnel responded in like manner, his voice trailing off as Jack strolled around the room, seemingly at random. Suddenly the major jerked at one of the bookcases. It obligingly moved several inches away from the wall, and he peered into a secret room thus revealed. He was just in time to see his cousin's skirts disappearing around the next to the last curve of a circular staircase set in the corner.

"Cousin!"

Jack pulled at the bookcase, widening the opening. Much more slowly then she'd ascended the steps, Mary returned to the bottom. Her feet dragging and her head hanging, she approached the opening. Finally she raised large, innocent eyes to meet his stern gaze.

"Yes, Jack?"

"I'll deal with this," said her husband. Grinnel stalked nearer, frowning from one cousin to the other. His voice was harsh when he demanded, "I would know how often you have hidden in my secret strong room, Mary, and listened to conversations that do not concern you."

Mary bit her lip, her skin paling. "I do not like secrets, my lord," she said in a small voice.

"You do not answer me."

In an even smaller voice, she said, "Quite often, actually."

"Mary, Mary." He sighed. "You are such a child! What am I to do with you?"

"You are not angry?" She brightened until she saw his expression. *Her* countenance then expressed abject misery.

"Of course I am angry. You've no business listening to conversations when those involved believe they are speaking in complete privacy."

She hung her head.

"Mary," said Jack gently, "you will not be ready to leave when I am if you do not prepare your children now."

"Yes, Jack."

She trailed back up the steps, turning her eyes from the men who watched her go.

"Mary," said her husband.

She stopped but didn't look around. "Yes, Grinnel?"

"You are never again to use this room to listen to what is none of your business."

"I hear you."

Jack chuckled. "My friend," he said softly to his lordship, "I suggest you make her promise. She doesn't break promises. Merely hearing what you say doesn't mean she's agreed, you see."

Mary threw her cousin a look pregnant with disgust.

"Promise, Mary," said Grinnel wearily.

She bit her lip.

"Mary."

She sighed. "I promise." She then went on, running her words together. "But I cannot *bear* it, I tell you, when people keep secrets from me!"

She scurried on up the stairs and disappeared. Jack saw tears as she turned away and checked to see if Grinnel, too, had seen them. He couldn't tell from his lordship's expression.

"I wasn't aware she made such use of the strong room," said Grinnel, pushing the bookcase back into place. He scuffed at the marks opening it had made in the carpet and, once they were erased, moved back to the fireplace. "I take it she knew things she shouldn't?"

"Bless her, yes. But she *will* fret at what she doesn't know. Will you take it wrongly if I suggest you give her a summary of what goes on in here when you've had company?" Humor in his tone, Jack added, "Or at least that part of what goes on which will satisfy her?"

"Excellent advice," said Grinnel. "Is there some part of what you wish to say to me now that I'm *not* to include in such a summary?"

"Yes." A vein throbbed in Jack's temple. "I've reason to believe a young friend of mine is in serious danger. I've asked your wife to invite the boy, his sister, and their mother to the manor in order to get them out of town. I'm off to France myself, but will leave Harry—you know my batman, Harry—to protect the lad. I don't consider it necessary, however, that Mary should be aware that there is danger. I will suggest that Lady Mordaunt tell her cousin she goes to Cornwall, and *not* that she visits in Kent. If, as I suspect, Mordaunt is plotting against the boy, he'll look for him in quite the wrong direction. I foresee no real problem . . . No *immediate* problem, I mean."

"Mordaunt?" Grinnel tipped his head slightly to one side. "We spoke of Wilmot Mordaunt when last you were here."

"The boy is a relative. The lad's father is the current baron and the boy his heir. Wilmot is next in line."

"Ah!"

"But he'll think Lady Mordaunt returns to Cornwall. He'll discover she has *not,* but he'll have no notion where she's gone. And I'll have returned from France long before he discovers her true location. I'm going to find Lord Mordaunt, you see, and bring him home. Then *he* can see to the boy's safety."

"When do you leave?"

"As soon as we can manage it. Today if possible, tomorrow for a certainty."

"I'll send a groom to inform our housekeeper of your imminent arrival."

Jack grimaced. "A very good notion. I seem to have forgotten the social conventions in my concern to forward my plan. I'm off now. With your pretty wife and offspring in tow. But not their nurse!"

Grinnel frowned. "I see Mary has complained to you. Why in the name of Heaven did she not rid herself of the woman if she does not like her?"

Jack widened his eyes in pretended innocence. "But, Grinnel, you told her the nurse was very well recommended. You insisted she was to be attended to on every and all occasions. Did you not?"

"I did?" Grinnel frowned. "Perhaps I did say some such thing. Mary was very young when I married her, and then became *enciente* almost instantly!" He looked up, a wary look in his eyes. "Jack, she was little more than a child herself."

"And you didn't trust her to take proper care of your heir," Jack finished for him. He debated saying more, but decided Grinnel was not a stupid man. He'd put two and two together and come up with a useful four. This would, perhaps, allow the couple to get back on proper terms with each other, on which they had *not* been for some time now. Guiltily Jack recalled it was something he'd noted before, but, in the press of duty, forgotten.

Constance warmly welcomed Mary's arrival in the park and then, with more caution, turned to Major Lord St. Aubyn. "I'd no expectation of seeing you today, my lord."

"And such a *pleasant* surprise, is it not?" said Jack smoothly, his eyes twinkling.

"Perhaps. Or perhaps . . . not?" suggested Constance, her dimple making a quick appearance. "You, my lord, are a tease."

"So I am. Mary will tell you I have been the bane of her existence. What's more, she'll tell you so at great length, so be certain you've settled into a comfortable chair before she begins. Have a pot of tea nearby and perhaps other refreshment."

"Jack!" Lady Grinnel crossed her arms and scowled mightily. She tapped her foot. "I will *not* be made out a bobbing block by you. By anyone, for that matter. You will retract your accusations at once!"

"But Mary," he said in a complaining tone, "it is often and often you have listed all my sins, starting from years and years ago. How can I think you do not do so when speaking to others?"

"Jobbernal!" She tipped her pert nose into the air. "As if I spoke of you to others at all!"

"Ha! That puts me in my place, does it not? Lady Mordaunt," said Jack, abruptly changing the subject, "my cousin has thought up a delightful scheme, and I have brought her cousin here to broach it to you."

Constance noticed Mary's startled look and rightly concluded it was not her notion at all.

"She wishes to invite you and your children to join her at Grinnel Manor, which is in Kent. You will be near to hand, you see, when I return from France with news of Lord Mordaunt."

"*You* go to France!" murmured Constance, frowning slightly.

"Mary," said Lady Grinnel tartly, "can speak for herself." She turned to Constance. "*Will* you come? Jack says he can escort you as far as the manor, leaving London just as soon as you are ready. He'd like to see you settled before going on. I know your children would like to leave the city. In fact," she said, her face alive with a sudden notion, "you'd be doing me a very great favor if you would take mine along with you. That way your Mrs. Willes can, if she does not object, look after all four." Mary caught and held Constance's gaze. "I must thank you. You gave me the courage to rid myself of that woman who ruled my children's nursery!"

"But, having done so," murmured Jack to Constance, "it is up to you to provide the solution for achieving some sort of answer to the resulting problem of having no nurse! Mary," he said, turning a scowl on his cousin, "you are outrageous!"

Lady Grinnel looked rueful. "Am I? I do sometimes speak without thinking. Would it be a terrible imposition?"

Constance chuckled. "We will ask Mrs. Willes, assuming I and my lot *go* to Kent. Lord St. Aubyn, may I have a few words with you? In private?"

"Secrets?" asked Mary, her eyes narrowing, her glance passing from one to the other and back again. "I will tell you right now *I do not like secrets!*"

"Not secrets," said Constance, realizing that she had done the wrong thing in asking to be private with Major St. Aubyn. "I wish to berate this cousin of yours, but it is my belief one should not scold a person where others can overhear. It is so demeaning, is it not?"

"Oh! A *scold.*" Mary relaxed and grinned. Her brows arched knowingly. "In *that* case . . ."

Amused, Jack offered his arm. They strolled toward a glade situated up a gentle slope covered in lush grass. When they'd gone beyond hearing he said, "You think I've been overly officious, suggesting you be invited to the manor. But Mary will like having you, you know."

"The problem is not that at all, my lord. It is that you assume I myself will not go into France to find Silly. It is unnecessary that you take time from your work or that you spend your money solving my problems. I will do quite well all by myself.''

"With two children, a nurse, and, at the very least, a trusted groom in attendance?''

Constance bit her lip. "The children are very well–behaved. I am sure it will be a broadening experience for them.''

"Possibly for young Valerian, but Miss Venetia is far too young. Too, I suspect the both of them would find such a difficult journey distressing. I can travel faster alone and return more quickly. Last but not least, in reference to your other point, I'd be on government business so will *not* be away from my work.''

"Perhaps," said Constance, digesting that, "your cousin would not object to the children and Mrs. Willes staying with her in Kent while I go on.''

"Alone?" he asked, bluntly interrupting. "You were born with better sense, I think.''

She glanced at his set features. "My lord, you have, it seems, taken an interest in my business. Why?''

Jack frowned slightly, stalking on for another few paces. "Damned if I know. Except, of course, that Selwyn Mordaunt *is* my business. Even if you hadn't arrived, bringing his absence back to mind, I'd very soon have had to travel into France to see what the graceless young idiot is up to!''

"I insist that it is my part to find him," said Selwyn's sister. "The war is over. He cannot possibly be your responsibility.''

"Oh yes he can. The fool could, by high sticklers, be thought due for court–martial! It *could* be said he has deserted! You see," continued Major Lord St. Aubyn more gently, "he has neither reported in, nor has he sold out.''

Frowning very slightly, he caught Constance's shoulder, stopping her. He stared down at her. For half a moment her steady gaze distracted him so that, although he put sudden and rather provocative thoughts aside, he finished rather gruffly. "Far better that *I* locate him," he said, "and determine what the problem is, than someone like the man with whom you exchanged correspondence be sent to do so."

Constance thought of Lord Packway's rambling letters, in which he'd done his best to put her off but had merely aroused both anger and curiosity. The man was more a fool than Silly would ever be, but it was not impossible that such a man would be a danger to her brother. She paled.

"You begin to understand," he said gently.

"Nonsense," she said, forcing herself to be strong. "I will go to France. I will find Silly and I will take him by the ear and drag him home. It is *not*, whatever you say, your business. You are merely being obliging."

Jack's eyes narrowed, lines of humor radiating from their corners. "Obliging others," he said rather dryly, "is not a trait of which *you* may be accused. Let us agree to disagree on this one point, but let us agree that you leave London as soon as may be and go to Grinnel Manor in Kent. We can argue more while we travel down to the country, may we not? *Will* your Mrs. Willes object to taking over Mary's nursery while my cousin seeks a nurse to replace the current one?"

"Willy likes children. She will gladly stitch two more into her roll of children."

"Her what?"

Connie's dimple showed for a moment. "Miss Willes has in progress a large embroidery. It is a sort of record of her life and the children she helps rear." Constance shrugged. "I do not see any problem there." She looked up at him, frowning. "But am I to understand you wish to leave immediately?"

"It is a mere three hour drive," he said. "We could leave as late as four or even five and still reach our destination well before we lose the light."

Constance consulted the watch pinned to her dress. "It is now ten thirty."

He gave her an assessing look. "If I send a carriage for you at four–thirty? Could you possibly be ready by then?"

Is he holding his breath? wondered Constance, eyeing him.

"Four–thirty," she repeated. "Yes, we could manage that." She glanced back to where Lady Grinnel watched them. "But Major, are you very sure you have not imposed us upon your cousin?"

"If your Miss Willes will take over her nursery you are doing her a favor!" he responded promptly.

Constance chuckled. "I see. So Lady Grinnel will travel with us?" When he didn't immediately respond she glanced at him and found his mouth a firm line, his chin jutting at a stubborn angle and a muscle jumping at the side of his jaw. "My lord, *what are you not telling me?*"

He glanced down at her and grinned at her stern expression. "Merely that Mary will not go down until Monday or Tuesday, and I am racking my poor brain to find a way to convince you it is best that you and the four children leave at once with my escort!"

Constance thought of her cousin, of how he hated having her and the children in his house. "It will not take a great deal of convincing, my lord," she said ruefully. "You are forgetting that I am not welcome here. It will be a very nice change for the children to find themselves where they *are*. Welcome, I mean."

"And you."

"I am going to France," she said gently.

"*You* are staying in Kent."

"We'll see." She heard an odd sound and looked at him. "Are you growling, my lord?"

"You, my stubborn lady, will have to learn that you cannot always do exactly as you please."

"Leaving! Nonsense," blustered Wilmot Mordaunt, his bulbous eyes starting from his head. He pounded a fist on his desktop. "Can't leave just like that with no warning! Not polite."

"You have wanted us gone from the moment we arrived, cousin. I'm certain you'll much appreciate our absence."

"Thought you meant to see the sights. Buy a gown!" he said slyly.

"*Thank You.* I'd forgotten the gown. If you'll excuse me I'll just send a note to the *modiste.*" She turned to leave the dark, musty room in which her cousin spent by far the larger portion of his waking hours.

"Cousin!"

"Yes?" she asked, turning back.

"Why such a change in plan?"

Constance thought quickly. She didn't understand why the major had asked that she allow Mordaunt to believe she was returning immediately to Cornwall, but she was perfectly willing to do so. "While in the park I met an acquaintance from home. I discovered there has been a fire. I must return at once to see that our tenant's house is properly repaired."

"If that's all, you may postpone—"

"All!" Forgetting her notion was a mere invention, Constance took heart. "You should know that good tenants will not stay where they are not appreciated. I can do no less than return at once!"

Constance reminded herself there was no fire and that her response to Mordaunt was mere playacting. She forced a return of her usual calm, which soon wavered when she found him staring at her, his eyes glittering in that awful way they had.

At last he nodded. "I will wish ye good travel now, so I need not bother seeing you off," said Wilmot.

Once again Constance turned to go.

"And, cousin! Send in Lester when you go through the hall."

Constance, her back to Wilmot, grimaced. How like the man that his last words to her were an order unaccompanied by even a pretense of politeness.

"Of course," she said sweetly and whisked herself out the door. *When and if I see the man,* she added silently, hoping she would *not* meet Mordaunt's oily butler any time soon.

"You, my stubborn lady," said Jack to Constance, "will drive me to taking up residence in Bedlam." Jack looked out his side of the carriage as they swept out of Grinnel Manor gates—the carriage which would take them to Dover, where they'd catch a packet for Le Havre. "You know I could make this journey far more expeditiously without you, do you not?"

Constance looked up from her lap desk, on which she was penning a letter, and decided his was a rhetorical question and that he did not really require a response. It had occurred to her that she'd forgotten to write her friend, Ada Wright, about Lord Temperance's demands. She had promised the man she'd discover what her friend wished done about his lordship's insistence that he be introduced to her child.

The carriage hit a rut, and a splatter of ink spoiled what she'd just written. Sighing, she rewrote the sentence. How many days, she wondered, would be required for a letter to move from Dover to London and from London to their tiny village in Cornwall? Possibly she'd have returned before Ada's answer arrived at the manor in Kent, and be gone again on her way home. If so, she would speak with Ada and send a message to Lord Temperance, but she'd promised to write and she would.

"Have you finished?" asked Jack politely when she folded the page and wrote the direction out clearly.

"I have finished."

"Then you can listen while I rant!"

"You feel a need to rant?" she asked. "You poor lad."

"Lad! I've not been a lad for a very long time, which is another thing! Are you always so careless of your reputation that you blithely, without even a *pretense* of concern, go off with a man unrelated to you on a journey of such a nature as this? Do you feel no qualms at all?"

"What nonsense."

Actually, Constance had felt several qualms, but she wasn't about to admit to them—especially not while the man believed her married! Ada was correct that a married woman received a deal more respect than an unmarried one. What her friend had forgotten to add was that a married lady could do things an unmarried woman would never have the courage to attempt! Constance reminded herself to tell Ada so. Despite her initial decision to ignore Ada's advice, Constance was very glad she'd been forced to pretend to be married.

"You are a gentleman," she added when Jack's scowl deepened. "I am happy to have your escort."

On the return journey, when he'd discovered her deception, she'd have Silly for chaperone and perhaps, given

Major St. Aubyn's temperment, have need of his protection. Oh, not that the major was likely to beat her, but he was *very* likely to berate her. And . . . perhaps to kiss her? It had seemed, once or twice, as if he'd like to do so. Constance suddenly wondered if she truly wished her brother's chaperonage.

"If you were *not* along," she continued, putting such thoughts aside, "I'd have been forced to hire a courier. Frankly, I don't know if I could afford one I'd find trustworthy."

"Are you so certain you can trust me?" he bit out. "I am a *man,* Lady Mordaunt," he continued icily. "And you, my dear, are an attractive woman. I may *hope* I remain a gentleman, but the conditions surrounding travel are not condusive to keeping a proper distance." His voice took on a silky note. "You, my dear, may find you must take the consequences of your rashness."

"Fiddle. You are merely unhappy that I won the argument and have accompanied you. You wish to punish me, and so you attempt to frighten me. You will cease to be so nonsensical, and will, if you must continue your rant, do so in some other direction."

"Ah yes. My rant. I could, you know, have found a means of crossing the channel which would take me far nearer to Fréhel than Le Havre. I might even have gone there directly had I had my choice of transport. But no. You insist you come, too. Which means we take the packet and suffer the aches and pains induced by exceedingly ill–constructed diligences which will be slow and not always convenient!"

"I had thought to hire a postchaise," said Constance quietly, looking out the window to hide a growing sense of being in the wrong.

"Had you indeed? It is a very good thing I *am* here to

escort you. It is quite obvious you haven't a notion how difficult it will be to hire any sort of conveyance whatsoever. France was utterly depleted by the past quarter century of war. *We* merely fought the *French*. The French, at one time or another, fought nearly everyone."

"So they did. Although I believe we sent substantial subsidies to French enemies, did we not?"

"My lady," said Jack, half exasperated and half amused, "you, as a mere woman, are not supposed to know such things. How may I rant properly if you have valid arguments from which you may form a rebuttal?"

"Should I apologize?" she asked, hearing the amusement and hoping perhaps he'd soon calm himself.

"No." He chuckled. "You, my dear, are a complete hand, although I should not say so, of course. I'd find it boring to argue with someone who has no responses, and boredom is worse than anything. Nevertheless," he added on a slight sigh, "it is very true you'll slow me down."

"Perhaps we could ride?"

His head came round so quickly his hat fell off. "Ride!" He threw the hat onto the seat across from them and pushed back his stubborn hair.

"You know," she said in a falsely encouraging voice. "One has a horse on which one has placed a saddle. One sits in the saddle and—"

"Rides! Yes. But you haven't a notion how far we must go."

"Perhaps you would tell me, then."

"Well over a hundred miles. Nearer two hundred," he responded promptly.

After a thoughtful pause, Constance said, "Three long days. How long would it take by diligence?"

"Heaven knows." He eyed her, saw she was determined,

and added, "But you cannot ride sixty or more miles per day!"

"Of course I can, although I suspect," she said shrewdly, "you've exaggerated the distance merely to frighten me."

He grinned at the hit, saluting her perspicacity. "Perhaps a trifle, but a hundred and fifty miles is still more than you should attempt."

"Major St. Aubyn," she scolded, "I am not one of your society ladies who lies about the parlor on her *chaise longue* all day long. I spend hours in the saddle in all sorts of weather, overseeing the Mordaunt estate. I have, actually, missed doing so while in London. It will do me a great deal of good to have the exercise!"

"I insist that you cannot ride so far!"

Even as he argued, Jack suspected she would, again, get her way.

They left Le Havre as soon as Jack was able to hire horses. It had been too late in the day to go far, and Jack had settled them into a wayside inn well before dark.

The next day they travelled nearly seventy miles, and had nearly that much more to do the next day. Not for the world would Constance admit how difficult it was to rise from her bed after that long day of riding with another equally long day ahead. Still, today would see them into Selwyn's village. Tonight she would beg, borrow, or steal a bath and plenty of hot water.

And *tomorrow* she would not, for all the tea in China, rise from her bed before noon!

"I still say I should not have allowed you to ride so far," said Jack, that afternoon, looking across to where, her back straight, Constance's mount paced his.

"You think me so foolish I'll not tell you if I must stop?"

"You are not foolish. In some respects, at least. But stubborn? Yes!"

Jack's admiration for Constance had risen with every meeting. Now, watching her uncomplainingly endure the long hours in the saddle, admiration was turning to something warmer. Something much warmer. Something he'd never previously experienced.

It was not a simple increase in the intensity of that initial attraction which he'd already acknowledged before he realized she was married. He'd had trouble with those feelings ever since. No. This was something far more complicated.

He wasn't certain just what it was. He was, however, convinced he must not allow her to know how he felt, assuming he could puzzle it out so that he himself knew. No, she must not discover it. She'd be shocked. She'd accepted him as a friend, and she treated him as such. Not only would it be unkind to burden her with his feelings, whatever they might be, but to do so would very likely end, instantly and forever, even the friendship she offered.

And, although he knew he could have no more, he'd no intention of losing what little he had!

In the distance the spire of a church announced the existence of another village. "We will stop there to dine and rest our mounts," he said a trifle abruptly, not liking the direction his thoughts had taken.

The sun was very close to the horizon when Constance roused from a deep and restful sleep several hours later. She blinked, looking around. She felt a rough blanket under her fingertips and noted a building made of gray stone . . . a table with benches . . . a vine growing up and over an overhead trellis which cast shade over the area.

A grapevine, she thought drowsily, turning her head—*and Jack Durrant, Major Lord St. Aubyn, sitting there and watching me.*

Constance was instantly awake.

"You let me sleep too long," she said accusingly, and immediately yawned. "We'll never make it so far as Fréhel in the hours of daylight remaining."

"Then we'll arrive tomorrow," he responded quietly. "And earlier than we expected, with that much more of the day in which to discover what there is to discover."

"You said you'd wake me."

"If you recall my exact words, I said you needed a rest and that I'd see you didn't sleep forever. I have guarded you carefully, my lady," he said, a whimsical note in his voice, "and you see that you have not slept forever!"

"Bah!"

"The host has rooms," he added, ignoring her bad humor. "They are not fancy, but unlike last night's they are clean. I've taken them for the night. You will not object to our trifling delay in reaching our goal. After all," he added, his eyes narrowing with humor, "you made it impossible for me to reach it in the most expeditious of manners!"

"So it is all my fault! I will not have it!"

"That we stay here tonight?" Jack refused to think about why he wished to do so, why he wished to put off the inevitable meeting between this amazing woman and her husband.

"What I will not have," she said firmly, "is you blaming me for the decisions you make! I would gladly have ridden on."

"Yes, but will you also admit that you were tired and needed the rest? It is not as if another day will make any great difference."

"Perhaps. But I dislike leaving the children for longer than necessary. They have never before been parted from me."

"My cousin will see they are well cared for."

She waved a dismissive hand. "Oh, *cared for*, of course. Children need a great deal of love and attention, and I do not see your charming cousin giving them that. No, it is necessary to find Silly and take him home as quickly as possible. I cannot allow you to allow me to dally along the way as if I'd no responsiblities anywhere in the world."

A muscle jumped in Jack's jaw. "We will see about getting home once we've found your husband."

Constance turned away, biting her lip. She was becoming very tired of maintaining the charade that she and Silly were anything other than brother and sister. Why it seemed important that this particular man see her as unattached wasn't much of a mystery. She'd been fool enough to fall a little in love with the man in the space of time she'd watched him help Val to keep his hoop moving properly!

Unfortunately, that love had only deepened as they'd come to know each other. The hours riding, when they'd talked of everything under the sun, had not only been fascinating. They'd given her further justification for falling in love.

Jack Durrant, Lord St. Aubyn, was a good man. An intelligent man. A man who understood her rather odd sense of humor. Perhaps still more important, he was the sort who laughed *with* one rather than *at* one. He was honest. Honorable . . .

All this frightened her when she allowed herself to think of it. Major Lord St. Aubyn, a straightforward sort himself, would not be best pleased when he learned how the wool had been pulled over his eyes. In fact, he would likely be quite disgusted with her, consider her hoydenish if not worse, that she'd insisted on accompanying him without a vestige of a chaperone!

"There is, I'm told, a rather picturesque mill at the end

of the village," said Jack, breaking into her thoughts. "Will you walk with me to see it?"

Smothering a desire to wallow in self–pity, Constance turned toward him. "Of course, my lord," she said with a totally bland expression. "The exercise will do me good."

He chuckled as she'd meant him to do, and she felt a smile of her own form in response. She didn't move when he reached out a hand and, with a single finger, touched her cheek.

"That dimple, which appears far too infrequently, is a most delightful part of your features, you know," he said softly.

"That dimple," she said, instantly forgetting the pain of unrequited love, "is the bane of my existence. I have been teased about it forever."

"I would not tease."

"Would you not? Silly did." Her teeth clicking together, she closed her mouth before she could reveal the ending to that sentence, which was *even in the nursery.*

"Will you think me forward if I say that Mordaunt is a very foolish man?"

"Since I've revealed I hold to that opinion, I can hardly object that you do. But, let us go forward, Major. Present to me this picturesque mill!"

"You will, I have been assured, be exceedingly chagrined that you left your charcoal and paper at home, that you have no chalks or watercolors. It is *very* picturesque!"

"You have seen it?"

"Of course not," he said, smiling. "I merely quote our host. You forget. I've been far too busy guarding your sleep from dragons to hare off to the ends of the village!"

"Ah yes," she said, and her dimple flickered into view for a bare instant. "You were assuring that I did not sleep forever, were you not?" She pretended to frown, and pushed a long slim finger into his chest. "*You,* Major St. Aubyns, are a bigger tease than Selwyn!"

They were both a trifle startled when he caught her hand, lifting it to his mouth. He placed a kiss on the fingers bent around his own. For a long moment neither could quite look away from the other.

A flush rising into her cheeks, Constance broke away. It was, she thought, a very good thing they'd reach her brother tomorrow. At least she hoped they'd reach him, that he'd actually *be* where he was supposed to be.

Just what will I do, she wondered, despair leavened by just a touch of undenied hope, *if he is not?*

Chapter 6

Thanks to stopping overnight, Constance and Jack rode into Fréhel shortly after midday. Feeling satisfied that they'd finally reached their goal, Constance apologized nicely and admitted it had been a good thing for her to have rested as she had the day before. Before Jack could make the teasing response she saw was on the tip of his tongue, Constance asked, "Do you know where we'll find this inn of Silly's?"

"If my directions are correct, that is it just along the way." He pointed his crop at the sign hanging before a dark recess some yards down the narrow street, the only indication that an inn existed.

They were, at that moment, walking their horses alongside a high wall. From behind it came a loud, "Ouch!" Following that, in fluent and colorful French, descriptions of the ancestry of whomever had caused the pain. Constance, whose ear for the language had returned with their travel, found herself blushing slightly. But she also grinned as she pulled her mount to a stop, the tired animal quite willing to obey.

"It is a good thing, I suspect," she said softly, "that I do not understand all of that."

"A good thing indeed," said Jack dryly.

"Silly!" she said a trifle loudly.

Jack frowned. "Silly because I don't wish you to understand all that?"

"You are being very *silly,* I think." The words from beyond the fence ceased abruptly. Constance nodded toward the sign. "Jack, why don't you go into the inn and get our rooms?"

"While you stay here?"

She pointed a discreet finger toward the gate very near to where their horses stood. "I'll wait to see what you discover," she said, intending no such thing.

A muttered conversation could be heard beyond the wall. Finally, more loudly, the insistent order that someone, *"Go. At once."* The words, of course, were in French, but well within Constance's vocabulary.

"Very well," said Jack slowly.

He glanced around. There were no loiterers lurking in the street, so Lady Mordaunt would be safe enough even if she weren't allowed to enter the gate. And why *did* she wish entry? But that was easily answered: To have her first meeting with her husband alone, of course. Sighing, Jack rode on.

Constance watched until he'd dismounted. He no sooner passed under the sign, entering the building, than she slid from the back of her horse. "Selwyn Mordaunt, open this gate. At once!"

The gate cracked open and her brother, a scowl marring his features, looked out. "It *is* you." He reached for her wrist and pulled her into the garden. "I'm not returning to England," he said stubbornly before she could open her mouth to say a word. He didn't even wish her welcome!

"Are you not? May I inquire *why* you'll not, when you are so badly needed there?"

"Needed!" Selwyn limped on into the garden. Then, his leg crumpling, he lowered himself awkwardly into a convenient chair. He put his head into his hands. "She is impossible, Connie. I'll not return to be nagged at and ordered here and there and given demands for this and then that at every turn." He looked up, the scowl back in place. "I will *not* and you can't make me."

"I thought you had gotten over that sort of thing in the nursery," retorted Constance, her tone thoughtful. Her frown echoed her brother's. "You sound, you know, very like Val when he becomes stubborn."

Selwyn's eyes got a faraway look. "Val."

"You had forgotten your son, perhaps? *And* your daughter?"

He looked straight at her then. "A daughter?"

"Venetia Elizabeth." Constance's brows arched. "She is five, going on six. Silly, have you not received even a single letter since you left us?"

"Well . . . no." He flushed. "Or actually, I threw those from my charming wife on the fire and those from our irascible father into my case, which I lost in the Peninsula. If *you* wrote, then those I did *not* receive. I'd have read yours." He glanced around the inn's cozy garden, which ran from the road to low fence running alongside a placid looking stream. "Blast it all, we cannot talk here. And, Connie, I want you to know I'll not have you queering my game, so you and your husband will just have to find rooms elsewhere."

"Of all the . . . !" She'd also seen that mulish expression of his in the nursery. Often. "Silly, you don't understand."

"We'll talk, *but not here.*" Selwyn ran his hands through his hair and threw a harassed look toward the inn. "Look, take a stroll this evening along the road north of town. When you come to the first bridge, pass over and return in this direction. There is a small cottage with a flower–filled garden not too far upstream of here where a lady will offer you refreshment. I'll meet you there."

"Selwyn, the war is over." She resisted as he pushed her toward the gate, his bad leg hampering him just enough so that she was able to avoid being literally shoved from his presence. "You've no reason whatsoever—"

His hand cut off her words. "I *have* reason. As I said, I will not return to a nagging wife! Just do as I say, Constance. Just this once. We'll talk this evening." With that he managed to put her beyond the gate and shut it in her face.

"well!" as she glared at it, arms akimbo and hands on hips, she heard his dragging step hurry off. "Of all the . . . !" She paused, searching for the proper word or phrase.

"I agree with the unspoken part of that sentence," said Jack, who lolled against the wall, his arms crossed, one knee bent, the toe of that boot set in the dirt on the wrong side of his other foot. "In fact, if that was your husband I can teach you a few words. Assuming you'd care to learn them, of course. I've been told there is no room in the inn, and that English aristos, which it is assumed we must be, will be far more comfortable at the chateau on the north side of town."

"A chateau?"

"Formerly the home of an elderly aristo lady who, umm—lost her head." His brows rose up under the hair falling over his forehead.

"Poor lady. Do you suppose she deserved to?"

"She did not. My informant tells me the poor woman's

only sin was to be wellborn. At the time, that fact alone was sufficient. The chateau, however, has been put to much better use, and we will find excellent lodging and good food there.''

''Just who was your informant?''

''A lady almost as tall as you, almost as dark, and very, very French.'' Again the brows disappeared, but this time there was a twinkle in Jack's eyes. ''If you know what I mean?''

''A *coquette.*'' said Constance promptly.

His head tipped to one side as he considered. ''Actually—no.''

Connie wondered if she'd revealed the jealousy his words roused, and if that was why he frowned. She wondered *why* she should be jealous. Perhaps it was that she wished she herself were a bit more of a *coquette* so that she needn't feel it necessary to hold Jack quite so much at arm's length? She needn't have worried: Jack's next words revealed he was trying to decide how to specify what he meant.

''*Not* a *coquette,*'' he repeated. ''Not in this case. A *coquette* would, of course, be the extreme of what I mean. In its more natural form, it is something I can't quite explain. It is, however, a womanly quality which is very appealing to a man's senses.''

Constance wished even more that she had something of that quality, particularly since it appeared to appeal so greatly to this particular man's senses. Then she scolded herself. She was quite on the shelf, too tall and too independent, and would never be the sort a man like Jack would look at twice, despite his kind words on a few memorable occasions. After all, it had taken *days* to reach Fréhel and he had been the complete gentleman since leaving England, never once stepping over the line.

How she wished he would!

"Well," she said, breaking into his reverie after coming out of her own. "Shall we find ourselves this chateau?"

That evening Constance looked up from her dinner and smiled at their heavyset, faintly mustachioed hostess. "That was excellent," she said in careful but quickly improving French. "By far the best meal I've had for ages. Unfortunately, I've eaten too much." She glanced at Jack, who was enjoying the amber liquid in a small glass held between his fingertips. "Because of my greed, I'll need a walk. Jack? You will escort me?"

"As soon as I finish. It would be a sin to gulp this." He smiled a quick smile at the matron, who smiled back broadly. "It is quite the best cognac I've ever drunk," he added.

Their hostess's smile widened still more.

"Is there a pleasant walk if we go beyond the town? Perhaps along the stream?" asked Constance.

"River path. Other side," said the woman. "Bridge." She pointed.

"We should go north to the bridge and cross to the path?"

She nodded.

"Then that is what we'll do," said Constance.

As they approached the bridge Jack chuckled. "I see," he said, "that it runs in the family."

"What does?" she asked suspiciously.

"Nothing which need concern you, but I wish I'd met you back when I could have used a pretty lady with more wit than hair! I merely refer to how smoothly you pulled the wool over that poor woman's eyes. Asking where we might find a pleasant walk! Just as if you hadn't a notion exactly where we meant to go."

She blushed at his praise . . . if such it was. "It seemed a good idea."

"If Mordaunt insists his cover not be blown, then I suppose it was, although now the war is ended I cannot see why he *should*. However that may be, due to your machinations our landlady will not be suspicious that we have taken this particular route. Not when it was at her suggestion we do so."

"I wish I understood why Silly is so adamant he'll not return to England!"

"You will know soon. I can't believe it is merely that he refuses to return to a nagging wife."

When she asked just what else he might have heard, with a quick flick of her eyes, he grinned at her.

"I heard that bit clearly enough, but before it only a jumble of sounds." And he couldn't believe that Constance Mordaunt had ever been a nag. "Besides, I don't believe he'd allow his wife to continue in that fashion if he lived with her for any length of time." Jack scowled, staring straight ahead. He'd yet to hear Lady Mordaunt nag about anything—unless he counted her insistence she come to France. But even then it had been accomplished by calm assertion rather than argument. She'd go, she'd said, even if he didn't escort her.

Constance, aware he believed she herself to be Selwyn's wife, bit her lip. She wondered if there was a way she might talk privately with her brother, at least for long enough to discover the situation . . . and to tell him her own!

Selwyn *had* to return to England, if only to escort her there once the major realized she was Silly's sister! Then she remembered St. Aubyn's comment concerning desertion, and that Selwyn must sell out of the army. That, too, was a reason he must return, and a far more important one. He must *not* be considered a deserter, whatever else he became.

A muscle jumped in her jawline.

Return to England he would!

They'd arrived at the bridge and she paused in the middle, looking along the stream which flowed gently, a wood duck half hidden along one edge, feeding there. Nearer, the water splashed in the wake of a turtle sliding off a stone into it.

She sighed. There was no way to discover the situation except to ask, so she would. She laid a hand on Jack's arm. For half an instant the feel of hard muscle under fine wool interferred with her thoughts.

"Constance?"

She shook off the intriguing sensations. Now was *not* the time for such thoughts. "Jack, may I ask a favor of you?"

"You may *ask.*"

She felt new tension is the hard muscles. "It is only that I feel I must talk to Selwyn alone. At least for a few minutes."

"So you may nag him?"

"I've no intention of nagging him, but there are problems. Family problems which are private, and which I must discuss with him instantly, information he needs before he makes his final decision."

Jack's eyes narrowed, his gaze intent upon her upturned features. "You feel very strongly about this, do you not?"

"Very."

He sighed. Somehow the notion that she'd be alone with any man, even her husband, felt wrong. He swallowed. She was, however, a married lady, and he must not forget it. "Very well. I'll ask the woman who greets us to walk with me while you two talk."

Constance, remembering his reaction to some unknown woman at the inn, hoped this one would be ancient and grandmotherly. They strolled on until they came to the cottage where a tall, dark–haired Frenchwoman, her face an expressionless mask, awaited them.

"Monsieur? Madame?" she said. She continued in slow and highly accented English. "If you would be so kind as to stop in my humble garden, I will provide a nice wine for your refreshment."

They looked at each other. Jack's brows were arched in surprise, and Constance's expression asked a question. Since he hadn't a notion what the question might be, he turned back, smiled, and reached to open the gate. "We'd be charmed," he said in excellent French, "to enjoy your lovely garden and wine would taste very well after our walk."

"Come, then," she said, and they followed her around the house.

Under the arbor, Selwyn pulled himself up to his feet, grasping a nearby cross bar to aid him. "Constance. Do come sit. And introduce your—" His eyes widened. "But I know you!"

"I should hope so." Jack asked in English and lightly, "Are you, Lieutenant Lord Mordaunt, aware how close you have come to explaining yourself at a court–martial?"

Selwyn frowned. "Nonsense. You can't court–martial a man who has resigned."

"When?"

"As soon as the peace was signed."

"We've never received notice of it."

Selwyn's frown deepened, and a muscle jumped in a jawline that resembled Constance's. "I can't *prove* I sent it, of course."

Jack shrugged. "I received one of your early reports only a few weeks ago, so perhaps it will turn up."

"Damn! I see now why you've come looking for me. Constance—"

She held up her hand for silence and turned to the major. "Jack?"

He sighed. "Half an hour." He bowed at the French-woman and reverted to French. "I've not yet had quite so much exercise as I require. Will you oblige me by walking with me and leaving these two alone for a bit?"

The woman, who had stood to one side looking from one to another, her fingers twining together, glanced at Selwyn, who nodded. She took Jack's arm, a trifle reluctantly, Constance thought. From beyond the corner, Connie heard the woman's light laugh, so obviously Jack had already set the Frenchwoman at ease. She bit her lip. Then, realizing she'd brought their tête-à-tête on herself and that it had been necessary, she turned her attention to her brother.

"He is not my husband, and he thinks I'm *your* wife. I don't know what game you're playing, Selwyn Mordaunt, but don't you queer *mine*. I can't very well travel with him if he thinks me unmarried!"

"That you *have* rather sinks you beneath contempt, does it not?" asked her brother, growling.

"I meant to come alone. He'd not allow it. Since he'd already made the mistake of thinking us married, I kept up the charade because I assumed you'd be returning with us to act the chaperone once the truth was known."

He shook his head.

"Silly, you *must* come."

"To chaperone you? You got yourself into this mess. I should just let you get yourself *out*." He scowled. "Not only have I no wish to see my wife, but you *know* how badly I get along with Father." He looked up then, his anger clearing from his brow and a sweet smile appearing. "Besides—Connie, I'm *happy* here. I don't wish to leave." But then a helpless, hopeless, look settled over him. "Can't you just see me at home? Nothing to do, a wife who will not let me be, a leg which will prevent me doing the things I used to do? I'd be certifiably insane before the year was out."

"Two things must be said, and there is no time to work up to it slowly. Probably no way even if I had time. Selwyn, both your wife and our father are dead. *You* are Baron Mordaunt now, and you are needed. Your children need you, too. I've done what I could to keep your memory alive in your son, but your daughter has never even seen you. It's not right."

"My wife is dead?" he asked sharply.

"After Venetia was born she just . . . well, she simply faded away. We'd had no word from you, Silly. There was *official* word you'd been badly wounded and that you'd be invalided home, and then *nothing*. Father tried to discover if you were dead and was told no, but could discover nothing else. Your wife couldn't face life without you, Silly."

"She was . . ." He looked into space, guilt clear in his expression. He sighed. "You don't know how it was, Connie. Coming home that first leave . . . You wouldn't believe the carnage I'd seen. I needed . . . I don't know, something soft and feminine, and she seemed the antidote to all the horror, don't you know? But then it was time for me to go back, and she . . . well, you remember?"

"I didn't understand her either, until very near the end of her life. In her strange way she loved you, Silly. But it was a greedy, possessive love that wasn't, I sometimes think, quite . . . sane."

"Did you ever hear about her family? The life she'd lived?"

"I know her parents didn't bother to come to her funeral, and they've never answered the letters I've sent concerning their grandchildren."

"They are flighty, Connie. Utterly selfish. Totally absorbed in each other. I'd never seen anything like it. I can look back at it rationally now. I realize they pushed her onto me, and then both of us to the altar. They wanted her out of their lives." He ran trembling fingers across his forehead. "She stood in the way of their mutual absorption, I suppose."

"The sort of marriage her parents had might explain her expectations for her own, I suppose, her excessive need of you and her inability to adjust to the real situation. Which was in part, Silly, that your need for her overt affection vanished as soon as you recovered from your initial shock at what war was truly all about!"

He reddened. "I suppose there is something to that. The thing is, Connie, I *do* know what love is." Again he glowed. He stared sadly at the corner of the house around which Jack and the Frenchwoman had disappeared. "Now."

"That woman?"

"Hmmm. She is a widow. The war, you know. She's helped me at the inn from the beginning, needing the income to keep herself. Then, well, she began working with my leg. It's much better than it was, thanks to her. When I arrived here I was very nearly helpless to get around by myself. It was ridiculous. I could use crutches a bit, but I needed help to get up on them. Now, and thanks to her, I can manage for short distances, without them."

"You want to marry her?"

He bit his lip. "I've never thought about marriage. I couldn't, could I, when already wed." He whooped then, a wild glorious noise, as he realized he was free, could actually wed his love. "It's true. We can wed!" The joy faded. He glanced around the garden. "That is . . . if she will."

"There is some impediment? A reason she'd not have you?"

"I don't know, do I?"

"Whatever happens between you and your love, there is no question at all that you must come home, at least for a time. The letter of resignation you sent didn't arrive, so you must officially resign your commission. And the estate. Silly, I won't live the rest of my life as your agent, however much you may wish it. And last, but certainly not least, there are your children."

"*Two* of them," he said, musing. His gaze turned from vines heavy with ripening grapes to meet his sister's. "Have I thanked you for caring for them? Which I know you have. You and Willy. I haven't dared contact you since the war ended. I didn't want Father coming here to drag me home, where I'd have had to hold my lady wife's hand," he finished, wryly.

"Silly, you *will* come home?"

He sighed. "I . . . suppose I must."

There was a gasp behind them, sharp clicking footsteps, and suddenly a door slammed. They looked around.

Jack stood alone, staring at the door to the house. He turned to face them. "Of course you will return," he said sternly. "You are a fool, Mordaunt, that you hadn't told that poor woman you were already married. You hadn't, had you?"

"There'd have been no need for long explanations if you hadn't returned on little cat's paws," snarled Selwyn as he struggled to his feet. "Connie, you must come with me. She'll believe *you*."

"Believe what?" asked Jack, stepping in front of the younger man.

"That Connie is my sister and not my wife, as I assume

you told Felice! Now out of my way, St. Aubyn or even with this blasted leg I'll mill you down!"

Jack, flabbergasted, moved. He settled slowly into a chair as Selwyn, towing his sister, limped toward the house.

"Sister?" he softly asked a passing breeze.

And then, at the vituperative French flowing from the house, he grinned. He heard Selwyn trying to get a word in here and there, with little success. The voice rose to hysterical levels and was, suddenly, cut off. There was a pause and he heard Constance's voice, but not her words. Then his love appeared, closing the door quietly behind her.

"We'll be married as soon as I can get a licence," blurted Jack.

She sighed. "I feared you'd think some such nonsense necessary. You'll have difficulty wedding me when I refuse."

"But will you? I think not." He rose to his feet, coming to her, putting his hands on her shoulders. "You'll be outcast, my dear, if you do *not.*"

"I will not marry for such a reason," said Constance quietly. "We will speak no more of it."

"We'll speak of it a great deal more if you become stubborn!"

"Jack, we are friends, are we not?" she asked wistfully.

"Of course we are," he said, bewildered.

"Then be a friend. Forget this nonsense."

His lips compressed. "It is not nonsense."

An uproar from inside the house interrupted them. The argument, in French, was far too rapid and far too colloquial for Constance to follow, and it escalated still further even as they listened. She turned under Jack's hands to face the house. "Oh dear. And they were getting on so well when I left them!" She listened a bit more. "Can *you* understand what they are saying?"

"I think the problem is that she's just discovered he's English," said Jack who had followed enough to have a notion or two.

"There isn't much he can do about *that,* "she said. "Poor Silly."

Jack was still listening. "There's more. He's an aristo, and Madame Beugnot will have nothing to do with such, and it is insulting that he offers to make her one, and how could he have deceived her so?"

"Your French is surprisingly good, Jack."

"My mother as well as my *grandmére,* who lived with us until she died, are French," he said. "They were determined someone should speak with them in their own tongue. I was nominated since my father and paternal grandfather, an uncle, and my two brothers were incapable of getting their tongues around the language! My sisters and aunts are bilingual, but they are mere females and the English female does not, claim my mother and my grandmother, have good sense. Even my sisters." He eyed her. *"You* they'll like."

"I assume that is a compliment. What are we to do?"

"Mordaunt will have to settle his own problems, Constance. There is nothing we *can* do."

"To the contrary. We seem to have done much harm."

"I have great faith in your brother. He is not one to fail when he's a goal in mind."

Constance bit her lip. The tirade seemed to have become less vicious and she could hear her brother's voice, could even understand that he was speaking of why he must return, at least briefly, to England.

But then it escalated all over again. Even Constance

knew the meaning of *"Beste!"* which was the mildest of the insults Madame threw at her brother's head.

"What is it this time?" she asked when the speed and the vocabulary once again defeated her.

"It appears he abandoned his children, and how could he have been so cruel?"

"Hmm. If he plays that card rightly, he may talk her into marrying him just to see they are not made to suffer in future."

"He seems to be using that very ploy. You Mordaunts are an artful lot, are you not?"

"That sounds very much like an insult."

His brows arched. "To the contrary. That, my dear, was a compliment of the highest order. You forget you speak to a master spy, to whom such traits are exceedingly valuable."

"Not in peacetime."

"Oh, yes." He stared at his fingernails, turning his hand one way and then the other. "Even during peaceful times, except one calls it diplomacy then." He looked up, his gaze catching and holding hers. "A diplomat needs a wife who understands such things," he added nonchalantly.

"You are suggesting I look about myself for a diplomat who is looking about for a wife?"

"Yes," he said, promptly deflating her. "Me," he added, which instantly healed the wound his agreement had just inflicted.

"But you are not a diplomat."

He grinned. "I soon will be. I'd be bored out of my mind if I were to stay where I am with no war in progress. Castlereigh, in Vienna, has need of my talents, and will welcome you with open arms when he discovers how adept you are at the game."

For a very long moment Constance was silent, a frown

forming between her eyes. "I have heard," she said, "that Vienna has spies spying on spies, to the point no one trusts anyone and nothing gets done."

"I don't know *where* you heard that, but it is very close to the truth." He eyed her. "Actually," he said casually, "I'd be very interested in where you heard so much."

"Hmm?" She'd been listening again to her brother's voice. When he wasn't shouting, she found it easier to understand. "Oh, at Mordaunt's house. I overheard one of his visitors speak of such things when I was about to go into his bookroom to ask if I might . . ." She stopped and gave Jack a sharp look. "You appear overly interested."

"Oh, I am. Truly I am. Excessively interested. Do go on. I am all ears."

"You wish to know to whom he spoke. That I cannot tell you. But now that I think about it, I remember finding the bits I overheard a trifle surprising."

"Have you any notion why they discussed such things?" Jack picked at a piece of lint on his sleeve. "I only wonder, you see, why Mordaunt would be interested in such far-flung goings–on."

"I don't know exactly, but it had to do with exports. The visitor had an accent. I was curious as to exactly what it was. Hanoverian, perhaps? Or . . . Austrian?"

"Hmm. Well, it is worth checking. Thank you, my dear. You see why I think you'll be invaluable? You *must* wed me. I'll not allow you to escape me."

She glowered. "Bah! I'll do no such thing."

She hoped the glower would hide the hurt to her heart the necessity of resisting his cajolery caused. She would not marry him just because he felt honor bound to offer, having compromised her by travelling with her. Nor would she wed because he thought she'd be useful. Besides, no matter how well he wrapped it up, she'd *forced* herself upon him and it was that which had brought *him* to this point.

Actually, it hadn't occurred to her until they were well on their way that she was compromising him as well as herself. She didn't care about her own reputation, having long before concluded she was not the sort of woman men wished to wed, other than one ne'er–do–well neighbor who had thought she might manage his property instead of her brother's. When she'd told the man she must take care of the Mordaunt estate until Selwyn returned, he'd had the audacity to suggest she might do *both*.

But Lord St. Aubyn had no estate for which he required a manager. All he had were the gentlemanly impulses that forced him, gallantly if foolishly, to offer his name now that she'd ruined her own. She carried a heavy sense of guilt that the honorable man with whom she'd fallen in love should feel so trapped.

There was a solution. She must merely hold firm, and there was nothing he could do. Everything would be all right in the end—for him, at least. There was her heart, of course. She feared it would never be quite the same, although she'd eventually manage to patch it up and glue the cracks together. Some sort of healing would result.

At that point her thoughts were brought to an abrupt halt by the appearance of her brother, who limped toward them.

"I guess you'd better go. I'll stay here tonight. If you'll return in the morning we will speak again."

"You trust me with your sister?"

Selwyn eyed his superior officer. "If Connie trusted you to bring her here, then I guess I can trust you to take care of her somewhat longer." He turned to his sister. "Just see *you* behave!" He turned and limped back into the house, his leg obviously paining him rather badly.

"What," said Constance when he'd shut the door behind him, "did he mean by *that*?"

"If you don't know I don't know how I'd know."

"Well, I don't."

She eyed him, dithering. All was different now that he knew she was unwed and that, even so, she'd dared travel in his company. What was she to do? Could she continue to treat him as a friend? Would he do the same?

"I suppose," she said, deciding she'd no choice but to carry it through with a high hand, "that we had better seek our beds."

"Beds. I wonder. I did warn you, did I not," he said smoothly, "that my gentlemanly instincts were on a short tether?"

"Don't tease," she said crossly, and started around the house for the front gate. "I have had enough to bear with Silly acting like an idiot and his French love causing a scene." She glanced over her shoulder at his twinkling eyes. "And *you* pretending to rakish tendencies I'm sure you'd never wish to waste on a beanpole like me."

If she hadn't turned back instantly, she'd have seen the humor disappear completely. *Tout de suite*, as Selwyn might say.

"Fool," he said softly.

"An exceedingly tired fool," she countered a trifle ruefully.

He chuckled, his temper restored. "You have chosen the best way to defend your honor, my dear. I am unlikely to seduce a lady who is likely to fall asleep somewhere in the middle of my efforts. So you are safe. For tonight."

He took her arm and led her back the way they'd come. Arriving at the chateau he led her to her door, where he left her after nothing more than a single warm kiss.

The door shut, with him on the outside, and Constance

leaned back against it, her breath warming her fingers as they gently explored her lips. Perhaps a trifle *more* than merely warm?

"Fool, indeed," she whispered. "Oh, my poor lost and foolish heart! Ah . . . but I'd no notion at all a kiss could feel so wonderful!"

While sleep evaded Constance, her cousin in London was equally wide awake. "What do you mean, they haven't gone to Cornwall? Of course they went to Cornwall. Where else would they have gone, if not to Cornwall?" Mordaunt shook his cane at his cowering butler. "Tell me that!"

"Belgiam? Vienna? France, perhaps?" asked Lester quickly. "To find her brother?"

Mordaunt, preparing to beat the man across the shoulders, lowered his cane. His butler breathed more easily, although he feared he wasn't completely out of the woods.

"Couldn't go to the continent all on her own. That's nonsense."

"But if that officer she saw at the horse guards—?"

Mordaunt's eyes narrowed, practically losing themselves in his fat cheeks.

"More nonsense! He believed me when I told him . . . At least I *think* he did."

His mouth turned down at the corners as he considered, and he rubbed his hands together slowly, the dry skin rasping in a rather hideous fashion.

"Maybe I'll just go see him again. See if *he* knows anything."

"See if he's *there*."

"That, too."

"Then I'll tell your . . . hmmm . . . *agent* to await new instructions?"

"Hmm? What? Oh yes. Yes, you do that. Or maybe that he should poke around to see what he can see. Maybe he'll discover where the blasted wench hid the benighted boy!"

Thankful to have escaped with no bruises, Lester backed out of the bookroom and went to the kitchen door, where he informed Rhino Biggens that his new orders were to discover the lad's whereabouts and then return for instructions.

"Not without something on account." Rhino, his eyes again crossed thanks to his intense frown, folded his arms. Mr. Biggens resented that maintaining the style of life he considered proper was so difficult now the war was ended.

Lester had expected some such demand, and come prepared with coins filched from the housekeeping money. Very reluctantly, he dropped five golden boys into the would-be fop's dirty hand.

Chapter 7

A sullen Felice served breakfast under the arbor behind her house. She stared rudely from Constance to Jack and back again. "More aristocrats," she snarled. "Why do you have to be aristos?"

"I guess because we were born that way," said Jack calmly. "Is Mordaunt changed from the man you've known simply because he was born so?"

Felice exploded with one word: *"Yes."*

"Nonsense," said Constance. "He has always been something of a gallant fool, and I suspect he still is. Besides, he loves you."

The skin reddened over her high cheekbones as Felice glanced toward Selwyn and away. Arms crossed, she stared toward the trees backing her long, narrow garden.

"I do, you know," said Selwyn softly, maybe a trifle desperately, and not without an embarrassed glance toward Jack. "Love you, I mean."

"You would make me English, an aristo," said Felice, pouting.

"The mother of my children. Those I already have, and those to come."

"Children . . ." Felice turned back. "To have children—"

"My children," repeated Selwyn firmly.

Felice sighed. "But to leave my home, my country, all I know and all I love—"

"Except me, of course," inserted Selwyn slyly, never completely down.

"To go to my enemy, to live amongst them always, to speak the dreadful tongue–twisting English and never my beloved French, to live in the cold and wet and—have no friends."

Cornwall is well–known for its temperate climate," inserted Constance softly, so softly she wondered if she'd be heard.

"It is?"

Constance smiled. "We have high winds and storms off the ocean, but it is far warmer than elsewhere in England, and has less rain. *Much* the most pleasant part of the island!"

Jack suppressed a grin at that and looked as if he'd like to dispute her opinion, but merely picked up his coffee. He settled back in his chair, studying one Mordaunt and then the other with interest.

Because he was closely observing them, he noticed the likeness between the siblings, the bone structure and coloring, and kicked himself for not seeing it sooner.

"I'm slipping," he muttered crossly, too softly to interrupt the others. Silently, he added, *I should have seen the resemblance when she first appeared at the Guards.*

"We, too, have wind," Felice was saying. "I am used to storms off the water." She cast a calculating look toward

Selwyn. After a moment she said, "I will visit. That is what I will do. I will meet these poor, abandoned children who have lost their mother and whose dreadful father ignores them and I will see his house and his garden." Again she stared at the trees. When she finished her thought, her tone suggested a threat. *"I will see."*

Selwyn puffed out his cheeks, blowing out a long soft stream of air. Then, after a moment, he drew in a deep breath and let that out, an entirely different sort of sigh. Finally he struggled to his feet. "I must give orders at the inn, and you, my love, must close up your house. Connie will help you with that. If you *prefer* to do it alone, know that we've a day or two only to get everything done." Without waiting to see if Felice or Constance had objections to his high–handed suggestion, Selwyn added, "Jack? Coming?"

The two men walked off and Constance, hands on hips, sent a disgusted look after them. "Men!"

Felice's chuckle was low and throaty.

Constance glanced at her, one brow arched. "My brother is often a fool, but he has chanced onto something very special with you, Felice. May I call you Felice?" she added quickly.

"Since we are to be sisters, then I think yes?" said Felice.

"Are we? To be sisters?"

"Oh . . . I think so," admitted the Frenchwoman with a sly, little smile. "It is just that I think my Selwyn will value me more if he does not win me too easily?"

Constance laughed then, but she sobered quickly enough. "It's a brave thing you do, Felice, leaving all that is familiar to you to be with him."

"But it is that I love him, you see. I can do no less." Her eyes strayed to her garden. "If he were not responsible for an estate and his children, then perhaps I would convince him to stay here and forget he is an aristo and English and we could manage the inn and live in this house, and it would all be very pleasant, would it not? But . . . it cannot be.'' She cast a sad look at the flower bordered garden with a well–tended vegetable patch down the middle. She plucked a leaf from a potted herb standing on the edge of the patio, rubbing it between her fingers and sniffing delicately.

Constance looked around, as well. ''You know, Felice, the walled garden at home used to be a very pleasant place. My mother loved it, but I've had no time to pay it proper attention and it has deteriorated sadly. I wonder if Silly would not come back with you to take up cuttings and pot some pots and bring a bit of your home back to England with you . . . when you are settled, that is. At the Hall, I mean. He's a yacht that a friend has cared for, and . . .''

At the thought of Selwyn's yacht Constance's mouth dropped open, and she stared at nothing at all. Finally she closed it.

''Just you wait,'' she said, her voice low and angry, ''until I get my hands on that man! How *dare* he allow the youngest son of our best tenant to endanger himself!''

''Endanger himself?'' asked Felice politely.

Felice's question roused Constance from her preoccupation. Aware she should not have spoken aloud, she improvised quickly. ''I suspect Sel's friend, our tenant's son, has taken up smuggling, and Silly is helping him, perhaps even planning it all.''

She suppressed all thought of Jack's role as spy–master and Selwyn's work in espionage. If possible, that bit of information should be kept from Felice, who would not like it that she had fallen in love with a man who had actively worked against her homeland.

''Smuggling! An *aristo*? On top of all else he has been

engaged in *smuggling!* Ah, why do I care so much for the man? Why can I not be sensible and fall in love with . . . with . . . oh, with Gerard or René or . . ."

Felice listed several more men, ticking them off on her fingers, while Constance gathered the breakfast things onto a tray. A smile hovered around her mouth and the elusive dimple Jack loved flickered in and out. *This Felice will,* she thought, *lead Silly a merry jig! And good luck to her!*

When Constance turned to take the tray inside Felice broke off and hurried to open the door. The women found they worked well together, doing those chores which must be done before a house may be locked up for some weeks or even months.

Late that morning Constance looked up from the crate she was packing. "I am hungry, Felice. Is there a good cook at the inn?"

"What? A chef, you would say?" Felice chuckled. "If you care for plain country fare, then the cook is excellent. If you wish to dine properly, then you should return to the chateau in which you are staying."

"Let us go to the inn. I prefer country cooking for everyday eating. The food at the chateau is a special treat, something to be savored, but not to become commonplace by partaking of it day in and day out."

"I like that philosophy," said Felice. She picked up a stack of soiled linens to take to the inn, where a laundress would deal with them.

Constance hefted a second pile of laundry and they set off, not in the direction of the bridge but downstream toward the inn. "I've not told you how thankful I am that Silly found someone who knows how to help him with his leg," she said. "I fear he will be sensitive to that limp when he gets home. For instance, he is unable to ride, is he not?"

"He cannot yet ride for any distance, but he may drive and he can have a gig or a . . . what do you call them? A curry."

"Curricle? Yes of course." *But,* thought Constance sadly, *it won't be the same, not with the moors calling to him.*

Felice whistled shrilly, surprising Constance. She soon discovered the reason. A boy ran out the back of the inn and down to the water's edge, untying a boat and positioning himself in the stern with a pole. He crossed deftly to their side, helped the women in, and poled them back. There, young as he was, he equally gallantly helped them out again.

As they approached the garden Constance heard, ". . . is, legally, I suppose, the property of—"

"Silly? Lord St. Aubyn?" called Constance brightly before either could say something so blatantly obvious that even Felice, with her restricted English, must guess what had been going on at the inn during the war. "We've worked ourselves to a thread and have decided that, since we are starving, we'll join you for a nuncheon."

Jack strolled to the low wall, where he met Constance's eyes for a moment. He moved his chin in the barest hint of acknowledgement of what her interruption meant and opened the green–painted wooden gate for the women. "We, too, were beginning to think sliced ham and fruit sounded good."

"And a good loaf of bread and cheese and perhaps a bowl of Marie's sorrel soup," added Felice, her eyes going toward Selwyn, who sprawled along a bench, his back leaning against the inn's wall.

"Sounds excellent," said Selwyn, smiling his lazy smile.

His eyes said things to her that made the French woman's color rise. "I will see to it," said Felice quickly, and she laid her load on the table.

Constance put her pile next to it and sat on the bench across from Selwyn. "Have you finished organizing things here? Can we get away more quickly then you thought?"

"We can't leave yet." Selwyn frowned. "Jack, what is the date?" Jack told him. "Then, we may set out on the fourth."

"But that is several days yet, and it will take far longer. *Forever!*" When the men looked at her. "To return home, of course," said Constance crossly. Abruptly she rose to her feet and whirled away, running out the gate and along the river path before Jack caught her up.

"What is it?"

"The *children*. Silly can't ride. We must return by diligence. I will be away far longer than I meant. Jack, it will take days to reach Le Havre."

"We will return from a cove near here, Connie."

She turned on her heel and stared at him. *"His yacht,* you mean. That reminds me! I've a bone to pick with him! He'd no business drawing young Powery into his schemes!"

"But you will not berate him until you get him alone."

"You caught my hint that Felice should not know exactly what Silly did in France? I've suggested he was organizing this end of a smuggling operation. I hope you won't think that too awkward?"

"Masterful, actually. Quite up to what I have come to expect of you, my dear. I only hope Mordaunt can live with the notion his wife believes him to be, or to have been, a smuggler."

"Better that than that he was a spy against her homeland!"

"Ah yes, of course. It is entirely likely that would be the final straw to tear her from him, is it not? Shall we return?"

He held out his hand, but Constance pretended not to see it. She was, whenever she thought of it, deeply unsettled by the fact he knew she was unwed. And that kiss the evening before . . .

The memory drew her thoughts to when he might next kiss her, which led her to wonder about the evening, about their returning to the chateau. Alone. Together. She tipped a quick glance his way, only to find he was watching her with an affectionate look. Very quickly she returned her gaze to the path. But, *affection?* Much more likely he was laughing at her!

"It will be all right," said Jack softly.

"It?"

"You are a very bright lady, my dear. You'll figure it out."

"Bah!"

"I wonder if that means you think you won't, or if you think there is nothing you need unravel. If the latter, is it because you already understand exactly what I feel for—" His brow arched when she turned and raised her fists to beat him on his chest. He caught her wrists. "Now, why do you do that?"

"I cannot bear that you joke about such things."

He released one wrist, freeing a hand with which he tipped her chin up so he could look into her face. His thumb caught a tear falling from her lashes. "Is it so difficult to believe—"

"Don't. Don't pretend."

"But Connie—"

"And I don't believe," she said, recovering her dignity, "that I have given you permission to use that name for me."

"No, but—"

"Enough. We are hungry. And I have been under more than a little strain worrying about whether we'd find Silly. And now that we have, I am upset that we must delay our return. Please don't add to all that. I can't deal with you when I must sort out all the rest."

"Two things," he said sternly. "There is no need for you to sort out anything, my dear. Mordaunt and I will take care of everything, *which is as it should be.* You need not do a thing. As to your second worry, the delay, you'll find we arrive home at very nearly the same time by waiting for your brother's yacht—as if we'd ridden back up the coast, which we cannot do in any case—and then, arriving in Le Havre, were forced to await the next packet to England."

Constance struggled against the hand still holding her. "I do not *wish* that everything be done for me. I have taken care of myself for far too many years to enjoy mollycoddling!"

"I am certain you and Felice have much to do sorting out her home. You can see to that with all the energy I know you possess."

"The little lady must not interfere in manly things. She cannot possibly understand what it is they do!" she spat, sarcasm dripping acid from her tongue.

"Nonsense. I know you are more than capable of understanding all sorts of things as, I think, I've already told you. But in this particular case, it would be far more helpful if you were to keep your brother's woman where she'll not overhear something she should not learn!"

Constance rolled her eyes. She cast him a look of suspicion. "Well, why did you not say so? Or did that last just occur to you?"

"I just thought of it," he admitted, the slanting grin she loved creasing his face. "It is, however, true that it would be of help." He sobered. "It is also true that you no longer need shoulder all your cares yourself or bear the whole of any responsibility. Not only have you found your brother, my love, but you have me as well."

"I have asked," she said in a insincerely patient tone, "that you not tease me about that. We will forget all you've said on the subject of marriage, if you please. Or even if you do not. Not only is it unnecessary that you martyr yourself, but I will find you a dead bore if you do not stop referring to it."

Jack stared down at her, a frown creasing his brow. "You, my dear, are going to be a difficult woman to woo. However, if you insist, I suppose I might restrain myself from discussing marriage until we've returned to England and you see that Mordaunt's children are in good hands. Perhaps then you can begin thinking about your own."

The thought of having children of her own smote Constance like a blow. The thought of how those children might be achieved roused an entirely different sort of emotion. Using every ounce of will she possessed, she pushed both notions from her mind.

"It will take," she said, "some time for them to accept that their father has been returned to them, to say nothing of the fact they've a new mother. They will need me for several months, I should think. Therefore, you may return me to England and go off in good heart, knowing I am needed and busy."

Jack's lips compressed and a faint line drew his brows together. "Stubborn wench."

"So I am. See that you remember it," she finished with a pertness she didn't truly feel. "Now, do you suppose our luncheon is ready? I was hungry before. Now I am ravenous."

"Arguing gives you an appetite?" he asked, matching her lighter tone with one of his own. "I must keep that in mind and refrain from arguing with you when we may not feed you!''

"You promised—"

"Oh no!" he interrupted. "I am much too canny a soul, as a Scottish friend is wont to say, to promise what I cannot do. I did not say I'd refrain from teasing you. Only that I'd not mention the one subject you have denied me. And don't," he added, when she opened her mouth, "suggest any other topics I may not raise. I am, as I've warned you, a man with all a man's failings. One of them is a disinclination to refrain from flirting with an attractive woman. Which you are."

Once again she struggled against the hand holding her. "Nonsense."

This time he let her wrist go, but not her chin. "You are not a classic beauty," he said thoughtfully, "not fashioned in quite the common mode, but that is an advantage. I've always had a liking for the uncommon."

She grimaced. "An oddity, you would say."

"No. You are a rarity, which is quite a different thing. An intelligent woman who was forced by circumstance into doing far more than should have been asked of her." He tapped her nose with one long finger. "I had a word or two with Mordaunt on that head. He claims he'd no notion his father was dead, so how was he to know he was needed."

"Besides, I was perfectly capable of taking over the estate business and seeing to his children."

"Capable? Oh yes. I have said so. But as a result you were denied a season, were you not? An opportunity to meet men who would have understood you, men you might have loved?"

He spoke lightly, but with a pensive undertone that had Constance's heart beating faster even though she *knew* she listened to a rogue.

"And now," he continued, "it is too late to give you that choice. *I* have met you. You'd best pray you find it in your heart to love *me,* my dear, since I'll never let you go to another!"

"More nonsense," she said, and sighed.

Jack might have been pardoned for thinking she sighed out of exasperation, but actually it was a sigh of despair at the knowledge she must not allow the wonderfully smooth and lying tongue of the man with whom she'd fallen in love to sweep her away from her determination to save him from himself.

But, oh, she thought, *how sweet it is to hear such honeyed words, for all that his tongue must have been polished with bee's wax that they slip off so smoothly. Even if they are no more than sweet sweet, lies, I love it when he goes on that way. . . .*

Later that evening in Felice's garden, hidden by the deepening dusk, Jack gave Constance a quick kiss, a kiss that startled her so that she was unable to truly appreciate it.

He kissed her, too, before he allowed her to enter her room at the chateau that evening, a kiss which, more private, lasted longer, and could be savored.

And was.

He kissed her once in the inn garden when he found her there alone, but it was only a quick, hard kiss she stowed away in her heart as she was stowing her brother's clothing into canvas bags for transport.

And finally, he kissed her, again quickly, on the boat that took them, in the dark of a moonless night, to the English coast, a kiss she found unsettling because there were far too many people around who might have seen him. Still, it was one more kiss she could add to those she knew she'd remember and take out and examine and savor again and again. She also knew that, at that latter date, she'd wonder that she'd had the courage to allow him such liberties.

It also crossed her mind that, perhaps, she might need to reflect whether it was *courage* or merely *desperation!*

When they were put ashore at Portsmouth she suspected there'd be no further opportunities in which Jack might steal a kiss. At the thought Constance had a hint of how awfully dull she'd find the world from now on. No more kisses. No more Jack. Just a cold, dreary world of duty and responsibility.

Scolding, she reminded herself her life had been quite satisfying before she'd met the rogue. She determined she'd make it so again. On the thought she fell asleep, and it wasn't until they were driving up the long, tree-lined drive to the Grinnel's country manor that she awoke to the new day. The first day of the rest of her life. Her lonely life.

Someone must have run ahead from the gate because Nurse Willes, Valerian, and little Venetia were waiting for them before the house.

"Connie," said Val, urgently pulling on her sleeve with the hand *not* extending from a splint, "I am not allowed to ride. Do tell them it was an accident, and that I am perfectly all right and that I *may* go riding!" Val hadn't even given his aunt a proper greeting before making his demands.

Constance, hugging Venetia, looked up at Nurse Willes. "Accident?"

Willy mouthed, "Later," before she looked beyond Connie to where Selwyn stood, a trifle uncertain, staring at his children. Nurse Willes eyed the woman on his arm. She glanced toward Major Lord St. Aubyn, who watched Constance with a smile as Connie and the children greeted each other.

A gentle anticipatory warmth filling her, Mrs. Willes wondered how long it would be before she'd have Connie's babes to care for. She glanced again at the silent, slightly moody–looking woman at Selwyn's side. Would there be more children at the manor?

On the thought, the nurse approached her old charge, leaving the children with their aunt. "Well, Selwyn," asked Nurse Willes harshly, "What have you to say for yourself, hmmm?"

Miss Willes had always covered her emotions with a stern demeanor, as the Mordaunts were well aware. "Duty, Willy," said Selwyn, grinning insouciantly. His eyes didn't leave his son, who spoke earnestly to Constance. "You taught us we were always to do our duty!"

"I also thought I taught you manners," scolded the Mordaunt nurse.

Selwyn dragged his gaze from the children, looked at Miss Willes, glanced down at Felice, and red crept up his neck. "Lord, I am sorry. Allow me to introduce Madame Beugnot."

Jack, more interested in the sister than the brother, moved nearer to where Val spoke to his aunt. "But Connie—"

"If you have been forbidden to leave the gardens except in the company of Lord Grinnel, then you must respect that order, Val. Especially when you are a guest, where you do not know what dangers lurk around and about. Come Venetia. Val? I wish to introduce you to your father, who has been in the army for many many years now. He is anxious to see you, and very much wishes to become acquainted with you. "Selwyn," she called.

Her brother turned toward them. "In a minute."

Her hand went to Val's head when the boy's eyes widened at Selwyn's ungainly gait. "He was badly wounded, Val," she said softly, "in battle. You will remember that battle scars are badges of honor."

"Like old Henry?" asked the boy, referring to a retired sailor living in a Cornwall village near his home. The man had been badly burned by an exploding magazine in the ship on which he'd sailed, his face a ruin that might have been frightening if Constance hadn't explained about honor.

"Yes. Exactly."

"There was danger?"

"A great deal of danger."

"Will he tell me?"

Connie hesitated. She'd never understood why, but she'd learned that quite often men didn't wish to speak of the battles they'd fought. "I believe so, Val, but perhaps not right away. You are not to tease him for the tale. I will ask him to explain to you, but if he declines, that is that."

"All right, Connie. Battles are not nice, I think," said the boy slowly, coming up with one of his very adult deductions. "I think soldiers don't like to remember them. Like nightmares, perhaps?"

"I think you may have hit the nail squarely on the head, Val."

Selwyn approached a few hesitant steps, and was joined by Felice.

"Now," said Connie, "let us go to them so you may make your bow to your father and to Madame Beugnot. You remember Lord St. Aubyn, I think?" she added, seeing Jack.

The amenities taken care of, everyone moved up from the drive to the terrace fronting the Grinnel manor house, where Lady Grinnel and her husband awaited them. The Grinnels had had the tact to allow the family to greet each other first.

When the further introductions had been made, Lady Mary pouted, and glowered at her cousin. She had not liked learning that the woman she'd thought Lord Mordaunt's wife was not. The tale concocted to explain the error, one in which Constance was another Mrs. Mordaunt, might have appeased her if it hadn't included the information she was widowed.

"The widowed Miss Mordaunt," Selwyn had teased when they'd put the story together.

As well as pique that Constance was not safely married and therefore *was* a danger to her Jack, Lady Grinnel's welcome to the Frenchwoman contained more than a trifle of reserve.

And, finally, Mary turned her back on Jack himself, her usual manner of punishing a person for their sins, real or imagined. It was not the easiest of situations for any of them.

Everyone followed Lord and Lady Grinnel into the house and through the cool hall to a welcoming salon which looked out over a soothing northern prospect. There they found Lord Temperance who, upon seeing Constance, approached her hurriedly, thrusting out a sealed letter. "This came while you were gone," he blurted and added tersely, *"Open it."*

When Constance stared at him, openmouthed, his ears turned bright red.

Giving an abrupt and surprisingly ungainly bow for such a man of the town, he began again. "Lady Mordaunt, I must know what Ada has said to you. If she will not see me you must intercede. I must—" He mopped his brow, cast a glance at Jack who had come to Constance's side, looked to where Lady Grinnel's mouth was primmed into a disapproving line, and cast a further glance around at everyone else in the salon. His eyes shut, the skin over his bones tightening, he fought for control. "Lady Mordaunt . . . *please?*"

"It means so much to you?"

"*Yes.*"

There was no disbelieving the sincerity of that explosion, so she excused herself to the others and, with little Venetia holding her skirts, moved apart. She broke the seal and opened the single page which was not only crossed but *recrossed.*

Constance despaired of deciphering even the half of it. She moved to a table near the window and drew out a chair. Then, seating herself, she absently pulled Venetia into her side and began work. She didn't notice when Lord St. Aubyn took a sweating Lord Temperance by the arm and led him from the room to where Grinnel kept a decanter and glasses.

"I caught a glimpse of the unfolded page," he told Temperance. "It will take Connie some time to find the meaning in it," he added.

"If Lady Mordaunt would only allow me—"

"You recognized the writing on the address?"

"*Yes.* I must find her. The Mordaunts are from Cornwall. Where?"

"I know you may find that information easily enough, Temperance, but do you not think you should abide by your lady's wishes?"

"If I am forced to believe she truly wishes to never see me, then yes. But if she has been forced by her parents into isolation and convinced by them she is a pariah who must never darken the morally spotless doorsteps"—there was a wealth of sarcasm in that phrase—"of London's *ton,* then I will do whatever is necessary to convince her."

"Convince her?" repeated Lord St. Aubyn.

Temperance straightened and cast St. Aubyn a belligerent look. "That I have never forgotten her, and that I still wish to wed her. That if she has borne my child, it is my right and her duty to marry me!"

"I don't know that it *is* her duty, but I agree that if she still has any feelings of a positive nature for you, or even if she only has no negative feelings, it would be to her advantage for the two of you to wed."

"You would suggest a marriage of convenience," said Temperance after a moment. "I hope it will not come to that, but if it does, so be it. Nevertheless, whatever Ada decides concerning me, I must see my child, I must care for it."

"You admit to making Connie's friend *enceinte?*"

Temperance spoke stiffly. "I will admit that it was a possibility and, from Lady Mordaunt's description of the child I conclude that it could have no other parentage. I did not know she was breeding when I left with my regiment, and no one informed me. Nevertheless, the child must be mine. I will have it!"

"Though you must remove it from its mother? You are not so cruel."

Temperance again closed his eyes, and this time slumped down into a chair, his hands hanging down between his knees, the wineglass dangling from one. "I am going mad, I think. I have always loved her, but her family only laughed at the notion. As a suitor, I mean. I was not good enough for their daughter. Then she and I . . . oh, the devil! You know how these things happen. She'd been sent home from London in disgrace when she refused a marriage her father arranged for her. I was due to leave for the army."

He sat up. "I do not try to excuse my responsibility in this," he said firmly. "She was young. She was innocent. But we loved each other."

"I understand, although I admit I can't approve. I suggest you wait here while I try to help Connie with her . . . hmm . . . decoding." *I am, after all* he thought, *supposed to be an expert in decoding.* "Do not come back to the salon," he added, thinking of his last look at his cousin's expression of outrage at Temperance's behavior. "I will bring you word here."

Considerately, Jack moved the decanter nearer Temperance's elbow. He left the desperate man alone, returning to where he found his cousin speaking trifles to Felice, politely, if a trifle reservedly, and Mordaunt and Grinnel deep into some subject to which Valerian, standing nearby, listened avidly.

Connie remained at her table. Venetia had crawled into her aunt's lap. The child sat perfectly quietly, and Constance had one hand free to trace the words where they were particularly obscured. Jack grinned at the frown furrowing his love's brow, found paper and a pen in his cousin's writing desk and joined the duo at the table.

"I will write down what you tell me, leaving blanks where you cannot decipher it," he said. "That way, when you've managed to work out the most of it, we can go back and attempt to fill in any important holes."

"An excellent notion. I wonder why I thought I had to have every word as I went along. Particularly when it is such a mishmash of nonsense."

She softly read the opening parts which had been written with a steady hand and Jack transcribed them. When she began having difficulty, he moved his chair to her side and she pointed out how many words she could not read and he left space for them.

"Will you never be done?" asked Lady Grinnel, inter-rupting them. "Whatever is in that to have destroyed our Lord Temperance's manners? He arrived day before yester-day, discovered there was a letter for *Miss* Mordaunt, and then simply settled in to wait for her. When he heard you'd arrived, he must have gotten the letter from Lummy."

"Lady Grinnel, as I told you in London, it is not my secret," said Constance, glancing up from the page. "When I've finally discovered my friend's wishes, I will inform Lord Temperance and he may tell you what he wishes."

"Oh, please," begged Lady Mary, her fingers winding around each other. "Tell me *something*. I cannot bear secrets. *I cannot.*"

Constance looked at Jack, who sighed. "Mary, I assure you the woman who wrote this letter doesn't even know of your existence. Don't you think you have become old enough now that you need not worry that someone is making plans for you against your will, or that they are saying things about you which you will not like?"

Mary's skin paled to ashy white. She drew in a deep breath and turned on her heel. Allowing only one sob to escape, she ran from the room. Jack rose to his feet and watched her go. He saw Lord Grinnel turn a sharp look his way and moved to his cousin–by–marriage's side. He apologized for what he'd said to upset Mary, and *didn't* suggest Grinnel go soothe his wife

He didn't need to. Grinnel, sighing, apologized for the necessity of leaving his guests to their own devices and removed from the salon. Felice and Selwyn looked at each other and then at Val. Val gave his father a hopeful look.

Selwyn grinned. "Why don't you show me this garden, Val, to which you are bound?" Taking Felice with them, father and son left by way of the low windows opening onto the terrace outside the salon.

"What have we got?" asked Constance soon after.

"What we have is a yes and a no and a yes and a no and a yes and a no." Jack's brow arched. "Need I go on?"

"But what do I tell Lord Temperance?"

Jack grinned. "A yes and a no and a yes and a no and . . ."

Constance playfully growled and then hugged Venetia, who looked up at her.

"You, my good sir, are no help at all!"

"Neither is your friend!"

"Oh dear, how very true. I haven't a notion what to do."

"He wants to marry her," said Jack quietly.

Constance gave him a startled look and then stared thoughtfully at the letter. "Jack, what do you know of Lord Temperance?"

"From all reports he was a very good officer. From what gossip I've heard since he inherited he's been acting the butterfly, and there are wagers in all the club betting books concerning whom he will finally choose for a mistress."

"Whom he will finally choose," repeated Constance slowly. "Which implies, does it not, that he has not yet chosen, which is what your cousin said of him when we first met."

"So?" He waited in vain for her to go on. "Do you think him worthy of your friend?" he finally asked.

"I . . . don't know."

"You wish to keep him on tenterhooks until you know him better? I don't believe you'll see his best side. He is too impatient, too . . . needy?"

"I don't believe you should have said that last to me," said Constance, her tone more absentminded than scolding. "But I do see what you mean. He saved Val from harm once." She smiled and described the incident.

Jack instantly frowned. "I wish you'd told me that before we left for France."

"Why? What do you mean?"

"I . . . don't know." Jack had nearly forgotten his suspicions of Rhino Biggens and a possible connection to Wilmot Mordaunt which this bit of information might confirm. "Not for certain. I must talk to Temperance and then discover more about the, er, accident which resulted in the boy's broken arm."

Connie's eyes widened. "Jack, surely you aren't suggesting the accidents weren't accidents?"

"I don't know. On the other hand, when we arrived, I noticed an awful lot of gardeners out there!"

"Guards?" asked Constance, startled.

"I wouldn't be surprised. Which means you need not concern yourself, does it not? I set my batman the task of watching over Val before we left. I must discover what happened to cause Grinnel to set extra guards." He rose to his feet. "Connie, if you'll excuse me I'll see what I can discover. I'll start with my batman. While I'm gone, you may decide what to do about that letter, such as it is."

Much to Constance's surprise, he didn't wait for her agreement, but disappeared out the same window Selwyn had used some fifteen minutes earlier.

"So. Deliberate sabotage," said Jack unsmilingly. He'd just heard the tale of Val's accident. Harry, along with Lord Grinnel had been working with the boys, overseeing their jumping practice, when Val's saddle came off. "What did his lordship say?"

"He was as furious as I," snapped the batman, who hid

under the gruff manner his concern for the youngster he'd come to like. "That's when young Mordaunt were told he weren't to ride again without Himself along. Didn't take too well to that," grinned Harry. "Boy likes his riding, and his lordship's a busy man. Boy's very good for so young a one, by the way. Better'n Lord Grinnel's boy, and that one's rather older, you know."

"I can see you've taken a shine to the lad. He undoubtedly learned to ride well following his aunt around their estate in Cornwall."

"Aunt?"

Jack grinned and explained how he himself had mistaken Miss Mordaunt for Lord Mordaunt's wife and that she'd allowed him to retain that belief . . . until they found the truant in France and the truth came out. "We are calling her Mrs. Mordaunt now rather than Lady Mordaunt."

"She went off with you without a chaperone?" Harry's outrage was deeper and more real than that Lord Mordaunt had expressed. After all, Selwyn knew his sister's stubborn nature. "You'll find yourself tied up in parson's mousetrap afore you can say the words!"

"Don't I wish!"

Harry's mouth dropped open. He blinked. "You do?"

"Harry, I am aware you are something of a misogynist, but as you well know *I* am not. In Miss Mordaunt I've found exactly the woman for whom I've searched, even though I didn't know I was looking! Now I've only to convince her *I* am what *she* wants!"

That had the batman's mouth gapping. "She's turned you down?"

Harry's emotion was so obviously one of disbelief it was balm to Jack's somewhat lacerated sensibilities. He hadn't expected to be rejected, and although he'd hidden it it had hurt.

"From what she says, I believe she thinks to protect me from myself," explained Jack lightly. That he believed exactly that was the only thing that kept him from joining Temperance and the bottle, *several* bottles, in Grinnel's study!

"*Women*. Can't live with 'em, and can't live without 'em."

The hoary old chestnut brought a laugh to Jack's lips and he set off on his next errand, which was to speak with Lord Mordaunt about the more than probable danger his son faced. He didn't want the man thinking the boy was safe as houses merely because they were living in the middle of the placid Kentish countryside.

Then, once he'd warned Selwyn to have a care for the lad, he must talk to Temperance about what had happened in London. That is, he would if he could get the man to think of anything but his Ada. And then a few words with Lord Grinnel, assuming Mary had come down off the high ropes and her husband was available. Finally, he must concoct a plot whereby Valerian could be made safe so they could all stop worrying about him.

The plot, decided Jack, must not only protect the boy's life. It must also implicate the unbeloved, to say nothing of unlovable, Cousin Wilmot. It was apparent from what he'd learned that the man had made a fortune selling shoddy goods to the army, but that, at this point, would be exceedingly difficult to prove. So, proving the man was guilty of intriguing to kill Val would result in punishment which could also stand for his earlier crimes.

There were two reasons for coming up with a means of proving Mordaunt's guilt. The safety of the boy was paramount, of course, but the second was also compelling.

At least, it was to Jack: Because, the instant Constance

realized her nephew was in real and continuing danger, she would be unable to turn her mind to romance. And, for Jack, turning Constance's mind toward sweet romance was a personal need of equal importance to Temperance's need to find and woo his Ada.

Chapter 8

Major St. Aubyn stared down at the man sprawling in an overstuffed library chair, his legs wide and a fatuous smile on his face. "Temperance, get out of your lady's bed—even if you are only there in imagination. I need your attention!"

"Hmm?" Lord Temperance blinked owlishly and then tried to stand. He sat back with a thump and looked disbelievingly at the nearly empty decanter. "Bed, you say?"

St. Aubyn sighed and resigned himself to the necessary struggle to get Temperance to make sense. "My lord, cast your mind back . . ."

Jack finally managed to remind his heartsick lordship of the day he'd trailed Constance and her charges away from Lord Grinnel's townhouse, the day he'd saved young Mordaunt from a possibly fatal fall before a team of horses. But, even when he had the proper memory separated from those of his Ada, Temperance remembered little about the man who, perhaps accidentally, had brushed against

Val. His description of a smallish man, nattily if not quite tastefully dressed, fit Rhino all too well, however, and Jack started for the door.

"Wait!"

Jack turned, backing away, impatience stamped in every line. "Yes?"

"What did Ada say? What was her decision? Surely Lady Mordaunt knows the truth by now?"

Jack's mouth primmed, but his eyes danced. He wondered if he dared. A self–deriding, exceedingly wry smile momentarily distorted his face. *Of course* he dared.

"Your Ada says yes."

Temperance lit up like a lamp.

"And no."

Temperance's smile faded.

"And yes and no, and yes."

Bewilderment blossomed.

"And no and yes, until one's head goes round." Jack's eyes lost the glint of humor so common to him. "I've no notion what Mrs. Mordaunt will tell you. She is having a deal of trouble deciphering the *real* meaning behind the mishmash of contradictions that letter contains." He ducked out the door before Temperance, obviously beyond bewilderment and now quite angry, could make his weaving way across the room.

In the hall Jack found Miss Willes. "Aha. Just the one I must talk to next." He offered both a charming smile and his arm and led the bemused nurse from the house. "Now, tell me what you know about the accident when young Val broke his arm."

"No accident, my lord. His tack was tampered with. His saddle came off because the cinch had been deftly weakened."

Jack had heard of the sabotage from his batman, but

had forgotten to discover exactly what was done. "Do you mean it wasn't, as I assumed, an obvious cut?"

"I believe when Lord Grinnel inspected it it was only by chance he noted that the occasional stitch attaching the cinch to the saddle had been cut rather than worn. Jumping, which the lads were doing under Lord Grinnel's eye, strained the remaining stitches until the cinch parted from the saddle."

"Thank you Miss Willes. You give a very good report. Perhaps I should bring you into the army to train our young officers in the way of it."

Miss Willes blushed with pleasure, demurred, and told him he was a great tease. She curtsied and moved briskly into the house.

Jack's mouth compressed, and his eyes narrowed as he considered his next move. When Mordaunt, Val in tow, came into sight around the corner of the house his decision was made for him. Regretfully, he put aside his initial and more appealing plan of finding Constance.

"Mordaunt! A moment."

The three came together, and Jack looked down at Val. "Lad, do you think you could bring yourself to part from this rogue for a few minutes?" Val's features lost their animation. Jack put a hand on Val's head. "Valerian," he said gently, "I've business with your father."

"Val," suggested his father, "Aunt Connie is in the drawing room with Madame Felice. When St. Aubyn and I are finished, then we'll see the ponies."

Val huffed a bit. He dragged his feet and looked back more than once, but he obediently removed himself from the terrace and disappeared into the drawing room through the window. Jack felt a twinge of jealousy that the boy would be entering Contance's presence when he himself could not.

Not quite yet.

"The boy is in danger," said Jack bluntly. "The accident here was not the first."

He repeated the conversation he'd overhead between Rhino and the servant. He described how Val had been pushed into the Serpentine, which was, he thought, an amateur effort on the part of Wilmot's servant, and that the later shove into the street was a far more serious attempt. Finally, there was this problem with the girth.

"The lad should be warned," finished Jack.

"He is too young to be burdened with such knowledge," said Selwyn slowly, a frown creasing his brow. "Besides, I can't believe it true. Why would anyone do such a thing? What would be the gain?"

"The fact you didn't return after Waterloo was, I believe, the initial inspiration for the notion."

Selwyn cast Jack a startled look.

"Your sister arrived in London searching for information about you. It appeared as if you were lost, dead, gone forever. Only a handful of men knew differently. Do you think it impossible your heir presumptive decided he deserved to come into the barony, and *would* if only he could rid himself of young Val?"

"You mean my father's cousin, Wilmot, do you not?" Selwyn's frown deepened. "M'father would have nothing to do with the man."

"Your sister learned of his existence when going through your father's papers. When she needed to come to London she couldn't, with propriety, go to a hotel, a female alone. In any event, she put aside her qualms as to the man's character and wrote him. What do *you* know of him?"

Selwyn grinned a quick, flashing grin. "My father threw the fellow in my face when I demanded I be allowed to go into the army. He said that if I died the man would inherit, and that that would be a disaster. But I would not be dissuaded, having then that arrogance of the young, that belief that nothing bad can possibly happen to one's own precious self." Selwyn lay a hand on his bad leg and grimaced. "This wound might well have done for me, but by then Val had been born so I felt I'd not totally failed my father. When I was closest to death it was a comfort to me."

"But you survived and immediately put yourself into further danger."

A flush of embarrassment reddened Selwyn's cheeks.

"That is no longer relevant, I suppose. It is my belief the boy should be warned, so that he does nothing foolish. He's already chafing at the restraints put on him, primarily the order that he is not to go beyond the gardens unless Lord Grinnel is with him. I cannot see such a sprited youth long accepting such limits." Jack caught Selwyn's gaze and held it and added on a sarcastic note, "As *you*, of course, *would* have done at that age, would you not?"

Selwyn looked away, not exactly admitting his rebellious youth, but not denying it either. "I will take him about with me," he decided. "In that way, he need not be kept so close. But to tell the lad someone wishes to kill him? I'll not have the boy fearing such a thing. Especially since we do not, for certain, know it is true."

"I've no real proof, except that the saddle girth was deliberately damaged." Impatient, Jack pushed the hair back off his forehead. "It is only bits and pieces of information I've put together which make me believe it deep down in my bones. I've learned to trust that feeling. I think you, Mordaunt, are one of the few who understands what I mean by that."

"Lord, yes!" Selwyn grinned. "I don't know how often that odd sensation has saved my skin." He sobered. "When

I've mentioned it, I've been told to get a hold of imagination, that I'm merely superstitious, and ordered to stop spouting nonsense. I cannot explain such intuitions, but I don't deny they exist.''

"Then beware for your son.'' With that final warning, Jack turned on his heel and left Selwyn standing, one hand unconsciously rubbing his thigh, thoughtfully staring after him.

Constance looked up from where Val spoke rapidly, excitedly, and was rewarded by finding Jack standing just inside the window watching her. His expression was one of fondness, and she felt the warmth of response flowing up inside. She set Val away from her, absently hushing him, her eyes never leaving Jack's. Why, she wondered, did it seem hours since he'd left her there working on Ada's letter?

A quick glance at the clock proved it had actually been much less than a single hour. "What have you been doing, my lord?'' she asked softly.

"Worrying about the jackanapes mostly.'' He glanced down at Val, who sat on the floor fiddling with a ball and jacks he'd had in his pocket. "You?''

"Worrying about an entirely different imp, my lord.'' When he looked a question she added, "A female imp. My friend's daughter. I cannot decide what to do for the best.'' She fiddled with the papers she'd stacked before her, the much crossed letter, her translation and, finally, the clean copy she'd written out when she decided she'd done as accurate a job as could be managed. "My lord, will you escort me into the library where I assume you left his lordship?''

"No.''

Constance's eyes widened. "No? Whyever not, my lord?"

"You wouldn't wish to see him just now."

"But I must talk to him."

"Not until the man sobers up!" He grimaced. "And that is my fault. I thought a drink would settle his nerves . . . but then I left him with the decanter." Very soberly, almost pensively, he added, *That* was a mistake on my part. I don't usually make such obvious errors of judgement."

Constance tried not to smile at his self–accusing, rather bemused, tone. But she happened to glance at Madame Beugnot, discovered her new friend was hiding chuckles behind her hands, and could no longer repress her own.

"I suppose I must wait, then. Felice, would you . . . ?" She glanced from the Frenchwoman to Val, and back.

"Mon petit garçon," called Felice.

Val looked up when Constance prodded him with her toe. "Madame is speaking to you."

Val scrambled to his feet. "Yes, Madame?" he asked politely.

"You and I, I think, should go to your father."

"But he said he'd come here."

"Very likely he forgot," said Felice. She offered her hand to Val. "Shall we go find him?"

Val hesitated. He glanced at Connie, who nodded, and back to Felice. He bowed. "Thank you, Madame. I would appreciate that very much."

"Ha! The makings of a cavalier, is it not? *En avant, mon petite cavalier!"*

Val tossed her a thoroughly disgusted look. "I am not a Cavalier. I am one of Cromwell's Roundheads!"

"Are you, then? I don't know this Cromwell. You must tell me of this one," said Felice, leading him to the window. So, as they exited, Val explained about his ancestor who supported Cromwell's fight against the Stuart papists.

Constance gave fleeting thought to the problem of Felice's religion, which was most likely Catholic, and decided that was Selwyn's problem. "Jack, I truly must talk to Lord Temperance. Can you not sober him up?"

"I am sober," said Lord Temperance from the doorway to the hall. "Tell me when I may see my Ada."

"I cannot tell you." Constance eyed the bleary–eyed man, his rumpled coat and the tie set askew under one ear. "My lord, *Ada* doesn't know. I think part of the problem is her fear you'll take her child. Part of it is that her father and uncle convinced her she can never again show her face to the polite world. And part of it, of course, is the fact you abandoned her." Connie held up her hand when Temperance would have expostulated. "I am sure that's not the case, but her letters to you were never answered, you see."

"I never received such letters," said his lordship intemperately. "I had no word of her from her or from anyone."

"From what I have guessed," said Connie gently, "I suspect her letters were never sent, that Ada was only told they'd been sent."

After a moment digesting that, Temperance asked, "What can I do?"

"The most difficult thing in the world. You can have patience. I will write Ada again and explain a number of things to her. I'll need to discuss some of them with you, of course, before I do so, so that I'll know what to say?"

"Now?" asked his lordship eagerly, starting across the room.

Jack cleared his throat. When Lord Temperance cast an impatient glance his way, Jack did no more than run his eye over the dishevelled man. One startled look and Temperance moved instantly toward an ornately gilded mirror hanging beside the fireplace. His hand flew to his throat and he attempted to pull his cravat into place. He rubbed futilely at his wrinkled coat, and finally sighed.

"Later, my lord?" suggested Constance gently.

Lord Temperance bowed, turned on his heel, and left the room.

"His valet will have words to say," said Jack, laughing.

"I very much doubt the poor fellow will have the courage to say them to his lordship, however," said Constance, tacitly agreeing.

"Oh I don't know about that," mused Jack. "You've no notion how much the tiger a valet can become when his wardrobe has been abused."

"*His* wardrobe, my lord?"

"You called me Jack a while ago," he said suggestively, coming closer and taking her hands.

"I should not have done so."

"I liked it . . . Connie."

She felt a blush fly into her cheeks. "I think I do as well, my lord, but . . ." She tugged at her hands.

"When will you wed me?"

"You must not ask. You only do so because you feel you've compromised me. I'll not marry for such a reason."

"Then wed me because you've compromised me," he said, teasing, and realized instantly he'd made an error. Constance gasped, jerked free her hands, and ran from the room.

"Damn."

"Woman trouble?" asked Lord Grinnel. Just entering, he had politely held open the door for Constance, who passed him, head averted.

"My damnable sense of humor!"

"Said the wrong thing for the right reason?"

"Said the wrong thing, at least. I won't swear to the reason, right or wrong. It just came out."

"Yes, we do that." Lord Grinnel grimaced.

"Mary still in one of her snits?"

Lord Grinnel's throat turned bright red and flags flew in his cheeks, but he nevertheless uttered the embarrassing words. "She is . . . vulnerable. I don't know what to say, how to convince her that I love her."

"Telling her isn't enough, is it?" said Jack sympathetically. "It never was."

"Damn," said his lordship.

"Women!" responded Jack, glumly.

The two men, needing no discussion, took themselves off to the library where the observant Grinnel butler would soon be required to refill, again, the nearly empty decanter.

A very tired woman, her face heavily veiled and her child's bonnet brim pulled well forward, sat in a stage which would take the two of them the last miles to their destination. The woman huddled in a corner. Her daughter, although too big, snuggled onto her lap and held close. They spoke to no one, pretending to sleep or whispering quietly. Both mother and child hoped the terrible journey would soon be at an end.

Grinnel Manor, their destination, was situated just outside the village of Wych Cross, several hours from London. When they arrived there, the woman climbed down stiffly, then lifted the child out after her. She smiled at the guard for finding her portmanteaus. He was so bemused by her sweet manner he didn't even curse when she failed to tip him.

Mrs. Wright, checking that her veil was in place, entered the small inn, her daughter's hand in her own. She found the innkeeper and asked if he'd a boy who could carry a note to Grinnel Manor and if she and her daughter could have a room in which they might rest while they awaited a response.

"An answer, is it? Will you be needin' a room for the night, then?"

Ada bit her lip. "I do not know." She thought of her slender funds and hoped she would not. "The stage, I understand, does not return today?"

"Not 'til Thursday," said the landlord.

Ada's eyes widened. "Oh!"

The man's eyes narrowed and a muscle jumped in his jaw. "I'll be wantin' something on account."

Ada's color rose at the implied insult but she compressed her lips. With great care, she counted several coins into the man's ready paw. Then, head high and Clarissa's hand held tightly, she followed his directions to the small room tucked under the eaves which he'd seen fit to give her.

Her message to Miss Mordaunt arrived at Grinnel Manor just as a much improved Lord Temperance reached the main hall. For some reason there was no footman in attendance when a dirty lad, a young groom by the looks of him, peered in the open front door and glanced around.

"Yes? You looking for someone?" asked Temperance, going toward him.

"Message for Miss Mordaunt, my lord," said the boy, handing over the note Ada had had prepared in advance to give to the innkeeper.

"*Miss* Mordaunt? I'll give it to her." Temperance flipped the boy a coin and took the folded and twisted paper. He glanced at the direction and stilled. "Boy!" he called after the retreating lad.

"Yes, my lord?"

"Where did you get this?"

"Why, at the inn, my lord."

"In the village?"

The boy cast him a look that asked what other inn there would be, but he answered politely enough. "Yes, my lord."

"Thank you."

Once more Temperance took the stairs to his room to change clothes. He accomplished this far more quickly than he was used to doing, this time donning riding gear. He returned to the hall where, unlike earlier, he found a footman.

"Where may I find her ladyship?" he asked, biting off his words crisply, a tone very unlike his usual drawl.

"Lady Grinnel is not available," said the footman, his nose in the air.

"I must speak with her." Lord Temperance rubbed *his* nose with one finger. "I'll write her a note," he decided. "She'll accept a note?"

"I will take it to her maid, my lord," said the footman, not exactly answering the question asked.

"Very well."

Temperance returned to the hall with a hastily scribbled note and then followed the footman up the stairs and along the hall to the master suite, where Lady Grinnel had barricaded herself within her private rooms. He paced as he waited, wishing he could simply rush in and demand to speak with the spoiled beauty. He'd a sinking feeling that Lady Grinnel would not like his request that he bring an unknown woman into her home and, if she had accompanied her mother, the woman's daughter as well, but he didn't know what else to do.

"Her ladyship will see you now," said a maid, opening the door to the sitting room.

"My lord!" caroled Mary as he entered. She held out her hand to him and he saluted it perfunctorily. She looked disappointed. "My lord?"

"My dear," he said, pacing up and down in front of the fireplace, "I've a great favor to ask of you."

"A favor?"

He sighed. "Lady Grinnel"—he stopped and stared sternly—"can you keep a secret?"

"I am very good at keeping secrets." Mary, always interested in secrets, was intrigued. Her mood, which had lightened when she'd thought Lord Temperance had come to flirt with her, then darkened when he did not oblige her by doing so, lightened once again. "Jack knows. Ask him if you do not believe me."

"This secret could be the ruin of a lady," he warned.

"Oh. Merely gossip." She shrugged. "Still," she added, wishing to hear what he had to say, "if you do not wish it told, then I promise I'll not tell."

For a moment Temperance debated the wisdom of confiding in a society matron, but, feeling he'd no choice, he began. "Just before I entered the army I fell deeply in love with a young woman I'd known for many years. I'd known her all my life, of course, but . . . not known her."

"She grew up," suggested Mary.

"Why, I believe that must have been the case," said Temperance thoughtfully. "I was both lucky and unlucky. She fell in love with me, too, you see, which was lucky, but her family would not accept me as a suitor, which was a very unlucky thing, indeed. They took her to London for her season. When she refused a very acceptable offer she was sent home."

"Her family would not relent and accept you?"

"They would not. She was to consider herself in disgrace." Temperance sighed. "I had just been bought my colors and was spending a few weeks at home before leaving for Portugal to join my regiment. We discussed eloping but she feared the scandal, and finally we decided we must wait until I proved myself in the army and try again to convince her family of the sincerity of our feelings." He fell silent.

"I do not see how that caused her ruin," said Mary a trifle pertly.

"I am having trouble admitting to the despicable behavior on my part which ruined her. I seduced her. My lovely innocent. My love . . ." He got a faraway look in his eyes

A terrible jealousy took hold of Mary. Why did it sometimes seem that every woman in the world was loved except herself?

"You should not tell me such things," she said on a note of prudery.

"It is necessary," he said, ignoring the warning signs. "You see, I left for Portugal to join my regiment very soon after. My Ada suffered the consequences of my impatience all by herself."

"Why did she not write you?"

"I am told she did. I suspect her letters were never sent. Her family, you see. They decided to bury the incident under the rug, and Ada as well. She was told she could never again appear in polite company. That she must hide herself and her . . . mistake . . . away. And that she must never ever tell anyone what she'd done."

"So how have you discovered all this? Ah! She read of your inheritance and wrote you and threatened you."

"No. Never would my Ada do such a thing! You see, Ada's child has eyes like mine." He recalled the address on the note from Ada. *"Miss* Mordaunt—"

"Mrs. Mordaunt," said Mary absently.

"Mrs. Mordaunt saw my eyes when I visited you in London. She couldn't hide her surprise. I accosted her when she left you and demanded an explanation of her. Loyal woman that she is, she would not give it me. Instead she wrote Ada, asking if I could visit her.''

"So?" Lady Grinnel was not stupid. Her eyes narrowed. "Ah ha! That letter that came here for Constance. You knew what was in it. That was why you would not go away.''

"Yes. I am desperate, you see, to find my Ada. And . . . I believe she is as close as the inn in the village!''

"So why are you here? Why do you not go to her?''

"I require your permission to bring her here," he said with such simplicity Lady Grinnel almost missed that this must be the favor he wanted.

Mary bristled. "A fallen woman? You would have me welcome her to my home?''

"You have welcomed me, my lady.''

Mary had to think about that one. "You mean," she said slowly, "that you are as much at fault?''

"Far more at fault. She was an innocent.''

Mary frowned. "I do not see how I *can* welcome her. It is not done. Her family has the right of it, you know. Such a woman is not acceptable in polite circles," said Mary primly.

Temperance lost patience. "Such hypocrisy! That I may walk where I please with no stain to my reputation and she, poor dear, must suffer! I will find her and take her away and marry her, and we will live hidden away at my estate if that is what we must do!''

"Oh!" Mary's eyes rounded. "You wish to *wed* her?'' Her disbelief was obvious. "Even now?''

"You think I should not simply because she has borne a child, you mean? Lady Grinnel, it is *my* child!''

"But . . .''

Mary had a great deal of trouble dealing with the conflict between the deeply ingrained rules concerning proper behavior which she'd imbibed at her overly rigid mother's knee and, as well, had beaten into her by her governess, compared to the very different views held by Lord Temperance. He should not, she felt, wish to wed a woman who had borne a child out of wedlock. He might take her as his mistress, in which case she would not be welcome at the Manor any more than she was now, but if he were to wed her? Then she'd be Lady Temperance, and one didn't wish to snub the future Lady Temperance.

"Sir, I must ask Lord Grinnel to guide me. You see, if she has her child with her," said Mary earnestly, "she would be forced to bring it to our home as well as herself. And if I were to bring a love child into our nursery"—she spread her hands—"well, I do not know what Lord Grinnel would say!"

"Let us find him. I am impatient to go to my Ada."

Mary remembered she was angry with her lord. She turned away, her nose in the air. "I am not speaking to Lord Grinnel. He is a beast."

Lord Temperance sighed. "Then have I your permission to speak to him myself?"

"You mean ask him if you may bring that woman and her love child here?"

"Yes."

Mary gasped. "He would ask why you did not ask me."

"I would tell him I did."

"Oh dear."

"Lady Grinnel, she is a very sweet woman."

"She may have changed!"

"Yes. She may have. It would not be surprising, would it? I must discover how my ill-considered behavior has damaged her, must I not? But I cannot do so unless I may be with her again."

Lady Grinnel scowled. "You will not bring your mistress under my roof!"

Lord Temperance's eyes narrowed. "That was insulting to both my love and myself, my lady," he said quietly.

"But you said—" Mary felt her throat and cheeks heating.

"Ah." Enlightenment dawned. "I said I wished to be with her. I only meant that we'd be together in innocent ways. Days when we may get to know each other again. Walks where we might talk. Evenings where we may entertain and be entertained. Meals together. And my child." He smiled sadly. "I hope the girl *is* with her. She is my *daughter*, Lady Grinnel, and I have never seen her."

Mary might pretend to be a hard-hearted society hostess, but underneath were both a kind heart and many insecurities. "Never seen her?"

"I didn't know until that day in London that she existed," he said.

Mary sighed, Then she brightened. "I may be making a terrible mistake, but no one need know any of her background, need they? Yes, bring her here. I'll order a room prepared and warn the nursery they may have another child added to the rest."

With plans to make and things to do, Mary forgot her pique and bustled, from the room in a housewifely way, followed by his lordship.

Temperance, following, said, "I will bring her here, my lady, but do you not think a note from yourself—?"

"I should have thought of that, should I not?" She hastened down the stairs and into a small parlor where she kept a desk for her personal letters. After dashing off a note to Ada Wright and sanding it, she gave it a twist and handed it to Lord Temperance. "You must take the carriage. She will not wish to arrive here in your curricle, I believe."

"Thank you. That had not occurred to me."

As his lordship went through the hall he gave a footman Ada's note to Miss Mordaunt, something he should have done much sooner. Holding it, he'd felt closer to the woman who wrote it.

Giving it up caused him a pang. But, he assured himself, he would very soon have the woman herself to hold.

He hoped.

Chapter 9

Ada Wright sat in a straight-backed chair, her hands folded in her lap, and stared at her sleeping child. Fear, replacing hope, had entered her mind only as they approached their destination. It churned her stomach into knots.

What would she do if dear Miss Mordaunt were not at Grinnel Manor? What could she do? She'd so little money. It had been utterly foolish to take the very last of her allowance, which was to keep them for another month, and spend it on her panicked flight to Miss Mordaunt's side, seeking her advice, much in need of her comforting common sense. Only when her only friend left Cornwall on her own odyssey had Ada realized how much she depended on Miss Mordaunt.

Ah, but such an ill-considered journey on which she had come. What had she thought to accomplish? What had she thought would come of it?

Her attention turned from the internal to the external.

What was that noise? What a terrible hullabaloo! Was this, after all, *not* a respectable inn? What had she done!

Doors banged open along the narrow hall, the host's deep voice expostulating and another, much less genteel, protesting vehemently. Finally, her own door slammed against the wall. Very slowly Ada, eyes painfully wide, rose to her feet.

"Ada," breathed the man she'd long thought never to see again. "My Ada."

Ada slipped gently to the floor in a dead faint.

Constance, a frown marring her brow, hurried along an upstairs hall, attempting to locate her hostess. "Ah! Lady Grinnel, have you a moment, please?"

"Mrs. Mordaunt!"

Once again Constance debated telling Lady Grennel it was Miss, and not Mrs., but embarrassment that she'd dared travel alone with a man held her tongue.

"Is it not a great thing?" gushed her hostess. "*So* romantic!"

Connie bit her lip. "Romantic?" she asked cautiously.

"Yes. Lord Temperance's romance. I have discovered why he is such a butterfly but never settles to any single sweetness. His lost love—His Ada. He has pined for her in silence and hidden his broken heart by making of himself an errant flirt, do you not see?"

Ignoring all the rest, Connie repeated only a name. "Ada?"

"He told me all," breathed Mary, clasping her hands before her breast and rolling her eyes.

Then Lady Grinnel glanced around the bedroom and told a maid in a far brisker tone that she'd done quite well but to please remove the cobweb from the corner above the windows before leaving the room. Then she nearly pushed Constance out the door.

"I must do flowers," she explained. "And quickly. He'll be back with her in no time at all."

"He?"

"Lord Temperance," said Mary impatiently. "With his true love." She frowned, her lips turning down. "And his daughter," she added, not half so happily. "We are not Foxites," she said sternly.

Connie shook her head at the non sequitur. "I'm sorry. I do not follow your meaning."

"Devonshire House," said Mary on a sour note. When Constance still frowned, Mary sighed. "I forget you are not *comme il faut* with the gossip. Except, of course, this is very old gossip. The fifth duke's nursery was said to hold the first Duchess's children, the second Duchess's children by the Duke—he didn't marry her until later, you know—and the Duke's child with a mistress from before his *first* marriage . . . or very early in it." Mary debated that point briefly. "Too, there was a French child. A mystery, that. I've heard the second duchess wished her children from *her* first marriage raised there, but I believe she did not gain the point. And I haven't a notion what flotsam and jetsam might have been kept there along with all the rest!"

"Are you saying you are aware Ada has come and has brought her child?" asked Connie, making a wild stab at Lady Grinnel's meaning.

"But of course. Lord Temperance has driven to the village to bring them here. He told me all." She brightened. "*Such* a romance. I have already decided he must go at once to Canterbury to see the archbishop." She frowned. "Or would His Grace be residing in the Palace in Lambeth? Oh well." Her frown faded. "Grinnel will know. Temperance will buy a special license and we will hold the wedding here. In the gardens. I will invite . . .''

Connie, wondering whether she would ever get a word in, watched her hostess's frown return, the ridges deeper than ever.

"Or no. Perhaps I will not. It will be a private wedding but a very special wedding. The *children* should attend, I think, do not you? Lord Temperance's daughter will like to be there, I know, and she could not if the rest were forbidden to come. That would be quite unfair, don't you agree?'' Mary glaced at Connie. "Why are you looking at me like that?''

"Did Lord Temperance also receive a note from Mrs. Wright?'' asked Constance.

Mary stopped dead in her tracks. *"Mrs.* Wright? She is already married?'' she wailed.

"No, no, it is a courtesy title. But, Mary . . . Lady Grinnel—''

"Oh, please. Do call me Mary.''

"Mary, I have just received a note from Ada. I was coming to ask if I might bring her here, but, frankly, hadn't thought of poor Clarissa. Of course Ada must have brought her. She'd have had nowhere to leave her. Still . . .''

"You wonder if I'll mind having her in our nursery? Lord Temperance will adopt her, of course. It is so silly, is it not, that he must do so when she is his own daughter? But that will make all right and tidy, so we will ignore the current irregularity. In fact, no one need know of it.''

"But they will. Everyone who sees Clarissa will recognize her as Lord Temperance's daughter. She has his eyes, you see.''

"Oh dear. I had thought it could be kept from—''

Lady Grinnel broke off and cast Connie a sideways glance. Constance shook her head, and her ladyship heaved a sigh so lugubrious Connie had some difficulty refraining from a laugh.

"If it cannot be, then I suppose I must face my lord and explain what I have done and somehow bear his scold. Then, after all that, I must convince him I have done the right thing. Lord Temperance is to wed this Mrs. Wright." She gave Constance a worried look. "It *would* be very wrong to snub the future Lady Temperance, would it not?"

"Once you meet Ada, you will not wish to snub her for her own sake. She is a very gentle woman who was badly used by her own family. So unfair." Constance smiled a slow smile, her face lighting up. "Oh, yes. Do support the wedding! It will be such a slap at her family that she is married from a stranger's house!"

"I never asked. Just who are her family?"

"Hmm?" Constance's eyes widened. She giggled. "I'd not realized it before, but I haven't a notion! I only know they treated poor Ada without so much as a smidgeon of understanding or kindness or, to be frank, the least little bit of good sense when there such was a simple solution! They should have taken her to Portugal, where she'd have wed Temperance and only have been considered imprudent and *not* an outcast forced to live her life in obscurity, which is what they did do. I have the notion it is because they were overly proud and could not bear to admit they'd been wrong to deny Lord Temperance's suit in the first place."

"How very sad." Lady Mary, always senstive to mood, dragged her feet for a few steps, but then continued more briskly. "Flowers. I must pick flowers and make a bouquet for her room. And I've yet to warn the nursery . . . how old is the child? I forgot to ask."

"Clarissa must be eight, or nearly so. Shall I tell Willy she'll have Clarry here at any moment?"

"Please do. What is the time? Oh dear. So late as that? Any moment, indeed!"

But it was not "any moment." In actual fact, it was not any *hour*. The missing couple had yet to arrive as evening approached . . .

Mary had wandered the house and garden, coming back again and again to stare down the drive. What had happened? What *could* have happened? Even word that Lord Temperance had quit the inn in company with Mrs. Wright and the child did not settle her mind. Mary fretted.

Still later, Lummy twice came to the drawing room to announce dinner and twice found his mistress shaking her head. Mary moved to where Constance and Jack stood a little separated from the rest of the company, who had gathered nearer the long windows.

"What am I to do?" she asked. "Cook will have a tantrum, and I have never known how to deal with her megrims. Worst of all, she will not cook a decent meal for days until she comes out of her snit!"

"Then by all means, let us eat," asserted Jack, grinning. "I cannot abide burnt offerings. You know I like my eggs just so."

"Don't tease. Mrs. Mordaunt? What do you advise? Should we wait just a little longer?"

Constance wished, for the second time that day, that she had *not* agreed to the charade that she was her brother's widowed cousin. At the time it had seemed a way of protecting Jack from himself, obviating the need for them to wed. After all, widows had at least as much freedom as married ladies had. But it proved so irritating, being called by the wrong name.

"Mrs. Mordaunt? Constance?"

A solution! "If I'm to call you Mary, then please do call me Constance." She put her mind to the actual question. "Well . . . we know they left the inn together, and the innkeeper said they seemed quite happy. Lady Gri . . . Mary, I mean, I think we should dine. If they arrive later they will either have eaten on the road or Cook may fix them a tray."

"Excellent decision, my, er, friend," said Jack, giving a quick glance to see if Mary had caught what had nearly been a disastrous slip of the tongue. His cousin was already turning away, tripping lightly across the floor to the door to the hall. She was off to inform the butler they were to eat, and Jack, at least, was quite ready.

"You will cause a scandal yet, my lord."

"If you were not so stubborn, dear girl, we could wed and you could stop frowning whenever someone calls you Missus!"

"I admit I do not like it, but there is no alternative. At least, not until we have parted and I am once again safely ensconced on Mordaunt land."

Home. Alone. Constance placed her hand on Jack's offered arm and, as a tremor ran up through her hand and into her body, wished *they* were alone rather than going into dinner. Alone together. Why could she not get enough of his kisses? But, on the other hand, why did she allow them, as she *had* only the evening before, when he'd taken her for a walk in the shrubbery?

Actually, her body reminded her, he'd done just a trifle more than kiss her. He'd touched her where no man had ever dared to lay his hand. She felt her breasts swell and admitted she wouldn't object if he were to do it again. Reprehensible as the knowledge was, she could not deny that she'd liked it!

The company was seated around the large table and had

just completed the soup course when, a widely grinning Lord Temperance swept into the dining room his arm around Ada's shoulder and a hand guiding Clarissa. Their appearance startled a footman so much that he tilted a dish of escalloped oysters so that its contents slid to the floor with a dull plop.

"Ladies. Gentlemen," said Temperance. "May I introduce Ada, Lady Temperance. My *wife*. Oh." He smiled down at the girl. "*And* my daughter, Clarissa, as well."

"Wife? Oh no," exclaimed Mary, pouting. "It is not fair."

"Not fair?" asked a bewildered Lord Temperance, his arm tightening protectively around Ada.

"I had *such* plans. A garden wedding, you see. You were to be married under the copper beech, and there were to be masses of those wonderful new flowers, the dahlias, you know, arranged behind you. And little Clarissa was to be a bridesmaid, and I thought perhaps the other children might learn a song to sing and—"

Lady Grinnel broke off at the sound of her husband clearing his throat. She cast him a mischievous glance and rose to her feet.

"Lummy, do close your mouth and set two more places," she ordered. "As you see, Lord and Lady Temperance will be joining us for dinner." She walked gracefully to Ada and embraced her gently. "Our very best wishes, my dear Lady Temperance, and welcome to our home."

She turned in time to catch a look of approving pride in her on her husband's face and blinked. For once, it seemed, she'd done the right thing and she hadn't even been thinking about pleasing him!

Among the company, only Constance looked at Clarissa. Poor Clarry was looking rather frazzled, very tired, and more than a little confused. Connie went to the child and, kneeling, spoke quietly. "Clarry dear, Val and Venetia are in the nursery. Would you like to join them? Willy is there, too, you know."

Clarissa gave her a grateful look, but then glanced wistfully toward her mother. Ada, very nearly as bewildered by the happenings of the day as her daughter, was allowing herself to be urged toward the seat the butler held for her.

"When dinner is over I will bring your mother up to you, and even if you are asleep, which would be very sensible of you, my dear, she will kiss you goodnight. Come, Clarissa. From now on, everything is going to be very well with you and your mother," promised Constance. Silently, she promised *herself* she'd have a word with Lord Temperance to insure that that was so!

Several days later Constance and Jack strolled through gardens bright with late summer flowers. Constance saw Ada and her brand new husband cross their path. The two lived in a world all their own, which they'd have blushed for if they'd noticed how often their hostess wished them elsewhere. Poor Mary was racked by confused emotions that ranged from taking pleasure in the pair's happiness to green jealousy that she herself hadn't such a relationship with her husband.

Jack commented on Mary's conflicting feelings as they watched Ada stare up at her husband. Temperance watched his wife's path, seeing that she did not fall when she stumbled, which she did every so often since it seemed she could not take her gaze from his face to pay attention to where she was going.

"Mary has never understood she is truly lovable," finished Jack.

"How sad for her. I have seen how Lord Grinnel looks at her. I believe he loves her."

"If only one could convince Mary of that!"

"Perhaps I could say something."

Jack gave her a quick look. "Perhaps you could," he said noncommitally, and wondered if a relative stranger's words might not have more power over Mary than her family's observations ever could.

"Ada has never been so happy," said Constance, and didn't know whether she was happy for her friend, jealous like Mary, or both. Most likely it was both, she admitted ruefully.

"She glows with it," agreed Jack.

In another part of the extensive gardens they heard the children's voices raised in play. Constance heard Clarissa's trilling laugh. "Little Clarry never laughed so often, either, I think. She, too, will be happy. It is a great thing."

"You made it happen."

"I?" About to deny it, Constance paused. "Perhaps, but one could as easily say *you* were the means by which it came about."

"How do you conclude such a ridiculous thing?" he asked, startled. "I had never heard of your Mrs. Wright, and I had at that time had only the briefest of introductions to Temperance."

"But *you* got me the invitation to visit your cousin. I'd not have met his lordship but for you."

Jack slanted a twinkling look her way. "Then we must mutually congratulate each other, must we not?" He glanced around, seemingly idly, and ascertained that they were alone. Using a skill developed in his salad days, he'd maneuvered Constance between tall hedges where they were, for the moment, safe from other eyes. He reached for her.

Constance, noticing his deft maneuvers, did her best to cooperate without appearing to do so. Once alone, she didn't pretend. She moved close to him, spurning false coyness, and encircled his neck with her arms.

In only a very few days her brother meant to begin their journey home. They would stop in London—at a *hotel* and *not* at Mordaunt's house!—only so that Selwyn might go to the Horse Guards to sell out, interview the family solicitor, and, lastly, regularize things with his father's banker. And then, as chaperone to Madame Beugnot, who had not yet told Selwyn she would wed him, Constance would keep them company on the long trip to Cornwall.

A trip into a long, lonely future, she thought.

She put all thought aside and simply enjoyed the forbidden sensations she'd never know again. There was the feel of him close to her, the scent of him, his hand warm against her neck where it supported her head, his other hand lower on her back, the fingers spread wide. There was his mouth gentle against her own, against her cheeks, near her ear.

Constance turned her head. She wanted, needed, his kisses. Those deep, drugging kisses. Teasingly he refused to oblige her, moving to taste her throat on the other side.

"Bad man!" shouted Clarry. *"Let him go!* Don't you dare to hurt Val!"

"Get away, girlie, or it'll be bad for you," warned a voice with pretense to gentility.

At the noise from beyond the hedge Jack's head came up.

"No, no, no!" came Clarissa's panicked voice. "You stop that!"

For a fraction of an instant Jack's arms tightened. Then Constance was free and, his steps nearly soundless, the major raced toward the entrance to the winter walk which had protected their tête–à–tête.

Constance didn't recover so quickly as Jack had done. Her head was still full of stars when he disappeared. Then she heard a gasp and harsh breathing along with a crude word, then pounding steps running off. She displaced some branches and peered through the leaves. Little Clarissa was holding Val, who had his hands to his throat. The harsh rale of difficult breathing was coming from him. He'd been hurt!

"Oh no," whispered Constance. "Val!" In turn, she ran out of the shrubbery and around to where her nephew was quickly recovering. She put her arms about both children. "What happened?" she asked.

"A bad man," said Clarry. "Major St. Aubyn chased after him."

"He *hurt* me," said Val, his was voice raspy, but Connie was reassured to note that it held more a note of outrage than one of fear.

"Let me look," said Constance gently, but her heart pounded and the fear the boy should have felt filled her. Her Val! "I think you are a heroine, Clarry," she said as she touched the red where the "bad man's" fingers had gripped her nephew's throat. "If you had not been here, Val could have been hurt severely indeed."

Compulsively, she pulled Val into her arms, wishing to protect him, keep him safe. Hearing a noise, she turned her head around. Clarry was smiling, so surely it wasn't new danger. Ah. Definitely *not* a danger. At least, not to her nephew! Perhaps to herself?

"Jack?" she asked.

"The damn . . . er, dratted eel eluded me. I wasn't so very far behind him but he slipped around a shed, and when I reached it he was gone. I haven't a notion how he did it, except there is a spinney there in which he might have hidden a horse.''

Constance smiled at the major's show of pique, but sobered when he glared at her. She removed the smile from her face. "Did you see who it was?'' she asked soberly.

"Oh, yes. Exactly who I thought it would be. I can at least give the authorities a name and a description.'' He caught Val's gaze. "But until the rat is caught, you, my boy, cannot be allowed out alone. Not even in the garden. Do you understand?''

"He might come back?'' croaked Val. Finally experiencing something which could be called fear, his eyes widened. He stepped nearer to Connie, grasping her hand tightly.

"Yes, Val, he might come back. I'm sorry. You know now what can happen, and you'll not foolishly go off on your own, will you?''

Val, shivering, shook his head. He glanced at Clarry.

"The major doesn't mean,'' added Connie, "that you may just have Clarry or your new friends with you, Val. That is not sufficient protection, no matter how brave Clarry was today.''

"Clarissa could not protect you if the rat came near again. Worse, she might be hurt herself,'' elaborated Jack. "What I meant was that you cannot go out without adult supervision, preferably your father or myself.''

"Someone bigger than that bad man!'' said Clarry, shuddering, her eyes wide with remembered horror.

"Good girl,'' said Jack, patting her head. "That is *exactly* what I mean. Ah—Temperance. I am very sorry to interrupt your idyll with your love, but will you escort the children and Miss Mordaunt back to the house? I've some errands to attend to.''

"Jack.'' Connie felt herself blush at using his name before the others. "Major—''

"Miss Mordaunt," he said, forgetting in the pressure of the moment for the second time to pretend she was a widow, "you will help most if you find your brother and tell him what has happened." He took her hand, lifting it to his lips. More gently he added, "My first step is to send off a message to Bow Street."

"Bow Street!" Temperance, his attention still on Ada, had been smilingly agreeably, but at that became more alert. "Just what *has* happened?"

"Miss Mordaunt will explain," said Jack and, for Connie's ears alone, he said, "Watch over yourself as well, my love." He turned and headed toward the stables.

"Connie?" asked Ada fearfully. "My brother?"

Constance shook the last remnants of the fuzzy emotions roused by Jack's kisses from her head and answered Ada as best she could. "Its nothing to do with you, Ada. Or with Clarry. Children? Come along now. We'll find Willy, and you must all return to the nursery until we may get things organized. Val? You'll remember what Major St. Aubyn said?"

Val nodded vigorously, remembering his brief panic when, for an instant he couldn't breathe. As soon as he was free anger had covered the fear, but, looking back, he knew he'd been very close to something very very bad . . . something he never wished to experience again.

Willy was soon informed and, clucking, she shepherded her charges into the house and up the stairs, where Val became something of a hero as his bruises came out and were admired by all the nursery party.

Everyone but Jack gathered in the salon, and Constance told the tale. "It is my fault," groaned Selwyn, his head in his hands. "I told St. Aubyn the boy would be safe in the gardens, that we'd protect him when away from the house.

How could the murdering bastard have gotten past the guards? How did he make his way out again?"

"In that *I* am at fault," said Lord Grinnel. "I set guards, but haven't checked them with any regularity. They must have slacked off."

"It has, I'm sure, been boring duty," said Selwyn with a sigh. "Bored men become inattentive. I saw it again and again while in the army."

"They won't do so again!" promised Grinnel.

Jack strolled in. "No they won't, because they won't be on duty again. I sent them all away." He immediately searched the room until his eyes met Constance's gaze. He smiled tenderly at her worried frown, but, when Grinnel growled, looked back to his host. Jack grinned. "You would say?"

"Blast you, Jack!" said Grinnel. "This is *my* house. How dare you dismiss my servants?"

"They won't be needed because the boy won't be here."

"Why?"

"Because Master Val will be moved to Castle Durrant. At once." As he talked he edged toward Constance, although he spoke to his hostess. "Mary, I am sorry to deprive you of your nurse, but Miss Willes must, of course, go as well."

"And I," said Selwyn, rising to his feet.

"Oh yes. And Madam Beugnot and Miss Venetia." His glance slid warmly over Constance. "And our Mrs. Mordaunt, of course."

Constance smiled, but her frown remained in place. She was torn between her fear for Val, and her love for Jack. If only he loved her, too.

"Why Castle Durrant?" asked Selwyn.

"Because when the drawbridge is up and the portcullis

down, it is as safe now as it was centuries ago. At least, against this sort of marauder!''

Lord Grinnel grinned appreciatively, but asked, ''Your father will allow the castle to be sealed?''

''He isn't there, and my mother is very understanding.'' He turned to Constance and asked, ''How soon can you be ready to leave?''

''Half an hour,'' she replied promptly, but her eyelids flickered as she realized she'd soon be meeting Jack's mother.

''Impossible,'' exclaimed Lady Mary, throwing up her hands in amazement. ''Why, that leaves no time at all for packing!''

''When you've as little with you as I have, one cannot call it packing!'' said Connie cheerfully. ''The only thing with which I must take any care is my new London gown!''

She looked at Felice, who nodded her agreement and the two rose to their feet. The Frenchwoman had brought very nearly as small a wardrobe with her as Constance had.

Then Constance recalled she meant to have a talk with Lady Mary. ''Will you come with me?'' she asked.

When they reached Constance's room, Connie pulled her box from atop the wardrobe and opened it on her bed. She glanced at Mary, who wandered from one part of the room to another. ''You are so very lucky, I think,'' said Connie.

''Lucky?''

''To have two loving children and a husband who dotes on you.''

Mary turned a startled look on her guest. ''Dotes! Why, what can you possibly mean?''

''Perhaps it is more obvious to a stranger?'' asked Connie, pretending a reserve she didn't feel.

"But what can you possibly have seen which would sug-gest—?"

"Oh, the way he looks at you and smiles. The way he always looks out for your comfort." Constance shrugged. "Little things, of course, but they mean so much, do they not?"

"He is always involved with his work. *Always*, it comes *first*."

Constance put on a surprised look. "But of course. He is a man, is he not? His work is a large part of how he defines himself, you see."

"If he loved me he'd . . . he'd—"

"What, Mary? Wait on you hand and foot? Give you your every wish, even if it were not a wise wish on your part? Let you go your length and nod and smile and tell you what a good girl you are? That isn't love."

Mary looked bewildered. "Then how does one know one is loved?"

"By the little things. That he smiles when he sees you come into a room. That he touches you when he doesn't need to do so." Connie tried to think of other little tricks she'd noted in Lord Grinnel's behavior.

"By worrying about me? And trying to teach me the best way to go on?" asked Mary, scowling.

"Of course. Do you not worry about your children? Do you not try to teach them the best way to go on? Do you not scold when they do wrong?"

Mary's scowl deepened. "That isn't love."

"That *is* love. Surely you are too mature to think that you must be constantly wooed, even after you've been won? Of course you are. Such a relationship would become a dead bore."

Mary looked surprised. "It would?"

"Of course. Just think. When would one have time for living if one were always playacting at loving?"

"Playacting?"

"Isn't that a lot of what goes on during a courtship? Each on his or her best behavior? Each hiding one's faults, for fear the other will be put off by them? Such nonsense when one must live with the real person."

Mary was silent for a long thoughtful moment. "Did Grinnel put you up to this discussion?" she asked, suspicious.

"Lord Grinnel? Of course not. I believe it began when I told you how jealous I am, and how lucky you are to have a man who dotes on you so." Constance took down the London made gown, the last item to be packed and, very carefully, using a great deal of blue paper, folded it to lay on top of her other things in her box. "There. I am finished. Shall we see if we can help Madame Felice?"

Actually, it was Selwyn and Jack who held up the party. Jack had had his batman go up to London for proper clothing when they'd returned from France, and Selwyn had brought nearly all he owned with him, anything which still had a decent amount of wear in it.

For once it was not the women who slowed up the men.

Chapter 10

The journey to Castle Durrant became something of a rare show for the children of the villages through which they passed. Lord Grinnel had had his head groom choose and arm six outriders. The groom himself rode guard on the box beside the driver of the closed carriage in which Lord Mordaunt, Madam Beugnot, and Val rode. Ahead of them was another closed carriage with Nurse Willes and Venetia. It had been planned that Constance ride there as well, but she had other notions.

"I do not like riding long distances in a closed carriage my lord," she said. "I will ride with you."

The major frowned. "My dear, I fear for your safety."

"Nonsense. With all these armed men around us the rabbit you have described will not dare to attack. It is perfectly safe."

"What if I said I did not wish your company?"

"Do you not?" she asked in a small voice. She realized

how revealing that had been, and scorned herself for using it.

But Jack didn't pretend not to understand. "I want you beside me now and forever, my dear," he retorted promptly. "I wish to hold you, to kiss you, but when I cannot have that, I like it that you are near me." His grin faded. "Still . . ."

His words made Connie brighten. "Hmm," She smiled wickedly. "If you do *not* allow me a place in your curricle, I will ask Lady Grinnel to order me a horse and I will ride."

"You'd do it, of course."

Her eyes widened. "Of course, I would. I *never* threaten what I will not do."

Since it was one of his own character traits that he never made empty threats, Jack could hardly object. "You may ride beside me. I'll feel better about that than that you make a target of yourself on horseback."

In the end, both were pleased by the arrangement. At the manor they'd been unable to be alone together except for brief intervals. For the first time since their long ride through France they talked, arguing about some things, supporting each other's notions in others, and generally learning still more to like about each other.

Too, there was always that growing tension between them, sensations Constance only understood in theory, although she guessed they were very important to the sort of relationship of which she'd dreamed. Even though they could not indulge in the sadly immoral behavior which beset her when asleep in her bed, always awakening abruptly *just* when their dream behavior grew most interesting, she wished to experience whatever Jack would allow.

And that was true even when it was nothing more than conversation. She craved his nearness—every instant she could manage. However unhappy her deepening feelings would leave her when he'd gone alone to Vienna, she'd have as many memories as she could manage.

"Lady Durrant, I wish to apologize that we arrived this way, with no notice," said Constance, her eyes following Jack as he left the room behind the others—to see, he said, to the raising of the drawbridge.

"Nonsense." The countess bit off the word and waved away any more attempts at apology. "That jackanapes I must call son has ever been thus, a whirlwind blustering over or around anyone in his way, as I'm certain he did when he insisted you come here."

"He heard no objections from me," admitted Connie ruefully. "Not in this case," she added. As Jack disappeared, she turned her attention back to her hostess. "Val has bruises where that fiend had him by the throat, a constant reminder of his danger."

"Ah, that poor boy. To have experienced such a thing!"

"We must remember that, although he experienced it, he *lived*. That is the important thing."

Lady Durrant chuckled. "Oh yes. One cannot argue that point. You have been looking at my hair, have you not?" she finished, changing the subject abruptly.

Connie made no attempt to deny it. One could hardly avoid staring at the mass of pure white hair dressed high in an old-fashioned style, a long curl laying over her ladyship's shoulder. "It is quite beautiful, but with your youthful complexion it looks a trifle strange."

"It is a family trait, the premature whitening of the hair. We don't yet know if Jack's will turn. Occasionally it passes a generation by, and we should know within the next few years." A quick, flickering smile lit her face briefly. "My husband will not allow me to cut it, and to say truth, I don't know if I would in any case." She lowered her voice to a confiding tone. "I admit to a trifling vanity where my hair is concerned."

"As you well might. It is lovely." Constance tried to imagine what Jack would look like with pure white hair. He'd allowed the sun to bronze his skin a trifle more than was quite acceptable in polite society, and Connie thought that might look very well with white hair.

"You like my son, do you not?" asked Lady Durrant softly.

"Very much," said Connie, still thinking of Jack with a head of pure white hair. Her words penetrated her preoccupation. Blushing, she glanced up to meet her hostess's eyes. Her color deepened as she added, "He is easily liked. Surely there is no one who could not like him."

"I prefer your first, unthinking, response." Lady Durant laughed. "Jack wrote that I am to tell you all his good points, and am not to mention any bad habits. He said he is having difficulty convincing you he truly wishes to wed you."

"That foolish man, to mention such a thing with you!"

"You frown most fiercely, my dear. Has he been plaguing you?" asked her ladyship sympathetically.

"It is only that he *doesn't* wish to wed me. He merely thinks it is the proper thing to do." Constance's chin rose a notch. "I will not have him sacrifice his freedom and any future happiness with a woman he can love when it is quite unnecessary that he do so!"

"You do not suggest you'd be sacrificing *your* happiness if *you* were to wed *him,*" suggested Lady Durrant perceptively.

Connie sighed, wondering how they had become so very intimate on such short acquaintance.

"You think me rude and overbearing to push you as I

am, do you not?" asked the countess. "Well, perhaps I am. Still, if I correctly understood what my son said of the last few years of your life, you've had complete responsibility for your nephew, so I think you can empathize with a mother's concern for her son's happiness."

"Your son, Lady Durrant, could charm the birds from their nests," retorted Connie with asperity. "I fear he has used that smooth tongue to convince you of what cannot possibly be true."

"Not so. We made a pact a very long time ago. If there is something Jack does not wish to discuss with me, he says so. Or he will skirt around a truth he doesn't wish to say. Or he will simply not come home until he feels he can talk to me." Lady Durrant grimaced. "In which case, I worry until he *does*. But, Miss Mordaunt, *he does not lie to me.*"

"I cannot understand it." Bewilderment surged through Connie. "He must have met far greater beauties than I, far more interesting women, and far younger. He cannot have fallen in love with me."

Her ladyship paused for a moment, eyeing Constance closely. She sighed. "I will not lie to you any more than I do to my son, since I hope that I may soon call you daughter. Jack did not say, in just so many words, that he loved you. What he said was that he'd finally met the woman with whom he wished to spend his life, a woman with a sense of humor and a quick mind to whom he did not have to explain every little thing. A woman who would be of aid to him in the diplomatic world he is soon to enter, and not a millstone around his neck. A woman to whom he'd entrust the rearing of his children . . . oh, and many more like things. No, he did not speak of love, but such words imply it, do they not? And men, bless them, find difficulty with the word, do they not? He is impressed with you, Miss Mordaunt. As am I. You have, I believe, lived a very busy life with heavy responsibilities for some years now.''

"I have done nothing alone. We've an excellent bailiff.''

"Modesty as well as all else! A paragon, indeed." Lady Durrant's brows arched, and she smiled a crooked smile. "Yes, I believe Jack *has* found the woman he will wed, so beware, my dear. Willy–nilly, he will wed you. I know my Jack, you see.''

"You would say he is stubborn," suggested Connie.

"Stubborn as an old goat," was the prompt if inelegant reply.

"I myself have been described as stubborn, and *I* have decided I will not allow the man to sacrifice himself.''

Lady Durrant's eyes narrowed. "Do not sentence my son to a living hell by making the wrong decision, my dear. Nor should you cut off your own nose by refusing to change your mind. Stubbornness *can* be an excellent trait, but I will consider it sinful if you end up hurting Jack, to say nothing of yourself, because you cannot bring yourself to admit you might be wrong." She waited for Constance to respond. When she did not, the countess sighed a tiny sigh. "My dear," she said, "you will wish to see how your niece and nephew are situated. Shall we go up to the nurseries?''

Connie thanked Heaven the personal interview had ended. She'd been on the verge of losing her temper for the simple reason she was required to argue against her own inclinations—as Lady Durrant had correctly guessed.

If there *were* a hell in all this, as the countess feared, it was *she* who would live it. But was it possible Jack truly admired her good qualities, and to such a degree? Did he really think she'd make him a good wife? Lucky marriages were based in something so moderate as *affection*. It was a lucky couple *indeed* who found true love with each other. Constance, who had observed the abiding love between her mother and father, had sworn she'd accept marriage only if such love existed. Could she break that vow?

Except . . . there *was* love, was there not? But could she bear living with Jack, as his wife, knowing the love was on only one side? Her side.

She and the countess reached the nursery just then, and Venetia ran to her, clutching at her skirts and sobbing. All thought of Jack disappeared when she discovered Val was nowhere to be seen.

"But where is he?" asked Connie, holding Venetia close. Venetia, tears running down her cheeks, buried her face against her aunt's thighs.

"Lord Mordaunt and Major Lord St. Aubyn came for him. They are giving the boy a tour of the castle defenses," said Miss Willes gruffly, with a quick glance of irritation toward Venetia, who had not liked her brother leaving her behind. "Do not mollycoddle the child, Consta . . . Miss Mordaunt, I mean. Venetia is merely throwing a tantrum that she was not allowed to go as well."

Lady Durrant smiled at that. "They mean to show the lad he is safe here. That is well. Perhaps he'll not have nightmares from his experience." Her ladyship moved gracefully toward Constance and Venetia. "Good afternoon, young lady," she added, stooping down to the child's level.

Venetia turned her head sideways to look at this stranger. *Still another* stranger in her life.

"When your brother returns, my dear, ask him if he was allowed to watch the portcullis let down. It is quite an interesting sight, and I promise you that tomorrow we will raise it up again so that you, too, may watch it go down. Would you like that?"

Constance was certain Venetia hadn't a notion what a portcullis might be, but, like any child, she nodded agreement that she would like the treat.

"You have found the doll's house?" asked Lady Durrant when Venetia moved a little away from her aunt, although not yet releasing a good hold on Connie's skirts. The girl glanced toward the corner, where a very large doll's house stood open, the two halves swung apart so that the inside rooms were revealed. "It is, I think, a very nice doll's house," continued the countess. "I hope you enjoy it. Now, my child, I must take your aunt away and show her to her room, which is just next to Madame Beugnot's. They can come to see you when you are ready for bed and listen to your prayers," she finished when Venetia turned from her and clutched one of Constance's legs.

Venetia, her eyes again damp, looked up at her aunt with a pleading expression, silently begging her not to disappear.

"I will come and listen to your prayers, love, and perhaps read you a story," said Constance with sympathy for the child's confusion. Children, she decided, should not be dragged from pillar to post as they'd done with these two. Poor Venetia! "Madame Felice," she added, "will come as well. Willy's here with you, love, and Val should return soon. He'll have a tale to tell you, I'm sure."

Reluctantly Venetia returned to Willy, leaning back against her nurse. Almost as reluctantly, but showing it not at all, Constance followed Lady Durrant from the day nursery and down a winding stair within the thick wall. She feared she might be let in for another catechism, this time on the proper way to rear a child. Therefore she felt exceedingly relieved to find herself settled, alone, in a room in which two tall windows had been cut, the thickness of the ancient walls forming window seats beneath them.

Lady Durrant left her there after pointing out the connecting door to Felice's room. For a long moment Constance hesitated to disturb her French friend. But then, her thoughts returning to Jack despite her determination they would not, she knew she must have distraction.

She knocked. "Felice?" she called.

"I am here," was the answer, and the door opened. "Ah. You look like the mouse the cat will not allow out of his hole."

Connie, startled by the image, chuckled. "And how does such a mouse look?"

"Angry and aggravated and unhappy," responded Felice promptly. "Has Lady Durrant been urging you to marry her son?"

"What made you think she might?" asked Connie.

"I heard Major St. Aubyn telling my Selwyn he meant to enlist his mother's aid in pursuing his suit."

"He has told *Silly* he is wooing me?"

Felice nodded. "For me, I would take the man if I were not in love your brother. He is besotted with you, and what more can a woman ask?"

"Besotted?" Constance's pulse throbbed at the notion. "Surely are mistaken!"

"As are you with him," said the Frenchwoman, nodding.

"I am not." Constance's mouth firmed, her eyes narrowed, and she frowned, forming a shuttered expression.

Felice laughed. "You do not wish to admit it? Ah well, the time will come when you cannot deny it. As it did for me and Selwyn. Have you seen the children?"

Constance wasn't quite certain that she wished to change the subject from the interesting notion that Jack might actually be in love with her. Nevertheless, she allowed the new topic. She was far too shy of her own feelings to asked why Felice thought she was enamored of Jack, and even more reluctant to ask on what basis Felice had judged that Jack was enamored of her. She was too afraid she'd discover it wasn't true, and she wished to believe it might be for a little while.

Instead, she told Felice of her visit to the nurseries.

"Ah yes. They left some time ago with the boy. I can empathize with little Venetia. I, too, wished to see the castle defenses, merely out of interest, you know. But Selwyn said it was just for the men." Felice smiled, her eyes damp at the memory. "He glanced down at Val, who looked up at him and then looked so proud to be included among the *men* that I could not bring myself to tell them that was nonsense and make demands that I be included."

"There will be a moon. Perhaps Silly will show you the ramparts by moonlight."

Felice instantly sobered. "But no. They are to make use of the moon to ride tonight. To London. I tell them they cannot make so many miles in the dark, but they say they must reach the city as quickly as possible. They hope the little rat who hurt Val will have been caught and that he may be forced to tell who hired him. They wish to be there if your cousin Mordaunt is accused."

"Why does no one tell me anything?" complained Constance.

"Why should they have told you?"

"Because I am the only one who knows our cousin," she said, sorting through the thoughts roiling around in her head. "Because of that I must go with them. I believe," she added even more slowly, "that I will know how to approach him." She looked up, her eyes twinkling with mischief despite the seriousness of the situation. "Perhaps I may be able to trick him into an admission of guilt." The plot which entered her head was quite choice. She was certain it would work, and became even more convinced as she outlined it to Felice.

"Hmm. Perhaps it would work. You can tell it to your Lord Major, hmm? Because I do not think they will allow you to go if you cannot convince them of that little thing."

"*Allow* me!"

"Mmm?" Felice chuckled. "What is this, then? You do not give them the right to make such decisions for you?"

Once again Constance fell back on anger to cover her confused and confusing emotions surrounding Major St. Aubyn. "I have been making all the decisions on my brother's estate for far too long to allow *anyone* to try to force me to sit back and do nothing. Especially when there is something I can and should do!"

Her scowl well in place, Constance stalked from the room, determined to find Jack and have it out with him. Halfway down the hall toward one of the many circular stairways, though, she realized she hadn't a notion where she'd find him. She wasn't even certain she could find her way to the ancient entrance with its huge double doors made of ironbound wood. Lady Durrant, upon leaving the salon, had taken her up one staircase to the nursery floor and then down another to her room, and through a maze of halls in between. She could, she supposed, return by the same route, but that seemed very much out of the way.

Half an hour later she wished very much that that was what she'd done. She hadn't a notion where she'd gotten to, except she could not seem to retrace her steps. That surprised her. Usually she'd a very good notion of where she'd been, but the inside of the old castle, built around at least two courtyards which she'd glimpsed more than once through inner windows—*different* inner windows, with halls going off in unexpected directions, some ending in blank walls where she'd fully expected to find a door—well!

Constance marched on, frustration at her situation rising to the point she was very nearly ready to scream. Or laugh.

How *could* she have lost herself so thoroughly? But lost she was. She admitted it as she poked her head into a room, found it one which overlooked the outer defenses, and decided she'd had enough. She'd stop and stay put. Someone would come looking for her. Of that she was certain. She'd just have to swallow her embarrassment that she'd put the servants to such trouble.

Or Jack? Would Jack search for her? Yes, he would. Although it was quite irrational, somehow she was certain it would be *Jack* who found her. She entered the room, leaving the door open.

There was a book of etchings on a table. She took it to one of the ubiquitous padded window seats and curled up with it. Every time she wondered where everyone was and whether she should try, again to find her way, she remembered her father's advice to her as a very young girl, when she'd lost herself on the moor. Her father said that if she were ever again so stupid as to do such a thing it was best she remained in one place so that those seeking her could find her. She sighed and turned the page.

Nearly an hour later a harassed looking Jack poked his head in the door and then followed it into the room.

"So there you are," he said.

She looked up from the bucolic scene depicted on the page before her. Warmth filled her. Jack. He'd found her. Although she knew she'd a fight ahead of her, she also realized that in his presence she was suddenly and completely relaxed, at ease with herself and her world. It was a thought to put away and take out again when she'd time to think about it.

"Connie?" he asked sharply when she didn't instantly respond.

"Hmm?" she asked. "Have you been looking for me?" she added, mischievously.

"I suppose you will tell me you are not at all lost and did not need every able-bodied man in the castle set to searching for you?" he asked, his brows arching up under hair which was, as usual, lying over his forehead.

"Why should I tell you what is untrue? Of course I am lost." She smiled benignly and shrugged. "I knew you'd find me." And she had, somehow, *known* he'd find her.

"I will always find you," he said earnestly. His mood shifted as he crossed the room to seat himself beside her. Taking her hands, he said, "You cannot hide from me, my dear. You mustn't try, although I sometimes fear that is what you have in mind once we settle young Val's problem."

Connie looked at their hands, hers long-fingered and slim, and his, tanned and strong, the nails beautifully kept even though they'd been through so much in the last few weeks.

"Ada, Lady Temperance I mean, invited me to visit them after Silly and Felice are wed," she admitted, seemingly idly.

Startled, Jack's hands tightened around hers. "They've decided to wed?"

"Drat." Constance sighed. "Please do not tell Selwyn. Felice has not admitted to Silly she will wed him, so do not reveal that I've been so indiscreet as to break a promise of silence." She looked up, meeting his eyes. "I have told you you do not wish to wed me. You must admit it now. If I cannot keep this private secret, how can you trust me to keep much more important government secrets such as those a diplomat would know?"

"It is only that you trust me that you have told me, not that you would become a gabble grinder to just anyone," he said soothingly.

Constance admitted to herself the justice of his comment, and wondered that he understood her so well.

"I will not tell your brother," he added, "although I wonder that Madame has the courage to deny him for so long."

"She says she will not tell him yea until they have arrived in Cornwall." Connie's dimple appeared and then deepened. "She says that he will appreciate her the more if she does not give in at once."

"If you are trying the same tactic, my dear, let me warn you that it is impossible that I could appreciate you more than I already do!"

The dimple faded. "You are very convincing, Jack, but a spy must be convincing, must he not?"

"Blast and bedamned." Jack pushed Connie's hands away and stood up. He strode from one end of the small room to the other and back again. Running the fingers of both hands back through his hair, holding it there, he stared down at her. "How am I to convince you?"

"You are merely being stubborn. I said you no when you decided I would say you yes, and now it is only that you are determined that I say what you would have me say."

"I am not so perverse. If it were not that my future happiness is at stake I would not press you so. I was raised a gentleman, at least, and I know the proper forms. But I am convinced it is not a question of you disliking to wed me. It is merely that you have misread the situation." For another moment he stared at her. Then, dropping his hands, he said, "I will persist."

"I cannot see how the situation, as you call it, could be misread."

"It is simple. I erred in thinking that the easiest way of convincing you to wed me was to use the situation we were in. I made the mistake of pretending that it was important that we regularize our association by marrying. I used that as my excuse for proposing, when I have wanted to wed you, my dear, almost since I saw you arguing with young Redfield that very first day."

"You cannot have." Unable to think how to finish without actually asking if he had fallen in love with her so quickly as all that, she turned away.

"Have known so soon." He touched her hair. "But I *did*. Not that moment, although I was instantly attracted to you and distressed to discover you were, as I thought, already married."

"You couldn't have been ... attracted," she said, her disbelief evident. But there was hope in her heart.

"Not attracted to you? Yes, I was! That dimple, you know, is pure delight when it is not being elusive so that I cannot bring it to life." His grin was a trifle devilish. "Beware, my dear!" he warned. "I dream of ways of making it appear. You will like them, however," he added more thoughtfully. "My methods, I mean."

"You dream that," she said absently, "while I imagine ways of making your hair stay in place. I work and work and work at it," said Constance, dreamily, hope rising further with his every word.

He chuckled softly. "Sounds a dreary occupation if done only for that reason. I admit I would like the feel of your fingers in my hair, however."

"Hmm? Oh!" Constance felt heat flow up her body and into her neck and face. "How could I have said such a thing?"

"It is the sort of thing lovers say to one another, my dear."

"But we are not . . ." She broke off, unable to use the word.

"Not yet," he said so gently she very nearly missed the implication. "But soon, I hope," he added, assuring that she would not.

"Jack! Major!"

"When we are wed, I mean," he said with well–feigned innocence.

"Did you?" She eyed him narrowly.

He grinned, the devilish light reappearing in his eyes. "I am not so nice in my notions I would object to an *affaire,* but only on the assumption it would lead to our marriage. I have told you that I would live with you all of my life." He reached for her. *"Shall* I seduce you, my dear?"

"You shall not!" she said, but realized her words sounded rather breathless. Embarrassment had her on her feet and moving toward the door. "You will instead, and at once, return me to my brother."

"I doubt he and Madame would approve of you coming upon them just now," he said pensively. When she didn't respond he sighed. "Instead, but only if you insist, I will take you to my mother." Lazily, he rose to his feet and moved toward her.

"Tell me why Silly and Felice are alone together."

"I believe Mordaunt is explaining why he and I must leave you and at once head for London this very night, which is one of the reasons *I* came looking for *you.*"

Constance stopped so suddenly that he walked into her, his arms going around her to steady her. She grasped his wrists and pushed them away, then turned. *"That* is what I have forgotten. I must ride with you."

"You will do no such thing."

"I *must.* I believe I can trick Cousin Mordaunt into admitting his guilt. As it is, he will simply deny your rabbit's accusations, and who would believe a slum—reared rat over a fat and wealthy man of the world?"

"Any number of people. Anyone who knows anything at all of *how* he became fat and wealthy!" said Jack promptly.

For a moment Constance's curiosity got in the way of her determination, and she asked questions. For the first time, she learned that Mordaunt was believed to have made his fortune by selling low quality products to the army for full price although it was not proven.

"He is a true monster, is he not?" She ranted on a bit longer about his antecedents. "But that is not relevant," she said. "What *is,* is that I can, I am certain, force him to admit he wished to have Val killed."

"How would you do it?" asked Jack, more interested than he'd admit.

"I would sneak into Mordaunt House and pretend *I* wished to kill *him!* I would let my hair hang every which way and roll my eyes wildly, and wave a gun at him."

"And then? Even if he were to admit the truth to you, of what use would it be?"

"Hmm." She frowned, thinking. "You mean," she said, "you, too, would have to hear him say the words?"

"There would have to be witnesses, yes. Myself, of course, but preferably someone who has no interest in the case. A Bow Street Runner, perhaps."

Constance slowed her steps and frowned. "My cousin never leaves his lair unless he must," she mused. "It would be necessary to confront him there. But his servants might warn him. Jack," she asked after a moment's thought, "would it not be possible to take over the house? Then, if I were to go in to him, you, and perhaps others, could listen from the hall, could you not?"

Jack searched for holes in her plan and, unfortunately, could find none. He sighed. "I cannot bear that you risk being hurt. There *must* be another way."

"Perhaps there is."

His brow arched and he cast her a hopeful look.

"But you have not thought of it, so perhaps there is *not*. If nothing better comes to mind, then I must be there to play my role, must I not?"

Again Jack could find no flaw in her reasoning, no reason to deny her—except for his overwhelming desire to keep his love *safe*. "We mean to ride."

"So?"

He recalled their journey on horseback down the French coast and grinned. "So I suppose you mean to ride as well?"

"Why not?"

"Because," he said promptly, "you'll find yourself much less tired if you are driven. I will drive my curricle. It will be very nearly as fast."

"There isn't room for three in a curricle."

"Your brother can ride."

"Jack—" She stopped and touched his arm, searching his eyes. "*Can* he? Ride, I mean? So very far?"

Jack stopped and frowned down at her. "His leg?"

"*Has* he ridden such long distances yet?"

"I'd forgotten his leg. Blast it." He caught her to him, pulling her close, and stared down at her, his features forming something which approached a pout as he stared into her eyes. "Damned if I wouldn't very much enjoy driving with you beside me, my dear. I can *feel* you sitting there, your thigh against mine, your hand touching me occasionally, your head leaning against my shoulder." He shook her gently. "Hell and damnation if you are not correct that your brother should not try to ride so far, even though he meant to do it.''

"He won't like it if we say he must not," she warned.

For another long moment Jack stared into her face, and then he sighed. ''I will inform your brother that you insist you will come and that, whatever I say to you, I cannot convince you to remain here where you'd be safe. You have, I will tell him, made me very angry. That you will not obey me, you see. Therefore, *he* must drive you.''

"I congratulate you.'' Constance gave him an admiring look. "That is a most excellent plot for saving his pride!''

"Minx!''

Jack looked up and down the hall before he pulled her close. Constance made no demur when he raised her face with his finger. Instead she reached her hands behind his neck and pulled him down, rising on tiptoe to meet his lips with her own.

As kisses went, it was a most satisfactory kiss . . . but very soon a mere kiss was *not* satisfying.

Jack took one more look around, lifted her, and entered the room beside them. It was, fortunately—or perhaps *unfortunately*—a bedroom, and he lay her back on the bed, coming down beside her, a leg crossing hers and holding her down. He needn't have worried, however.

Constance turned in his embrace and struggled to close the space between them, moaning softly, enticingly. Jack's hands moved over her body, and roused sensations she'd not have thought possible. Still more intriguing was the discovery that touching him added to her pleasure.

And most surprising of all, she'd just discovered she wasn't the least embarrassed by their growing ardor when, suddenly, he sat up and away from her, turning to one side.

"Behave yourself, my dear,'' he scolded, his tone

unsteady. "If you do not, you'll find yourself utterly and completely and truly compromised, since I cannot promise to retain control of myself a moment longer."

She reached for him.

"No, Connie. I mean it. Keep your hands to yourself!" He turned farther away from her and ran his hands up through his hair.

She smiled sadly at his back, wondering how she would ever find the strength to continue denying him. She wanted so badly to wed him, be bedded by him, discover finally and forever what it meant to belong to him.

Jack again ran splayed fingers back through his hair. "Connie, my sweet," he said after a moment, "should I apologize?"

"I think it is the same as before, Jack. I can't ask you to apologize when I have been just as . . . impulsive."

"You allow me all sorts of liberties with your person, but you still deny that you'll wed me, do you not?"

"I must."

"You must *not.*"

Connie sighed. "Jack . . . let it be until Val's safety is assured."

"Let it be." He sighed. "I don't know if I can. You have no notion of how I suffer!"

"I am not exactly happy myself, Jack."

He turned. "Connie—"

"No. We will go to London. We will do what is necessary to make Val safe. And then, perhaps, we'll have a few days before you must leave for Vienna. We will . . . enjoy them. But for now, I must pack." She looked up, her dimple flickering briefly into existence. "I assume someone will lead me to my room. Jack, did you never get lost in this monstrous building?"

Before responding he caught and held her gaze. Then

he looked away, sighing. After another moment he said, "Lost?" Speaking more lightly than she'd have thought possible, he added, "Quite often, actually. Mostly on purpose, of course." He grinned that quick, slashing grin. "Escaping from my tutor, for instance."

His brows climbed up under his hair. On this occasion it was part of an expression of unbelievable innocence. When she chuckled, he led her into the hall.

"Ah! There is a maid," Constance said. She rolled her eyes up to meet his. "Perhaps," she added in a whisper, "if you asked *her* to guide me to my room I will manage to arrive there? Without another detour?"

Jack smiled wryly, but by asking the maid to guide Constance he tacitly admitted there might be further delays if he were to do so himself.

Chapter 11

Durrant Castle was situated some five hours from London. That assumed, of course, that one had a fast team and excellent driving conditions. They had the team, but moonlight was not optimal. It took them closer to eight. Even so, they arrived on the outskirts of London in the early hours of the morning.

St. Aubyn led the way to the home of one of his fellow officers, a married man. He pounded on the door until he roused his friend, who stuck his head, covered in a tasseled sleeping cap, from an upper window.

"Ho, there!" called Jack. "Michael!"

"*You* is it?" muttered the voice from above. The head disappeared.

The travelers heard a clatter of footsteps on stairs, and soon the door opened. There were a few hurried words and Jack returned to the curricle, lifting Constance down and holding her a moment to steady her. "I must leave you with Major Morningside and his wife. We'll return for you as soon as we know what has happened. When we have a notion what we're to do next."

"You will not accost my cousin until you've talked to me?"

Jack grinned wickedly, crinkles appearing beside his eyes and temporarily washing away dark circles of tiredness. "I promise you will not be left out of our plans—primarily because we haven't come up with a better plan than your own. Come, now. You need what sleep you may get."

But sleep eluded Constance. She turned from one side to the other, fretting that she might *not* trick a confession from her cousin. He'd bluster and blather and, she feared, refuse to say what must be said.

She turned back. A snarl of hair pulled across her chin, and she brushed it back, wondering if she'd ever remove the rat's nests from her hair. Not only was it wind–tossed by the drive, but now it was sleep–tossed as well. She rolled onto her back, staring up to where dim outside light revealed the thin line of a crack in the ceiling.

Sleep–tossed, she thought sourly. She rolled over still again, this time onto her side, and stared at the narrow strip of light where the curtains did not quite properly meet, and then back again. *That should rather be called sleepless–tossed, should it not?*

Finally she gave up altogether and simply stared up to where the oil–filled streetlamp outside made patterns on the ceiling in which she tried to see pictures. Unfortunately they didn't distract her from her concerns. Where had Jack and Selwyn gone? To Jack's rooms for a few hours rest, or directly to Bow Street? Was Bow Street open all night?

She yawned. If it were, would they discover that that awful Rhino Biggens with his crossed eyes and buck teeth had been apprehended?

She yawned again. If he had, what . . . ?

Loud knocking at her door roused Constance from a troubled dream in which a rabbit dressed as a man, complete with fobs and cane, tried very hard to hurt Val, who merely laughed and laughed and laughed at the creature.

She looked around herself, bewildered by her strange surroundings. The knock came again. "Yes?"

The door opened and a young matron peeped in. "I have brought you breakfast, Miss Mordaunt."

Who . . . ? Oh! Mrs. Morningside. The aroma arising from the tray filled Constance's mouth with saliva. Food! She was instantly awake and pushed herself up against the back of her bed as her hostess approached it with a tray. She wondered when she'd last eaten properly.

"Major Lord St. Aubyn is below and wishes to speak with you, but I told him he must give you half an hour, at the very least. I don't think he will mind." She smiled a quick, pert smile. "My maid is setting a meal before him while I see to you. That will hold him for a bit!"

"How wonderful this looks," said Constance. "Can you stay? Last night we exchanged no more than two words. I must thank you for taking me in, a waif in need of shelter!"

"We would do far more than that for Jack," said Dora Morningside.

Mrs. Morningside's words were said so simply that Constance knew there must be a story. She urged her hostess to tell it while she finished breaking her fast, and was rewarded with a tale of how Jack discovered a plot whereby another officer, a spy for the French, had attempted to put the blame on Major Morningside for missing documents, important plans for an upcoming battle, which the real spy had stolen.

"It is not possible that we can ever thank him enough," finished Dora Morningside. "Giving you a bed in the middle of the night, Miss Mordaunt, is a trifling sort of thing in comparison.''

"Still, I thank you. We had driven so far I felt as if my insides were tied up in bowknots!''

"In a curricle all the way from Durrant Castle! I do not know how you stood it. Night driving, too. It is never comfortable. Ah, you have finished. And here is Meg with hot water. If you need anything, simply ask.''

Mrs. Morningside smiled sweetly and left Constance alone. . . . with a dilemma. Did she or did she not brush the tangles from her hair? Did she or did she not dress properly? Should she adopt the dress of a crazed person now, or later? She dithered for as long as it took to wash away the dirt of travel. Then she decided she must speak with Jack. *That,* given she was in *deshabille,* might be difficult. She sent the maid to find her hostess.

"Did Major Lord St. Aubyn inform you of what is in the wind?'' she asked, not wishing to wash more of the family's dirty linen than necessary.

"He mentioned that you must participate in a very important charade this morning.''

Connie bit her lip, thinking. "In that case, I believe I must adopt my disguise as a madwoman . . . but I cannot be certain. Would you escort the major to me so I may speak with him?''

"Let me find you a wrapper, and then I'll do so,'' agreed her hostess.

Mrs. Morningside's cheeks took on a rosy hue as she flicked a glance over Constance's nightrail which, made of fine linen, was much too revealing. Her hostess's embarrassment had Constance feeling it, too.

"Yes,'' said Jack some minutes later, "do make yourself ready to confront Mordaunt.'' He handed her a long cape with a hood. "This should cover you thoroughly so you need not fear frightening the horses while going through the streets.'' He eyed her wild hair. ''Besides, we go first to Bow Street to discuss our plan with the runner in charge of this case, and you will not wish to alarm the poor man!''

Constance grimaced. ''It is ever thus. A man wishes a woman to look *just so* even when she has been tossed for hours in a curricle and then suffers lack of sleep at the end of it!''

He grinned. ''I wish you to look exactly as you do, my dear . . . but not because of driving into the wind *or* because you have slept badly! Certainly not from sleeping.''

''You, my lord,'' scolded Constance, ''may take yourself off if you cannot behave. You are shocking Mrs. Morningside!''

''Am I, Dora? I merely tease my bride to be a trifle.''

''Bride?'' Mrs. Morningside gave Constance's blushing face a long look. ''Yes, I think she is exactly right for you, Jack. She will not let you run completely wild, but it is obvious she will enjoy your larks and join you in them whenever she can!'' Dora's smile turned to a severe look. ''But for now, go away so she may prepare herself.''

''I believe,'' said Jack, instantly sobering when reminded of what must be done, ''that she might appreciate your aid. She is to look the complete madwoman, her clothes torn and hair wild.''

''For that she must stay in her shift, and you cannot want that. I viewed the insane once!'' Horror filled Mrs. Morningside's features. ''At Bedlam, you know? Some women wore nothing more than filthy rags. It was terrible.''

Jack's eyes teased the women. ''I believe we must do better than a mere shift. Not that *I'd* not prefer it, but I would not wish others to view her in such a state!''

Connie rolled her eyes. *''You* may go away.''

''Yes, unfortunately the manners drilled into me by my

nurse insist I go." He winked. "I'll be just downstairs, however, if you need me."

"Irrepressible," scolded Mrs. Morningside, watching him disappear around the turn in the stairwell. She turned to Constance. "I have known him for many years now, and I have never seen him so . . . so buoyant. So happy. Oh, he is ever jesting and is very good at keeping others in spirits, but he himself, underneath, you know, is always rather . . . dour? No, not that, exactly. And not sad. Serious, perhaps? But now, oh, he is so different. You must be a very special woman indeed, Miss Mordaunt."

Everyone but Constance herself seemed to think so. At least where Major Lord St. Aubyn was concerned. She allowed herself, just for a moment, to wonder if perhaps Jack were *not* pretending, if perhaps he might truly wish to wed her. Oh, if only it were so!

But that must wait for better times.

When she'd finished she stared into the mirror and actually studied the wild creature who faced her. She grinned. Jack couldn't possibly wish to wed *that hag!* With that thought, she put what must be wishful thinking from her mind, preparing herself for the coming confrontation with her cousin. For that, she looked just right!

"I don't like it," growled the Bow Street runner. "A moll to face the man? Go straight into the devil's den? 'Taint right, *I* say."

"I don't like it either," said Jack patiently. "But she is correct when she says that merely accusing the man, merely facing him with Rhino's confession, will do no good. He will deny he has ever had a thing to do with Biggens, and he would not in that be a liar. If Biggens did not lie, and that is one sin I do not lay at his door except when he feels it necessary, of course, then Mordaunt's man made all the arrangements."

"And even if Mordaunt's man confesses, that will be met with the same denials," agreed the runner sourly. "Our best hope is a confession from the man himself, then."

"And our only hope of a confession is to trick him into making one."

"But a moll." The runner shook his head. " 'Taint right," he repeated.

"Then come up with a better plan," suggested Jack.

"He might shoot her."

"She'll have a pistol herself."

"Can she use it?" asked the startled runner.

Jack grinned. "I've never asked." He turned to Constance, who waited quietly in a chair beside him. "Connie, can you shoot? A man, I mean?"

"If I have to. It was once necessary that I kill a horse that broke its leg. I didn't like it, but I did it."

"Was there no one else?" asked Jack softly, taking her hands and looking into her eyes.

"Not if the mare's suffering was to end quickly. It was only chance a pistol was in the saddle holster. We'd had word of escaped French prisoners, you see, from the prison in Devon, and our agent insisted one be kept there. But we'd heard they'd been caught, and at the end of that day I'd meant to return the pistol to the armory." She shrugged. "However that may be, it was as well I had it with me just then."

"I don't believe I've ever seen a lady's saddle with a holster," mused Jack.

Her brother, who knew her better, demanded, "You were riding astride?"

Connie studied him, realized how drawn he looked. She

wondered how much his leg hurt, but knew he'd not like it mentioned. She also thought she heard a note of criticism, and that she would not have!

"As you very well know, I wore your old britches when I was a child and rode astride more often then not, but then I grew up and did not." She scowled. "When you were not to be found after Father died and I took over, it meant a great deal of riding. Yes, I rode astride. If it will forestall the lecture I see hanging on the tip of your tongue, I will admit I had divided skirts made up for the purpose. They answered very well."

"I wish you'd had them on the ride down the French coast," said Jack quickly when Selwyn looked as if he'd still make some objection. "It would have been much easier for you, would it not?"

"Riding sidesaddle can, for some, be difficult to master, but once one learns it is not so much harder than riding astride." She saw he wasn't convinced and she wasn't certain enough of her argument to continue. "Besides, I'd left my riding skirts in Cornwall, so the point is moot. This is getting us nowhere. Sir," she said to the runner, "I will admit I don't know if I could aim a pistol at a man, even Cousin Mordaunt, and pull the trigger. I do, however, know one end of a gun from the other."

The man sighed gustily. " 'Taint right," he said once more, gloomily. Then, giving up further objections, he settled down to plan exactly how they would take over Mordaunt house, and how they might best protect Miss Mordaunt once she'd entered the study to confront the villain.

The Mordaunt butler was taken as soon as he was safely away from the house on an errand. When it was explained to him that Rhino Biggens had confessed and implicated him, he instantly broke and confessed. Then it was pointed out to the butler that his master need only deny everything and keep on denying it and the master would likely avoid prosecution, while the servant and hireling would likely be sentenced to hang. Lester, made bitter by the truth of that, agreed to do what he could to help trap Mordaunt into the necessary confession.

Constance did not trust the man, however. She was convinced that if Mordaunt saw him, his white face and shaking hands would give away the fact that the plan to murder her nephew had collapsed. "Use him to collect and settle the servants, but do not allow him near our cousin," she urged. After a trifling bit of discussion, the men agreed.

The house was soon secured and Jack returned to the carriage, where Constance waited to play her part. He took her hands. "Are you sure you wish to do this?"

She smiled, her dimple appearing briefly. "Does one ever truly wish to put a paw directly into a snare? I am, however, determined. I will not fail," she said, more to convince herself than him.

"Whatever you do, you do it superbly," he agreed, and she heard pride.

It was his pride in her which firmed her spine and helped her to walk without trembling through the side gate and into the Mordaunt kitchens, where her cousin's bewildered servants huddled around the table under the watchful eye of a pair of runners. She led the way up the stairs and into the entrance hall and then up the beautiful flight of stairs rising gracefully to the first floor, down which her niece and nephew had one day raced. . . .

Constance took off her cape. The runner boggled at her wild hair which she proceeded to ruffle still further, pulling part of it over one side of her face. She tore open the buttons at her throat and jerked at her crushed skirts until they rode at an odd angle around her hips.

When she'd finished disarranging herself she looked at Jack, who studied her dispassionately. He grasped the lace at the edge of one sleeve and ripped it so that it dangled. He studied her again and nodded. Handing her a long–barreled pistol, he warned her in a soft voice to be careful. "It's loaded. It hasn't what they call a hair trigger, but it requires a delicate touch."

Gingerly Constance took the weapon. She turned and hefted it, pointing it at the other end of the hall. She held it next in both hands and aimed it. That felt better. Turning back, she met Jack's eyes.

Jack glanced at Selwyn and the runner. Then, before anyone could say a word, he pulled Constance into his arms and kissed her warmly. "Take care, my dear," he muttered into her ear. "I could not bear it if anything bad happened to you."

She stared into his worried eyes, wondering at his willingness to show his feelings with other men looking on. "Nothing will happen," she promised.

"I'm sure that's what your brother said just before a ball caught him in the thigh." Jack sighed a trifle sourly. "Go, my dear, before I pick you up and carry you out of here to where I may know you'll be safe."

The men took up positions on either side of the entry to the study and Constance, after one deep breath and a short prayer, thrust open the door, slamming it back against the wall.

"Murderer!" she shouted, stomping into the room.

"The brat's dead, then?" asked Mordaunt, startled into that much of an admission.

"You killed him."

Mordaunt's sense of self–preservation returned. "Nonsense. I never killed anything in my life."

Connie leaned over the desk, placing her free hand on it. "You said you'd kill him. I heard you."

Mordaunt's eyes narrowed. "Come, cousin. Calm yourself. This is not like you."

"My Val! My boy. You murderer!" Connie saw him inching his hand toward a drawer and raised her pistol. She held it between both hands. "I'll shoot you."

"Here, now!" Beads of sweat popped out on Mordaunt's forehead. "Where'd you get that? Is it loaded?"

"Of course it is. I will shoot you. I will kill you dead." She remembered she was supposed to be mad. "Murderer!" she screeched.

"I haven't left the house for weeks," Mordaunt blustered, his eyes never leaving the pistol. "I can't have murdered anyone."

"With your money, then. By your orders. I will kill you."

His eyes skittered around the room and, glittering, slid back to meet hers. "Put that gun down and listen to me. I've a plan, you see . . . you'll like it," he added in a cajoling sort of voice.

Connie didn't put the gun down, but she lowered it slightly. "What sort of plan?"

"I'll marry you."

By his glittering eyes she knew he lied.

"You can have children. Your child will inherit, you see. When I'm gone, that is."

"Inherit?"

"The barony, of course."

"My brother—"

"Dead. His son, too. Now I'm baron. So I'll marry you and you can have children and—"

"I wouldn't touch you, you slimy toad," said Connie, momentarily forgetting her role.

"Don't need to," he said simply. "Find yourself a lover more to your taste."

He shrugged . . . and his hand once again inched toward the drawer where, she guessed, he kept his own pistol. Connie raised hers, aiming for his heart, and he moved his hand back.

"So?" he wheedled. "You like the notion? Make you a real lady," he said slyly. "You can have new gowns. You liked your London gown, did you not?" he coaxed. "Give you all the pin money you want. You can live in town. You like London."

"I don't know."

"Come now. You're a sensible woman. I'll purchase a license and we can wed immediately. Take you off the shelf," he added. He would never know how close he was just then to having Jack rush in and take him by the throat.

"I can have fine dresses?" asked Connie, pretending to think.

"Lots of them."

Connie made several more requests.

Out in the hall the three men frowned at each other. "It isn't going to work," whispered Selwyn very nearly silently. The runner nodded, but Jack put a finger to his lips.

"And how do I know you won't have me killed like you did Val?" asked Constance suddenly.

"Now you stop that." Mordant frowned. "I thought you'd forgotten that."

"I don't want to die," she whined.

"Don't know how I can make you believe me."

"You did it."

"So?"

Connie drew in a deep breath and adopted a sly look.

"Write it out. Sign it. I'll put it where it's safe, only to be opened if I die suddenly without explanation."

"And then you'll wed me and forget the whole thing?"

Connie paused. "I'll forget the whole thing." In her mind she added that she wouldn't wed him if he were to threaten her with boiling oil or one of the dungeons she suspected still existed at Durrant Castle.

"I'll be a complacent husband," he said in an oily tone. "Only want a pretty hostess. You are pretty when you don't look like a wind's been in a haystack."

Connie pushed hair back behind one ear but she didn't put down the pistol or allow her attention to stray. "You write it."

"What do you want me to say?" he asked. He reached for the drawer.

"Don't do that!" She shook the pistol slightly, holding it with both hands. "You've pen and paper right there in front of you. Now write."

"Tell me what to write," he coaxed.

"You know. What you did."

"What I did."

"Write."

"And then you'll shoot me."

"No. Then I'll think about marrying you. I don't trust you, but to live in London . . . to have London gowns and go to parties and . . ." She put on a dreamy expression but let it fade when once again he reached toward the drawer. She knew *he'd* not hesitate to shoot!

"I'll write it," he decided, but then glanced at her sharply. "I won't give it to you until you've married me."

Connie watched as he slowly filled a page with a dozen or so sentences. "Sign it."

He did so with a flourish.

"Turn it around."

He did that, too, moving it toward her side of the table. She glanced down, took in a sentence, and looked up.

"Don't touch that drawer or I'll shoot," she warned.

His hands returned to the top of the desk. She managed another two sentences and had to warn him again. When she'd read enough so that she was certain he'd actually written out a confession, she asked, "It is true, then? You hired that awful man to choke my nephew?"

"Choke him? That's what he did?"

Constance scowled. "It was your fault."

"Of course it was," he soothed. "Now let me have that paper. I'll give it back when we are wed."

"There's a problem," said Connie.

"What is it now?" demanded Mordaunt, scowling fiercely.

"I wouldn't trust you to give it back, you see. Besides, I don't think I want to wed you." She snatched the paper from the desk and backed away. "In fact, I think I'll just give this to the Bow Street Runner waiting in the hall. That way I won't have to worry about you killing me or anyone else. Selwyn, for instance, who is also waiting in the hall."

Jack, followed by the other two, strolled into the study. "I'd begun to wonder if you'd manage it, Connie, my love, but I should not have lost faith, should I? Well done."

Mordaunt stood, leaning both hands on the desk and glaring. He stared at Jack and winced slightly as he recognized him, then turned first toward Selwyn and then the runner. "Who are you? What are you doing in my house?"

"Michael Dewey, Bow Street Runner," said the Runner, stepping forward. "I arrest you in the name of the king for conspiring to murder the heir to the Mordaunt barony."

"And I," said Selwyn, "am the baron you thought to replace! Alive and well, as is my son, no thanks to you!"

"You are Selwyn Mordaunt? You?" A filament of drool

slid from the side of Mordaunt's mouth, and his eyes rolled. "He's a disgrace to the name!" shouted Mordaunt, pointing at Selwyn. "Arrest that man! A deserter, I tell you. Arrest him now! He must be court-martialled. At once!" Mordaunt's wandering gaze fell on the major and sharpened. "I know you," he said with no bluster at all. "You were at the Horse Guards."

"Yes," said Jack. "and I know exactly where Lord Mordaunt's been the past few years, and what he's been doing. He is not and never was a deserter."

"Bah. You look into it. You'll find he deserted. Or maybe he died? Yes, I think he died. I will be baron," said the obviously insane man dreamily. "What a cap to my career. Baron Mordaunt. Everyone will bow to me. It's an ancient honor, you know," he said confidingly to the runner who led him from the room. "One of the oldest in the kingdom. Still," they heard as he went down the hall, "it is only a barony. I must plan how I might enlarge it. To viscount, or perhaps an earldom? Yes, I will be happy with nothing less than an earldom. You!" they heard. "You must get me an appointment with Prinny. *He'll* see to it."

Connie, who had held herself rigid as Mordaunt was led away, collapsed, leaning one hip against the desk. "He is really gone?"

"Yes. You no longer need worry about Val."

"Thank Heaven," she said prayerfully.

"You did well, Connie," said Selwyn, patting her shoulder. "I'm proud of you."

"So you should be," said Jack. "And not just for her playacting here and now. I don't know how you could pretend you might agree to wed that slimy toad, Connie. I wanted to strangle him for suggesting it!"

"He just about did it, too," said Selwyn, chuckling. "I had to hold him back from rushing in and ruining everything." Selwyn dropped into a chair and rubbed his thigh. He yawned. "I don't know about you two, but I want nothing so much as to find a bed and collapse into it for about a week." He leaned forward and worked with both hands at the muscles in his thigh.

"I don't believe I'll need a full week, but I would certainly like some sleep," agreed Connie, wishing there were something she could do for her brother's pain. She, too, yawned.

Jack found himself yawning as well, as one did when confronted by yawns. "I think anything which must be done to wrap this up may be done later as easily as now. I'll take you back to the Morningsides, Connie. And Selwyn and I can go on to my rooms."

"If you won't need me once we've had some sleep, I think I'll return to Durrant Castle and retrieve my wife and children," said Selwyn as he limped from the room.

"She is not yet your wife," objected Connie.

"Not legally, perhaps. But in my mind and heart she's been that for a long time now."

Connie was impressed by the simplicity with which he spoke. "I am sorry for your first wife, Silly, but she was not right for you, and you were certainly not the man for her. I am sad she died, but perhaps it is for the best. She'd never have been happy, even with you home. Even now you are no longer a soldier, she'd have made life hell for both of you if she'd lived."

Selwyn turned sad eyes her way. "I wed her for the wrong reasons, and she—she'd never the least notion of what it meant to be a soldier's wife."

"We needn't speak of it again," said Connie. He pressed her hand in silent thanks.

* * *

The Morningsides' small house hadn't room for additional guests, so when Selwyn returned to town some days later with the rest of the party it included Lady Durrant and a number of servants. Soon her ladyship had enough of the Durrants' townhouse opened up so that everyone could stay there until Selwyn finished his business in London and they removed to Cornwall.

Connie introduced Madame Beugnot to the *modiste* who had once made her a gown, ordered another for herself, along with a new habit. She took Val and Venetia to see the sights, which she'd not done previously, being too preoccupied with discovering what had happened to their father. Lady Durrant insisted they must remain as long as they liked. She organized several small dinners and evening parties which, Connie very soon realized, were for the purpose of introducing her to family and friends.

"You must not raise false expectations," she gently scolded her hostess.

Lady Durrant chuckled. "My dear, you are taking so long agreeing to this marriage, I *must* do it this way. Jack is scheduled to leave for Vienna at the end of the month! You've no longer time for banns, so it must be by license, of course." She settled her chin in her hand and stared at Connie. "I wonder if you should not order more gowns." When Constance glowered, she quickly added, "If you do not, you may find a good seamstress in Vienna. I am told there are French *modistes* there who are very good indeed, although not quite in the English style, of course."

"Why will no one believe that what I mean to do is for the best?"

Lady Durrant smiled mysteriously and shook her head.

"I so fear he will be unhappy," Constance almost wailed.

"I *know* he'll be unhappy if you do *not* wed him!"

"But he said he must marry me merely because he'd compromised me! I will not have it."

When her ladyship, who had never heard the details of the journey through France, asked how Jack had compromised her, Constance told the tale of how they'd found Selwyn. "You do not approve," she finished, noting the darkening look on her hostess's face, "but I assure you nothing untoward happened. He believed me married, you see, and is too honorable to put horns on another man's head."

"Bluntly spoken for an unwed woman, my dear."

"Do you scold me for that, too? I won't apologize. I find the restrictions on maidens of my advanced age ridiculous."

"They are, of course, but outward appearances can be important. And the appearance of your journey with my son is not such as one would wish generally known."

"But no one does know!"

"Except that rattle, Lady Grinnel!"

"She will not speak of it. She is, actually, very good at keeping secrets. She knew Jack's role at the Horse Guards for much of his time there, but she told no one, not even her husband, whom she knew knew the truth. She listened to conversations between her husband and ministers in the government and again held her tongue. I believe she'll keep still about this minor *contretemps* as well, since it involves her cousin Jack."

"*Especially* since it involves Jack." Lady Durrant sighed.

Constance didn't pretend to misunderstand. "Her feelings are, I believe, merely the tag end of a hero worship she felt for him when they were growing up. She may not always think things through to a logical conclusion, but in the end she wed someone else, did she not? She knew, somewhere deep inside herself, that Major St. Aubyn was not a proper husband for her.''

''That sounds reasonable. Perhaps I've worried for nothing.'' Lady Durrant sighed. Then she looked sharply at Constance. ''But that is all wide of the mark. You *must* wed my son.''

''I'll not force him to the altar, and if he is forced there, I will not go myself.''

''You don't wish to wed?''

Constance paused. ''I suppose I have had my dreams, but those were childish dreams at best. I have long realized I must devote myself to my nephew and niece. And now that Selwyn is to rewed, there will be more children in his nursery. I will have a full life.''

Lady Durrant chuckled. She glanced at Constance and laughed more fully. ''My dear, you say that as if you were doing your very best to convince yourself. I do wish you would get it out of your head that Jack can be forced to do anything he does not wish to do. You will get along so much better, once married to him, if you realize that.'' Her ladyship rose to her feet. ''I have nagged and lectured enough for one day. Do come with me to Mrs. Burney's hat shop,'' she coaxed. ''I have heard she's a delightful new girl who trims the most delicious bonnets you ever did see!''

While Lady Durrant and Constance tried on one hat after another, Selwyn and Jack crossed the river and braved Lambeth Palace where, without half so much difficulty as they'd expected, each purchased a license.

''That went better than I'd thought it would,'' said Jack as they left. ''Now, do you know where your sister is ordering her new gowns?''

"A Madame Marie, I believe. She said she doesn't believe the woman has been nearer to France then the east end of London, but that she is a very good *modiste* for all that. Why do you ask?"

Jack pushed hair back from his forehead, a muscle jumping in his jaw. "Because whether Connie knows it or not she leaves with me for Vienna. I would have a trunk or two filled for her." He shrugged. "That is all."

"You would order clothes for her? She'll have your lights and liver!"

"Why, because I choose the style and colors?" Jack's mischievous look replaced his formerly grim expression. "I have a nice touch at that—or so I am told."

"My sister is, despite appearances, rather nice in her notions. She'll object to a man not closely related to her purchasing such intimacies for her," said Selwyn primly.

"Ah! But she *will* be closely related, will she not?" Jack patted the hidden pocket in which the license rested.

"You hope!"

Jack sobered. "Mordaunt, how am I to convince her I truly want to wed her?"

"You ask *me*? When I can't convince my own woman *we* should wed? I haven't a clue where you get the notion I'd know how *you'll* convince Connie."

Chapter 12

"Connie, are you going to marry Major St. Aubyn?" asked Val, looking up from the paper on which he was laboriously writing a letter to young Grinnel.

"Why do you ask?" asked his startled aunt.

"I don't know. But you are always cuddling, and I have noticed that people who cuddle get married. Like Betsy."

Constance felt her face flame. "Not at all like Betsy!" she exclaimed. Betsy was the nursery maid who had married the footman the previous year and, less than six months later, given him a fine son.

"Oh."

"Why so sad?" she asked.

"Hmm, I just thought it might be nice to have a little brother, but maybe Madame will give me one?"

Connie relaxed. She could speak of Felice and Selwyn's marriage far more easily than she could speak, or even think, about her own future. "I believe she will, Val. She has told me she'd like to have babies."

"Still—I think I'd rather you gave me a brother."

"The thing is, even if I were to have a child it wouldn't be your brother or sister, Val. It would be your cousin."

"Willy wouldn't mind," he said, looking up and speaking earnestly. "We'd love it even if it were just a cousin."

"I'm sure you both would," said Connie as she scrabbled for something, anything, which would change the subject. "Get on with your letter, Val, or it will miss the post, as will mine."

Connie bent to her own epistle, which was in response to one she'd received that morning from Ada. Lord Temperance, said Ada, had informed her family of the marriage. Ada was distressed that there'd been no response, but other than that she was blissfully happy. Or so she implied in a dozen different ways.

Your family is the loser if they continue to snub you, Ada, wrote Connie. *They haven't a notion of the delightful woman you have become and they will never know your children, which is always a great loss.*

Connie looked at her words and wondered if she'd said enough . . . or too much. And then, her disobedient mind straying once again into forbidden channels, she wondered about the children she'd not have if she didn't wed Jack.

Hurriedly she picked up Ada's letter and looked for distraction from such thoughts. She didn't find it. Ada asked *when,* not *if,* Constance meant to wed Lord St. Aubyn. Lord Temperance said they would come to London for the wedding if only they knew the date and that, in any case, he'd business he must see to. Too, he was aware his new wife wished to visit a *modiste,* to say nothing of many other shops as well. There'd been no mistress at the Temperance estate for over a decade, and much in the way of linens and hangings needed replacing.

The letter rambled on as if Ada and Lord Temperance

had been married for years rather than less than two weeks, and Connie discovered she was capable of feeling the greenest of green jealousy. She was jealous of Ada's happiness, which was an exceedingly foolish emotion and one she felt it wrong to feel. She should, instead, be happy for her friend, happy that after years of suffering Ada need never again feel ashamed or alone.

"Connie, I have finished," said Val. This time his voice was a welcome interruption. "When will Willy return with Venetia?"

"They shouldn't be long now."

"I don't see why she needs a new dress." He pouted slightly. "Or why *I* had to be fitted for new clothes. Do you, too, think fittings a bore, Connie?"

Constance chuckled. "*Definitely* a bore, Val, but do not say as much to Venetia. Some women enjoy the business, and she may grow up to be one of them. Do not prejudice her against what will be a necessary duty when, otherwise, she might in future like it!"

"Father took me to his tailor," said Val after digesting that advice.

Ah! thought Connie. *Silly is, perhaps, not so silly as he used to be? Or perhaps his Felice told him to do it?* Much more likely, she decided. Unless it was Willy. She would not put it past the nurse to chide an old nursling into doing right by a later one!

She sighed. There were, suddenly, so many to watch over these two precious lives. Very soon she'd be unnecessary to the children—unnecessary anywhere, for that matter— the unwed sister who must be accommodated, must be chaperoned, must have found for her the odd man so that the dinner table would not be unbalanced. . . .

Constance felt a chill at those notions. *Almost* it would

be a relief to give in to everyone's belief that she would
and should wed Jack!

Willy returned just then and, after listening to Venetia's
enthusiastic description of her new dress—an uncharacteristicly voluble Venetia—Constance left the nursery, found
an unoccupied footman to go with her, and departed for
her own appointment for one of the dreaded fittings.

With brotherly bluntness, Selwyn had informed her he'd
deposited several thousand pounds in an account for her,
some part of the monies she should have given herself
over the past years for managing his estate. More blight-
ingly then bluntly, he'd added that in his opinion she
should spend some if not all of it on her back, because
her clothes were shockingly out of fashion, from what he'd
seen of them.

This too seemed uncharacteristicly thoughtful, although
no less tactlessly presented than one would expect on the
part of the long lost brother she remembered. Whatever
Selwyn's motivation, Connie had, quite thankfully, gone
about the business of spending a great deal of the funds
he provided.

Not all of it went on her back, of course. Some, far more
than was necessary, went on her head. Constance, thanks
to Lady Durrant's tutoring, had discovered the delight of
wearing fashionable hats. Previously, she'd found them a
burden. She now had hats that ranged from one exceedingly practical everyday sort of bonnet, a sop to her practical side, to more frivolous *chapeaux* which were to be
pinned atop her piled up hair. In fact, she'd several of the
latter sort which were not the least bit protective of one's
complexion and certainly didn't guard one from the ele-
ments!

Then—as well as the lovely little designs that were nothing more than frivolous combinations of lace and feathers

and lengths of silk ribbon formed into flowers and one
excellent if slightly mannish beaver which could be worn
out riding in most any sort of weather—there were straw
hats with wide brims, and delightful bonnets with wide
bows which tied at her ear. She now had more hats than
she would possibly need for many years to come, and fully
intended choosing still another as a reward to herself—
assuming she managed to stand still at the *modiste's* and
not complain, even once, not even if he were stuck with
a pin.

She truly did find fittings a bore!

"So, *is* she ordering a new wardrobe?" asked Jack a trifle
anxiously.

Selwyn had made him agree to a plan in which the
brother provided money and incentive for Connie to order
new clothing, rather than Jack's more direct and totally
objectionable scheme of ordering them himself.

"I believe she is at a fitting this morning," said Selwyn,
looking over the top of his newspaper.

Since coming to London, Selwyn had discovered how
much he'd missed a daily paper while away from England.
He'd ordered that every daily be delivered while he was
resident at the Durrant's, and had almost decided on the
two he'd have sent to Cornwall along with three weeklies
he'd discovered were much to his taste.

Upon leaving France he'd wondered how he'd occupy
himself now that he no longer had a war to fight. Only a
few days reading had led him to conclude there was, here
at home, a war of another sort in which he might submerge
himself. The annual conflict between the King's party and
the Loyal Opposition in Parliament could become quite
heated, he'd discovered.

"At least, I am almost certain she said she'd be visiting her *modiste,* this morning," he added.

"So she is," said Felice, entering the men's sanctuary just then. "She has ordered any number of fine gowns. A new riding habit was her foremost wish, then morning dresses and walking dresses and that sort of thing, but only *two* which one might consider full evening dress. She will need more than that, will she not, Major?"

"At least three, just to be going on with. When we arrive in Vienna she'll find it necessary to order more, of course. They who speak of all the balls and parties with which everyone is entertained there do not lie. Until the orders she places there can be made up, she must have several from which to choose." He looked from Madame Felice to Selwyn, who was again hidden behind his paper. Turning back to Madame, he asked, "Have you a notion how you might convince her she should order more?"

"Not unless I tell her she will not wish to embarrass you when you reach Vienna."

"I doubt that will do the trick," said Jack dryly, "since she has yet to agree that she goes to Vienna. I wish someone would tell me how I'm to manage that, too!"

"Patience. All you need is patience," said Felice smugly. "Me, I have pointed out to her how very much in the way she will be when we go to Selwyn's home." She chuckled. "It is not true, of course. And if she does *not* wed you I must quickly discover how very wrong I have been to suggest it to her and convince her of my abject need of her advice and counsel!"

"I do not want her to wed me because she has no other option!"

"You know very well that is nonsense," scolded Felice. "Her greatest wish is to wed you, if she would but admit it." Felice tipped her head thoughtfully to one side. "Actually, I think she has admitted it. What she has yet to admit is that it is also truly your wish. So, until she does, she may think of how drab her future will be, a cipher in her own home, and in the end she will follow her heart.''

"That is the most convoluted thinking I have ever heard,'' said Selwyn, once again looking around his newspaper. ''By the way, did you not, somewhere in all that, imply *you* mean to marry *me*? I mean, there is only one reason Constance would find herself with no responsibility in Cornwall.'' His brows arched. ''She will be unnecessary when we reach home only if you are my wife? Hmm?''

Felice flounced to a chair and seated herself, a delightful pout pursing her mouth. Then she sighed. ''I suppose I should not be angry that you caught that little betrayal of my intentions, Silly. Your sharp mind is, after all, one of the things I love in you.''

Selwyn's paper went flying, and soon after Jack quietly left the room, closing the door behind him. He met his mother coming down the hall. Her brows arched when he put his finger to his lips and turned her away from the library.

''But I wish to find a book which I mean to lend to dear Constance!'' objected his mother.

''I assure you, you do not wish to enter the library just now. Madame has admitted she means to marry Mordaunt!''

''Ah!'' said Lady Durrant smiling delightedly. ''But then, I knew *she* would.''

''I don't think I like the sound of that.''

''That I knew she would, but I still wonder if dear Constance will wed you?''

''Yes.''

She sighed. ''You have chosen a very stubborn lady, my son.''

"I know," he said ruefully. "It is as well I am equally stubborn, is it not?"

Lady Durrant set down her sewing and eyed Constance. "I fear for my son," said her ladyship, breaking a long silence.

"Fear for him? But why?"

"He needs a hand on the reins," said the son's mother mournfully. She stared into the small fire she'd had laid in the hearth. "He was so wild as a boy and on into his early life as a young man. A wildness which had me fearing again and again for his very life. Now it is not the same sort of wildness, of course."

"You would say he jumps into a thing enthusiastically and with his whole heart?" asked Constance, hoping that her ladyship would not begin, once again, to urge a marriage between herself and Jack. It was becoming harder and harder to say no. Jack would leave soon for the continent. "He is an intelligent man, my lady. He will not allow enthusiasm to overcome his judgement."

"Do you, of all people, say so?" asked Lady Durrant, putting on an expression of shock.

"Of course I do."

"But my dear, if you believe he has sound judgement why do you continue to refuse him?"

Connie saw she'd almost trapped herself in a contradiction. "Because his determination in this case is that of an honorable man who feels he has contravened society's dictates and must now live with the consequences," she said, thinking quickly.

"Ah! Then you *do* think his judgement can be overborne!" Her ladyship's lugubrious expression returned. "I so dislike thinking that he will be in that bedlam which is Vienna, doing who knows what, and as a result very likely stepping on dangerous toes. There are men, not *English* of course, who have very strange ideas about how one deals with a political enemy! They have not our determination to avoid the more tyranical methods, you see."

Connie stared at Lady Durrant, horrified. "You would say that if he got too much in the way of some great man, the man night have Jack killed?"

"It is not an impossible thought."

Connie's hands crushed the fine lawn material which she'd previously hemmed and on which she was embroidering the Mordaunt arms. The handkerchief she was making for Felice might never lose the resulting creases.

"I feel no shame admitting," added her ladyship piously, "that I will be ever so much happier with you there watching over him."

That was rather overdoing it, decided Constance. "I thought," she said, "that it was my willingness to join him in his folly which was one of my charms for him?"

"Ah! But even though you are willing to join in, you think ahead to consequences. You admitted as much when you told me of your decision to join with my son in traveling through France to find your brother." Lady Durrant smiled. "You accepted that you might be ruined by it if you were discovered in such a prank, but that you felt it was your duty to find your brother and that that was more important. You see? You thought of consequences, balanced the various choices, and only then did what you thought best."

"And I am ruined."

"Nonsense! Engaged, yes, but not ruined."

"I don't believe I've entered into an engagement."

"Have you not?" The countess's brows arched. "Then what is the meaning of this . . . oh where is it?" Her ladyship laid aside her sewing and searched through the paper which she'd perused earlier. "Ah! Here." She thrust a page before Constance and pointed with one long, aristocratic finger. "Right there."

And there, in print and in just so many words, was the information that Lord Mordaunt was pleased to announce the engagement of his sister, Miss Constance Mordaunt, to Major Lord St. Aubyn, the marriage to be observed immediately.

Constance rose to her feet, never taking her eyes from the notice. Still staring at it, she turned and started for the door.

"How dare he?" she muttered. "How *dare* he do this?"

"Miss Mordaunt!"

Connie halted, but she did not turn.

"You are about to run into one of my favorite vases. If you wish to shatter it and that will help relieve your temper, then of course I will give you no argument," said the countess, humor in her voice, "but if you are simply overlooking it, then I'd appreciate it if you would go around it."

Constance lowered the paper and stared at the vase which was only a foot before her nose on a rather high and none too steady pedestal. Red with embarrassment, she veered, and this time watched her way as she stalked on toward the door.

"I will have his lights and liver. I will boil him in oil. I will . . . I will turn Felice from him!"

When Constance had slammed the door behind her Lady Durrant reseated herself. She allowed a tiny smile to play about her lips as she wondered just how soon dear Constance would discover her brother had had nothing to do with the notice.

Nor had Jack, who would be the poor girl's next guess.

So how soon would her future daughter–in–law realize that it was her future mother–in–law who had found the courage to cut the knots and do what must be done?

Jack was not the only Durrant to jump without thinking through possible consequences! Lady Durrant suddenly wondered, a trifle belatedly, how long it would take her daughter–in–law to forgive once she'd discovered the actual source of the announcement!

"Of course you did it! Why will you not admit it?" asked Connie, shaking the paper in Selwyn's face.

"I will not admit to that which I did not do. Jack!" he added as the major strolled in, "I must give you my congratulations! At least, I presume you have reached the conclusion that the only way of mastering my sister is to ignore her?"

Jack, startled, stared. "The last thing I wish to do is ignore her. To what do you refer?"

"This." Constance's suspicions turned to Jack, whom she had seen looking the most innocent exactly when he was *not*. Was that the case now, she wondered. She thrust the notice before his eyes.

"Ah! Did you send it in, Connie my dear? Is this your way of telling me you have changed your mind?"

"I didn't!"

"You didn't change your mind?" he asked sorrowfully.

"I did not send it in," she said, speaking each word slowly and distinctly. "Silly denies it was he. You suggest you know nothing of it."

"And I do not," he interrupted, "but I am delighted."

"Bah!"

"Connie, I do not see how you are to get around this,"

said Selwyn slowly. "We must arrange your wedding quickly, so that you may leave for the Continent with Jack."

Constance folded her arms and tapped one foot. "I will get around it quite simply, Silly. *You,*" she asserted, "will write a retraction and send it off at once."

"But I do not wish to write a retraction."

"Must I do it myself?"

Jack moved to her and put his hands on her shoulders. "My dear, will you allow me to discover who inserted this very welcome notice? Before you do anything rash, I mean?"

"The longer it is put off, the worse it will be for me." Her eyes had a wild look to them when she raised them to his. "Jack, truly, we must do nothing which you will regret. I could not bear it."

"You do not say you would regret it," he said softly.

Connie turned from under his hands and fled the room.

Jack ran his fingers through his hair, then again, and finally a third time, holding the hair back where it belonged. "What did I say?"

"Only the truth, I believe. Well?"

"Well, what?"

"Well, shall we go discover who the guilty party is, since I know it is not I and you insist it is not you?"

Jack's body went completely still. "Mother!"

Mordaunt cast him a startled glance. "You think Lady Durrant did this?"

"Since we can be certain Constance did not, who is left? If *you* did not and *I* did not, then it must have been my mother."

Mordaunt had no answer once it occurred to him that his Felice spoke, but did not write, English.

Jack sighed. "Before I face her with it, I'd better ascertain the truth of it by talking to the editor. Coming?"

* * *

Somehow the retraction did not get inserted, although Constance searched the paper for it day after day. And then her brother decided to wed before leaving London for Cornwall, fearing that his Felice might yet change her mind.

"I cannot believe it is my wedding day," said Felice looking into the oval standing mirror which had been brought into her room.

Venetia, very fine in her new gown, sat quietly on the bed watching the proceedings. Lady Durrant occupied herself with rearranging, for the third time, the posy Felice would carry. Occasionally she cast a glance toward Constance, who was not speaking to her. Connie had finally learned who sent in the notice of her non–existent engagement.

Hiding her jealousy and the sadness that it was not *her* day, Constance carefully buttoned another of the long row of tiny buttons above one of Felice's wrists. She didn't turn when a knock sounded, doing up another button as Lady Durrant opened the door and inch or two.

"Yes?"

"We are going now," Connie heard Jack say. "We will take Val and Mrs. Willes with us."

"Very well. We are nearly ready. We will join you at the church," said the countess.

The pain never far from Constance's conscious mind rose to fill her, and she stifled a sob. Why had she been so foolish as to fall in love with Jack? *And why*, she wondered with a flare of resentment, *could he not have fallen in love with her? If only he had. Oh, if only . . .*

Constance bit her lip and concentrated on the last button. She straightened. "There. I believe that is all." Somewhat urgently, she asked the question which had bothered her ever since her brother's plans had been revealed to her. "Felice, it is all right, is it not, that you will be wed by an English churchman?"

"But of course," said Felice. Then her brows arched. "Ah," she added, you believed me a Catholic. But of course you would. My family, my soon–to–be–sister, are of the Huguenot persuasion. What few of us remain," she added sadly. "I've some cousins, I believe, living near Rouen. But that is all."

"Excellent," said Lady Durrant. "I, too, wondered if there would be problems between you and Mordaunt when it came to rearing your children. Come along, Miss Venetia. We will go down now and see that the carriage is awaiting us. Constance, Felice? Do not be long, and do not forget the bouquets!"

Venetia tucked her hand trustfully into Lady Durrant's. As they turned down the hall, Constance and Felice heard Venetia ask, "May I call Madame Beugnot Mama after the wedding?"

Constance heard the wistful note in her niece's voice and turned to stare at Felice who, her bottom lip between her teeth, stared back. "I will do my best," said Felice, "to be a mother to them, but I am not. Nor am I *you*. I can only be myself."

"One should never try to be what one is not," soothed Constance. "You will do very well."

"I believe I will suggest they call me *Mamán,*" said Felice slowly. "It will be a reminder that I am someone different, and they will not expect me to be exactly like someone else."

"Venetia is too young to remember her mother," said Constance slowly. "At least, as anything other than an amorphous presence very much in the background. She became ill after the child's birth, and never recovered. It is very lucky that we had Willy, who is quite wonderful."

"Yes. I will like to have her care for my children, too," said Felice with far more shyness than Constance had ever heard from the Frenchwoman. "I should not admit it, but I think—her ears turned an even brighter red—"well, it is possible that . . ."

"You are *enciente?*" asked Constance, finishing the sentence her brother's love could not.

"I . . . have hopes."

Constance grinned. "Well, it had better be a boy, you know."

"I . . . rather thought a girl," said a startled Felice.

"No. Val has requested a brother. He will be quite disgusted if it is another sister. We had a long talk only a few days ago, you see."

Felice smiled fondly. "That child! He is almost as delightful as his father, is he not?"

"He is very much like his father at that age according to Willy, who had a hand in raising us, you know. She was actually a nursery maid then, but we turned to her rather than our nurse when we had a bump or our feelings were hurt."

A tap at the door and the appearance of a maid reminded the two women that they were wanted below stairs. Mutually a trifle embarrassed by their recent confidences, they went.

Lady Durrant had mentioned to only one or two people that her young friends were wedding. Secretly, it had been her hope that her son would also be celebrating his marriage, but it looked as if she were to be disappointed. Then, too, Constance had remembered to write to Ada on the same day she'd learned her brother's plans. Ada had responded that they would be there, and slyly added that they hoped to witness *two* weddings. In any case, the church had far more people in it than anyone expected—including Lord and Lady Grinnel, the latter looking happier than she ever had. Mary would not let go of her husband, smiling at him fondly and receiving fond smiles in return. It looked as if the two had, somehow, finally solved their problems.

Constance stood beside Felice, staring at nothing at all. Everyone, it seemed, including her brother who had taken a few minutes the evening before to tell her how stupidly she was behaving, believed she should wed Jack. Could she be wrong? Could he truly wish to wed her?

As Felice and Selwyn spoke their vows she turned to look at him . . . and discovered he was staring at her. He mouthed the words Selwyn was saying, his eyes never releasing hers.

He was, she realized, saying his marriage vows.

Even though they were not wedding, he was promising all those things a man promised before God when he took a wife. She felt the blood flowing up her cheeks, but she could not look away. She felt mesmerized. The ceremony continued, and she found herself mouthing, "I will," along with Felice. Then, realizing what she had done, she very nearly fainted.

Some moments later she found herself in a little room off the apse and in Jack's arms. "Did you mean it?" he asked urgently. "Oh, if only you meant it," he added before she could speak. "I have hurt you so much that you have refused to come to me." He removed her fingers from his lips. "I never thought love would hurt so much."

Her eyes widened. "Love? You *love* me?"

"Have I not said so?"

She drew in a deep breath and let it out in a huff. "No you have not, ever, said you loved me. Only that you thought I'd make a capable wife and you should make me respectable, and that sort of thing."

"For most women that would be enough," teased Jack, feeling more than little lightheaded as he realized that somehow he'd finally managed the trick, and his Constance *would* wed him.

"Not enough for me. But now you *have* said it!" She stilled. "Oh dear. You have waited until it is too late! Oh, Jack, why could you not have said so before?" she wailed.

Jack blinked. "Too late? But too late for what?"

"To wed! How can we when you must leave England in only a few days?"

"Quite easily, if you mean it. Connie, my sweet, tell me honestly, now. Did you mean that if I had, in so many words, said I love you, that would have been sufficient for you to say you'd wed me?"

"Yes."

"So you refused to wed for less than love . . ." It was his turn to frown. "But, my dear, have I not said it every time I kissed you? Have I not said it by asking you to wed me? Have I . . ." He shook his head, sighing, never taking his gaze from hers. "Women need the words, do they not?"

"They do. Oh, Jack, men kiss so very easily. They wed for so many reasons." She put on a stern look as she finished, "They very rarely tell a woman they love her when they do not."

"As simple as that. Well, my elusive love, if you have now agreed to wed me, let us go as quickly as may be right back to the altar and allow that very nice vicar to wed us."

"But how?"

She stared at the license he waved back and forth before her nose. "Oh."

"I bought it the same day Selwyn got his. A man in love never quite loses hope, you know."

"You bought . . ." she chuckled, a lightness filling her because, finally, she was to get her heart's desire. "Well, Jack, I am, I believe, a sensible woman, a woman who believes in being thrifty." She touched the license with one finger. Although her eyes twinkled, her voice was serious when she added, "Jack, I should perhaps warn you that I am very much against waste."

"In that case," he scolded gently, "you should have wed me weeks ago. We have *wasted,* I think, far far too much *time.*" And then, before he returned her to the altar he kissed her, one of those long ardent kisses which Connie admitted should have revealed to her the truth of his love for her long ago.

So, with a slight rearrangment in the positions of the four people who'd stood there some minutes previously, Jack and Constance were married in the sight of God, family, and friends . . . and those London idlers who got more than they'd bargained for when, out of curiosity, they'd followed a wedding party into the church!

Dear Reader,

I apologize to anyone who has visited France. Since I have never been to the region I used in this story, I know I erred in the description! I dislike setting a story where I've never been myself, but occasionally it is necessary. Sigh.

My next book involves an orphaned young lady who has recently lost her stepfather as well. Not that anyone minds *that*. He wasn't a nice man and they will go on much better without him. That is, they will if he hasn't chosen a guardian just like himself for Lydia's half-brothers and half-sisters.

The guardian is surprisingly young and handsome. He is not a skint or mean, as was the recently deceased, but he does have a dislike of mysteries. And the lovely "governess" he finds in his ward's household is very much a mystery.

Though she looks enough like the other children to be their sister, she insists she is merely their governess. To add to the mystery, the children are determined they will not lose her! But they won't. She promised she'll not leave them.

Which makes his lordship's pursuit of her a trifle difficult. And it is complicated by the fact he doesn't know if she's legitimate or the deceased's by-blow: Does he woo her? Or does he seduce her? Oh, his lordship does detest mysteries! Look for *A Love for Lydia* in September 1999.

Happy Reading,

Jeanne Savery

Letters sent to Jeanne Savery, P.O. Box 1771, Rochester MI 48308, will reach me. I enjoy hearing from my readers. The enclosure of a stamped self-addressed envelope will insure a response.

<u>BOOK YOUR PLACE ON OUR WEBSITE</u>
<u>AND MAKE THE</u>
<u>READING CONNECTION!</u>

We've created a customized website just for our very special readers, where you can get the inside scoop on everything that's going on with Zebra, Pinnacle and Kensington books.

When you come online, you'll have the exciting opportunity to:

- View covers of upcoming books
- Read sample chapters
- Learn about our future publishing schedule (listed by publication month *and author*)
- Find out when your favorite authors will be visiting a city near you
- Search for and order backlist books from our online catalog
- Check out author bios and background information
- Send e-mail to your favorite authors
- Meet the Kensington staff online
- Join us in weekly chats with authors, readers and other guests
- Get writing guidelines
- AND MUCH MORE!

Visit our website at
http://www.zebrabooks.com

ROMANCE FROM JANELLE TAYLOR

ANYTHING FOR LOVE   (0-8217-4992-7, $5.99)

DESTINY MINE   (0-8217-5185-9, $5.99)

CHASE THE WIND   (0-8217-4740-1, $5.99)

MIDNIGHT SECRETS   (0-8217-5280-4, $5.99)

MOONBEAMS AND MAGIC   (0-8217-0184-4, $5.99)

SWEET SAVAGE HEART   (0-8217-5276-6, $5.99)

ROMANCE FROM FERN MICHAELS

DEAR EMILY   (0-8217-4952-8, $5.99)

WISH LIST   (0-8217-5228-6, $6.99)

AND IN HARDCOVER:

VEGAS RICH   (1-57566-057-1, $25.00)

WATCH FOR THESE REGENCY ROMANCES

LOOK FOR THESE REGENCY ROMANCES